DOUGLAS SKELTON is an established .... en
oks including *Glasgow's Black Heart*, *Frightener* and *Dark Heart*.
has appeared on a variety of documentaries and news programmes
an expert on Glasgow crime, and is a regular contributor to STV on
ninal history. He has also interviewed many well-known crime
ters for festivals as well as appearing in his own right. His 2005 book
ian Peter was later adapted for a BBC Scotland radio documentary,
ich he presented. His first foray into crime fiction was the acclaimed
od City, which introduced Davie McCall. It was followed by *Crow*
014 and *Devil's Knock* in 2015.

Open Wounds

DOUGLAS SKELTON

Luath Press Limited

EDINBURGH

www.luath.co.uk

First published 2016

ISBN: 978-1-910745-33-5

The paper used in this book is recyclable. It is made from
low chlorine pulps produced in a low energy, low emissions manner
from renewable forests.

Printed and bound by
Bell & Bain Ltd., Glasgow

Typeset in 11 point Sabon
by 3btype.com

December 2002

FUNERALS IN THE SUN didn't feel right to him – even a bloodless winter sun that hung low over the trees and glinted off the hard, frosted ground. There should be clouds, he thought, and rain. People should be hiding under umbrellas, not squinting against the light as they waited to file into the crematorium.

There weren't many of them. Some wouldn't dare show up – not after what happened. Those who had were the ones who really cared, who mourned.

There would be no religious element to the proceedings. There would be a memorial stone placed after the brief ceremony, but it carried merely a name and dates. Simple. To the point. No other inscription, because what could you say? *Gone too soon? Sleeping with angels?* To hell with that.

He'd say a few words, for he was his closest friend. Who else would do it – Rab McClymont? No way. Big Rab wasn't even there, which was telling. He didn't like funerals anyway. He always said he'd been to enough to last a lifetime. Caused a few, too.

Some of the faces were familiar, others weren't, which was no surprise. They had been close mates, but for ten years they had moved in different worlds. To an extent, anyway. He smiled slightly, but it was a rueful smile. They had been pals but were so very different. One was quiet – shy, even – the other talkative, outgoing. One was dark, the other blond. But they both had bad memories. The Life left scars that never healed, lesions that continually seeped poisons to taint the blood, to shadow the mind, to murder sleep.

He felt a hand on his shoulder and he turned. First there was pleasure, then shock.

Vari.

He hadn't seen her in years. She was still beautiful, even with her eyes brimming with tears as she greeted him by name. They hugged, held each other for a long time, then broke. He looked for the words but they wouldn't come. He knew she would have questions, but he didn't feel like yielding to them. He didn't know what to tell her. He didn't know how much he *could* tell her.

He looked down at the boy holding her hand tightly and felt something hit him like an open-palmed slap. The kid was dark-haired, his face serious, but it was the eyes that sent his head spinning. He knew who the lad was even before Vari spoke.

'This is Davie,' she said.

I

Two Years Earlier

OLD JINTY WAS THE only one walking in the street that day, pushing her pram as usual, her bare legs milky white but lined with varicose veins that rose from her calves like a relief map of the Pyrenees. There was nothing in the pram, of course, hadn't been for many a long year. Not since her son choked on the eye of his teddy bear. But she still pushed it through the streets and talked to the baby as if he was there.

The sun burned in an unbroken blue sky and the street trapped its rays like a desert canyon, the red sandstone tenements rising on either side soaking up the heat, bleeding it back through the mortar. There was no cooling breeze and the air was heavy and hot and no-one moved, apart from Jinty. In the hottest summer to hit the city in over thirty years, many people chose to stay indoors and swelter in privacy, their windows open to invite the faint promise of cool air, fans whirling, cold drinks near to hand, the ice cubes in them melting so swiftly it was as if they'd never existed. Others thronged the city parks in search of an open space where they might find a pleasing breeze, where they could sit on cool grass and eat ice cream, where the sun worshippers could bake their bodies and burn out the pasty white of a Glasgow winter. The heatwave topped the headlines in print and on screen, while radio jocks dished out advice on staying cool, then segued into The Lovin' Spoonful singing 'Summer in the City'.

Jinty, though, seemed oblivious to the stifling temperature, for she wheeled her pram along the searing concrete pavement at her usual pace, muttering to herself as she always did. She was well known, and most of the adults – the ones who knew her story – tended to look on her with pity. But the youngsters were a different matter. To them she was a target, a figure to be followed down the street, her ragged appearance fodder for their cruelty along

with her empty pram, the constant monologue that only she
understood, and the pink carpet slippers on her feet. They had
once been fluffy but were now worn through; they were coming
apart at the seams and her toes poked out from the front, but she
scuffed along the pavement, talking to the empty pram and not
noticing anything that was going on around her.

Until she saw the man in the car.

Approaching from the rear, first she saw a dog sitting up in the
back seat, but as she drew level she noticed the two men inside.
The driver was young; a baseball cap perched on top of his head,
his scalp cropped to the wood at the sides, the first wisps of a
moustache tickling his upper lip and a fag dangling from the side
of his mouth, jerking up and down as he spoke.

But it was the other one who caught Jinty's attention. He was
nearing forty, his dark hair greying at the sides and also cut short,
but not cropped. His face handsome, but not like a pretty boy. A
thin scar ran down one cheek. And his eyes were blue like the sky,
but sad and cold. Jinty knew this man, knew what he was. And as
he turned those cold, sad blue eyes on her, she felt the air chill and
she was afraid. So she pushed her pram faster to get by, to get
away from that man, that car and that street. She wanted no part
of what was going to happen here.

The man saw her scurry past as fast as her footwear would
allow, then dart a look at him through the windscreen before
ducking down to reassure her non-existent child. He knew she'd
recognised him, feared him, but he was used to that. It was nothing
unusual.

The windows of the blue Rover were cranked open all the way
to prevent the interior turning into a furnace, but it was an exercise
in futility. He fanned himself with a copy of *The Sun* while beside
him, the boy talked. There was nothing unusual in that either. Like
many a Glasgow ned, Jimsie was garrulous. The man didn't mind
the chatter. It reminded him of old friends, long gone.

'I was watching this programme the other night on the telly, a
documentary. I watch a lot of documentaries, me. They're a lot
better than most of the other shite that's on, eh, McCall?'

Davie McCall said nothing as he moved his gaze from the mad old bat with the pram to the tenement door opposite. He knew his silence would neither offend Jimsie nor staunch the flow of words.

'Anyway,' said Jimsie, 'this one was on Channel 4, or BBC 2, or maybe it was the Discovery Channel – anyway, it doesn't matter. It was about these Eskimo guys, right? And when they need food they cannae just slip out to Tesco, know what I mean? So they go out and cut a hole in the ice and then they stand there with this dirty great rifle and wait for a seal or a fuckin penguin to stick its nose up. They can stand there like that for hours, so they can, waiting for something to show up. But when it does – *bang*!'

He shouted the last word loud, clapping his hands for extra emphasis. McCall glanced at him, just briefly, and returned his attention to the tenement.

'But see, the thing is, these guys are going deaf. It's so bloody quiet on those ice fields and it's something to do with the sharp sound of the rifle going off that's affecting their ear drums. What do you think, McCall?'

McCall sighed. 'I sometimes wish *I* was deaf.'

The boy looked hurt. 'You don't mean that. If I thought you meant that, I'd shut the fuck up right now. Is that what you want? You want me to shut the fuck up right now? Just say the word, I'll do it.'

'Jimsie, son, I want you to shut up right now.'

'Like fuck I will. And I'll tell you why – you need someone like me around you. Because you're too taciturn for your own good. You know what taciturn means?'

McCall did not answer. A small smile flirted around his lips, but because his head was turned away, Jimsie couldn't see it.

'You need me to bring you out of yourself,' said Jimsie. 'Because you're too taciturn. Look it up in the dictionary – right beside "taciturn" it says "Davie McCall". So where the fuck was I before I was rudely interrupted?'

'Deaf eskimos.'

'Aye, right – deaf eskimos. So there I was watching this thing on the telly and I was thinking, we're just like they guys...'

McCall twisted in his seat to look at the boy, his face a question mark.

'No, look – we are!' Jimsie insisted. 'Okay, we're no going deaf – no matter what some us might hope for – but we spend a helluva lot of time hanging around waiting for something to turn up. I mean, look at us now. What've we been sitting here for... what? An hour? Just waiting for this geezer to show up. So, see, he's the seal and we're the eskimos and that closemouth over there, that's the hole in the ice and we're just...'

Jimsie stopped talking and tensed. McCall didn't need to look towards the opposite kerb to know that their wait was over. A black Audi had pulled up at the opening to the tenement. Standing beside it locking the door was a balding man wearing an expensive dark suit and carrying a briefcase.

'Looks like grub's up, Nanook,' said McCall.

They waited until the man disappeared into the gloom of the tenement mouth before Jimsie reached down to spring the boot lock and they both climbed out of the car. The young man walked to the rear as McCall hefted a pair of long-handled bolt cutters from the well of the driving seat, then glanced over the headrest at the dog, who was standing on the seat expectantly.

'Stay, Arrow,' he said and the dog sat back down obediently. He was used to this. The windows would remain open, of course, and any little scroat with larceny in mind would have to deal with the dog. McCall thrust the bolt cutters into the folds of his long lightweight coat and waited for Jimsie, who slammed the boot closed and joined him, both hands in his pockets now, the folds of his own coat pulled tightly to his body as if he was cold. He crossed the road before McCall could say anything. McCall's eyes narrowed as if he was squinting against the sun. Something wasn't right here.

They paused in the shadow of the tenement opening to pull thick woolen ski masks over their heads. The flat they wanted was on the ground floor and Jimsie had already pressed the bell before McCall caught up with him, his gaze flitting over the young man. He was hiding something and McCall's instinct told him it wasn't something good. He was about to challenge him when they heard a movement inside before the door opened a crack and a woman's face became visible behind a security chain. All they could see between the door and the frame was her full, thick head of red hair, a face bearing the lines of middle age and a mouth puckered from sucking on too many cigarettes.

Jimsie leaned closer to the gap in the door and said, 'Afternoon, hen – Just wondering if you've found Jesus?'

The woman's eyes widened as they flicked to McCall and then she tried to slam the door shut, but McCall was already moving, thrusting the bolt cutters into the gap, working at the chain. The thin metal snapped and Jimsie shouldered the door open.

'Where is he, Bridget?' McCall asked, his voice low and even.

The woman tried a bluff, but it was half-hearted. 'Where's who?'

'Don't fuck us about, hen,' said Jimsie, a touch of irritation creeping into his voice. 'We saw him come in, so where is he?'

Bridget didn't answer, but her eyes darted reflexively to a room on her left. Jimsie grinned again as McCall grabbed the woman's arms and pushed her towards the door. The young man tapped it open with his foot and stepped inside. It was a bedroom, the curtains drawn against the sun in a vain attempt to cool the air. Jimsie's smile broadened when he saw the balding, overweight man perched on the edge of the bed hastily pulling on his trousers. The man looked up, took in the scene – Jimsie with his hands still not visible, McCall holding Bridget by the arm – and decided he'd try to bluster his way out of it.

'What's the meaning of this?' He demanded as he stood up, his imperious tone undermined by the fact that he was holding the waistband of his dark trousers round his bulging gut with one hand. 'Who are you? How dare you burst in here and...'

'Shut the fuck up, Henry, and listen,' Jimsie said, quietly, and the man's mouth snapped closed. 'You've been a naughty boy, Henry. A very naughty boy – and not just because you've been playing hide the Cumberland sausage with another man's wife.'

Jimsie turned to favour Bridget with a long, appraising look, his eyes lingering over her curves, before turning back to Henry, who stood shivering near the window, still clutching his trousers to his love handles.

'Sure, she's no a bad bit of stuff for her age, but that's no excuse. It's one of the Ten Commandments, Henry – *Thou Shalt Not Shag Another Man's Bird*. You're a lawyer, you should know that's a big no-no. But, bad though that is – and it's bad, Henry, really bad – that's not why we're here. See, there's a wee rumour that you've no been representin your clients to the best of your ability. In fact, we've heard that you've deliberately blown some cases just so's you can do the horizontal jog with your clients' women. Bridget here being a case in point.'

This appeared to be news to Bridget, who forgot her own fear to give Henry a suspicious eye. Henry caught the look and tried to wriggle off the hook. 'It's not true, Bridget, none of it. The evidence against Tom was compelling, there was nothing I could do.'

'Ah, see, that's not what we've heard,' countered Jimsie. 'We've heard there was a witness who could've cleared Bridget's man, but you didn't call him.'

'He was clearly lying! The jury would never have believed him!'

Henry looked back at Bridget as she jerked her arm free from McCall's grasp. She glared at Henry, knowing instinctively that what Jimsie was saying was the truth, the whole truth and nothing but.

'Bridget, you have to believe me!' Henry was pleading now. 'I did everything I could to keep Tom out of prison.'

'You bastard!' Bridget fired the two words like bullets across the room and lunged, but McCall caught her arms and hauled her back.

'Now, here's the thing,' Jimsie said, his tone still affable. 'Our boss thought Tom was an okay kinda guy and hasn't taken too well to the notion of losing him to Her Majesty's Prison Service. We could report you to the Law Society, but our boss is the impatient sort. He likes instant results, if you know what I mean. So, here's the choice…'

'Choice?'

'There's always a choice, Henry. First we have Mister Side-By-Side here.' Jimsie had cut holes in the pockets of his coat to allow his hands to hold the 20-gauge shotgun, the barrel sawn-off to about a foot in length. He let the folds fall back as he raised the weapon and pointed it straight at the wide-eyed lawyer. McCall had suspected it was there but now that he saw it he was still shocked. There was no need for this, no need at all.

But Jimsie wasn't finished.

'Or we have...' With the 20-gauge held in one hand, he flourished an open razor with his other. The lawyer took a step back, his back flat against the bedroom wall. 'Now, we can either do your legs with the shotgun, which is messy and painful but has the bonus of being quick, or I can have a go at your manhood with the Wilkinson Sword Special Edition. That takes longer, is even messier and nips like buggery.'

McCall wanted to say something but he knew he couldn't. Never show weakness – that could be lethal – even in front of a scumbag like Henry. He'd never have agreed to come along if he'd known what Jimsie had been planning. Give the guy a slap, that was all Rab had said. But this was more than a slap, this was much more.

If Henry had looked towards McCall at that moment he might have detected a slight change in his body language. A stiffening of the shoulders that signified discomfort. He might have realised then that, if he played his cards right, he could have an ally in the room. But Henry didn't look at McCall. He only had eyes for the two weapons in Jimsie's hands. 'You don't honestly expect me to choose between...'

'The clock's ticking, Henry.'

'Come on, you can't.'

'Tick-tock, tick-tock...'

'Look, we're reasonable human beings here!'

'Tick-tock, tick-tock.'

'Can't we sit down and talk about this, for God's sake?'

'Tick-tock, tick-tock... DING! Time's up, caller – it's make your mind up time.'

'Are you off your head? I can't!'

Jimsie lost his patience suddenly and screamed, '*Make up your mind or so help me I'll use both!*'

There was silence while Jimsie held out the shotgun and the razor. Henry looked from one item to the other, before glancing at McCall in a mute appeal for help. But the moment had passed. McCall simply stared back at him. The lawyer gave his would-be lover a pleading stare, but the look in Bridget's eyes told him she was ready to emasculate him with her bare hands. Sweat beaded on his forehead and his upper lip, but it had nothing to do with the temperature. Finally, Henry closed his eyes, swallowed hard and said, almost in a whisper, 'The legs.'

Jimsie nodded, took a couple of steps back. 'Wise choice.'

He didn't give Henry the chance to reconsider. He levelled the 20-gauge, and pulled the trigger once, then again to discharge both barrels. Henry shrieked as his legs were blasted away from under him and he clutched at the wounds as if he could hold back the pain. McCall let go of the woman, expecting her to help the injured man somehow, but she merely stood over him, her eyes leaking fury and hatred, her mouth a snarl as she spat one word.

'Bastard!'

Jimsie closed the razor, shoved the shotgun under his coat again and smiled over at McCall. 'Ain't love grand?'

They didn't waste any time getting out of the flat and back to the car. The shotgun blasts would've attracted attention and they got away from the street as fast as they could without drawing any more. They were confident that neither Henry nor Bridget would give the police any useful information. In their world, that was not done. As he drove, Jimsie rattled a spirited drumbeat on the steering wheel with his hands. McCall watched him, his eyes expressionless.

'What a rush, eh, McCall?' The young man's voice was filled with glee and his eyes sparkled.

McCall's voice was soft. 'Whose idea was that?'

'What? The choice thing? That was mine. Big Rab just wanted

him cut or his legs done, left it up to me. I thought I'd add a wee
flourish by letting old Henry decide. Don't worry, there was no
way I'd've done his balls. No way was I touching another bloke's
tackle.'

McCall felt the muscles in his jaw clamp. Rab knew he wanted
nothing to do with guns. The lawyer needed slapped, sure, and he
would've done it. If Rab had told him that he'd sent the boy out
tooled up, there would've been words. There would be now, anyway.
When Jimsie pulled the trigger he'd felt his gorge rising but he'd
disguised it well. He'd hidden it, just as he'd hidden many things
for many years. Jimsie's 'wee flourish' was also troubling. The boy's
tendency to go over the top was, to McCall, deeply concerning.

'Rab knows I don't like guns,' McCall said, quietly.

'Relax,' said Jimsie. 'It was only loaded with rock salt. It'll've
flayed the hide off him, maybe, but not much else.'

'Don't be getting to enjoy these things, Jimsie,' said McCall, his
voice soft.

'Are you kidding? Bastard is a right scumbag, so he is. He
deserved it.'

'Listen to me, son.' A sharp edge cut into McCall's tone that
made the young man stop short. 'Sometimes in The Life we have
to hurt people. Most of the time they deserve it, other times they
don't. We have to do these things because it's what we do and,
God help us, we're good at it. But never take pleasure in it. The
minute you enjoy it, you're lost.'

Jimsie shrugged. 'Listen, Davie, I like you and I respect you and
all that, but you're no Obi Wan fuckin Kenobi, you know what
I'm saying? You're no my teacher. I don't need you to look out for
me or to guide me – I've got my granddad for all that, okay?'

McCall sat back in his seat, satisfied he'd said his piece but
recognising that what the younger man had said was true. McCall
wasn't his mentor. He wasn't his father. Jimsie was young but he
was a big boy now and he'd learn the hard way that The Life wasn't
fun and games. For some people, the hard way was the only way.

Jimsie watched the traffic ahead and then another thought struck
him. 'Is that what happened to you? Did you get to enjoy it?'

McCall closed his eyes briefly, the images flashing uninvited.

A face…

A voice, pleading…

Screaming…

He forced them from his mind, pushed them into the darkest part of himself, where he knew there were other memories waiting to be released. Over the years he'd become very adept at keeping most of them locked away, but that one kept surfacing and he didn't know why. He turned away, leaving Jimsie's question unanswered.

'Just as I said,' Jimsie commented. 'Taciturn as fuck.'

McCall rested his head on the side window, the glass cool against his forehead, and watched the buildings, the streets and his life slide past.

The words had been painted on the cemetery wall with a brush, not spray-painted, as was usual. There were places where the white emulsion had run and long tails ran down the brickwork, and even as the car sped past McCall and Jimsie could see the brush strokes.

Jimsie asked, 'Who's Dan Miller, d'you know?' McCall shook his head. Jimsie puffed his cheeks and commented, 'Well, whoever he is, he's a dead man…'

McCall watched the words DAN MILLER IS A GRASS recede in the side mirror and wondered who Dan Miller had offended. Then Jimsie turned a corner and they arrived at the taxi office.

It was a low building in an industrial estate near the river. There was space for parking outside, a tall aerial on the roof and a high mesh fence around everything. No-one knew what the fence was for, because none of the local vandals or break-in artists would dare set foot near the place, not if they knew what was good for them. They all knew who owned it.

The heavy front door had been specially strengthened to withstand anything up to a nuclear detonation and the first thing McCall saw when he pushed it open was Stringer's bullet head. McCall may have been an old pal, but he was too much of a

maverick for Rab McClymont's liking. Stringer was Rab's right-
hand man, a powerful bloke of McCall's height whose muscles
started just below his chin and went all the way down to his
ankles. He was going bald, so he shaved what was left of his hair
right down to the scalp and that coupled with the fact he had no
neck made him look like a reject from *Masters of the Universe*.

'He's been waitin for you,' Stringer said in what was virtually
a soliloquy for him. McCall knew he was taciturn, but Stringer
was downright monosyllabic. McCall nodded and headed towards
the office at the back of the building. He wasted no breath at all
on Stringer. He didn't like the man, didn't like his methods, didn't
like the way he preened himself in front of mirrors, baring his
bulging arms to flex and extend his biceps. He knew the feeling
was reciprocated. Stringer had no time for him, mostly because he
was jealous of his long-standing friendship with Rab. McCall
walked past the small kitchen where three cab drivers were enjoying a break. A radio was on and Madonna was singing 'American
Pie'. He preferred the original.

McClymont's hulking frame bulged behind a desk as he studied
the *Daily Record* racing section, the tabloid looking like a
pamphlet in the brickies' hods he used for hands. McClymont was
very dark-haired and by lunchtime he sported a heavy five o'clock
shadow. That and his wide lower jaw made him look like Desperate
Dan. All he needed was a Stetson and a cow pie and *The Dandy*
would've been reaching for a lawyer.

Joseph McClymont was stretched out on a two-seater settee
against one wall, his hands behind his head, staring at the ceiling.
He was as tall as his father but not as thick-set, having inherited
his mother's slim frame. He was eighteen now, a thin-faced, sallow
youth with eyes like black holes that allowed nothing out. McCall
didn't think he'd ever seen the boy laugh. Those dark eyes flicked
his way as he entered, but the youth gave him a barely impercep-
tible nod.

Rab set the paper down on the desktop beside the oscillating
fan that pushed the warm air around then sat back in his swivel
chair, which creaked in protest. 'Joseph, give us a minute, eh?'

Rab shielded his son from how he really made his money, but McCall suspected the lad knew more than he let on. Rab wanted him to go to university and study Law, reasoning that it would do no harm to have a lawyer in the family. Save him on legal bills. Wordlessly, Joseph rose and left the office. McCall was relieved. The boy always unsettled him.

Rab waited until the door was firmly closed before he said, 'How'd it go?'

McCall dropped himself onto a wooden chair opposite the desk while Arrow followed his habit of padding round to let Rab give his ears a rub. 'Fine.'

'He get the message?'

McCall nodded. 'You didn't tell me about the shooter.'

Rab shrugged, stopped scratching the dog's ears and picked up his paper again. 'You didn't need to know.'

McCall felt cold rage build. He didn't like it when Rab spoke to him this way, but it was becoming all too common. Rab had changed over the years, especially since the death of his wife. For that reason, McCall reined himself in, as he had done many times in the past five years, but wondered how long he'd be able to do it. Arrow had returned to his side and stretched out on the floor before he spoke again. 'You should've told me, Rab.'

'You wouldn't've gone.'

'The man would've been just as punished with a slapping.'

Rab laid the paper down and leaned forward again. 'No – he wouldn't. He needed a right message, the liberties he's been taking.'

'Then you didn't need me on it. You could've sent Stringer.'

'I needed you there to make sure the boy didn't go too far.'

McCall saw the logic, even though he didn't like it. Stringer didn't know what too far was. But if Jimsie's 'little flourish' wasn't going too far, he didn't know what was, yet he'd failed to stop it. He wondered if he was losing his touch.

Rab circled a nag's name in the paper and asked, 'How'd Jimsie shape up?'

'He was fine. Talks too much.'

'A fuckin mute talks too much compared to you. I like the boy, though. He's got a lot to live up to. His auld grandfaither was some guy. Still is.'

McCall said nothing. He knew Sammy was 'some guy'. He'd known that since their time together in Barlinnie Prison, years before.

McClymont asked, 'He ready for the big stuff yet?'

'He needs to learn how to get in, get the job done, get out. He's been around Stringer too long.'

'What you got against Stringer, Davie?'

'I don't like him.'

'He does what he's told.'

McCall said nothing and McClymont smiled. Not for the first time, McCall felt the big fellow enjoyed this needle between him and Stringer, even promoted it, perhaps believing it kept them on their toes. That annoyed him. He didn't like to be manipulated like that, especially by an old mate. But then, Rab had stopped being a real mate when the four-wheel drive erupted in flame. He'd stopped being a lot of things then.

'Jerry O'Neill's out,' said McClymont, changing the subject. McCall waited. 'Bastard's still shooting his mouth off. Still sayin I fitted him up for that MacDougall job. Now that Criminal Cases Review Commission has been listenin and he's out on bail pending an appeal.'

McCall remembered very little about the case. O'Neill had been sentenced to fifteen years for his part in a dramatic raid on the home of a successful bookie in 1994. The gang – at least four of them – got away with over two hundred grand, which was never recovered. Only Jerry O'Neill, fingered as the ringleader, came to trial. As soon as he was in jail, McClymont took over his security company, adding it to his already growing list of legitimate enterprises, all showing a profit, all dwarfed by Rab's real moneymaking empire.

'I've heard he's talkin to anyone who'll listen,' said McClymont. 'Tellin lies about me. I need him sorted, Davie.'

'I'll talk to him,' said McCall.

'It'll take more than talking. Take Jimsie.'

McCall looked across the desk, his face blank but his voice firm. He didn't want a repeat of that day's bloodbath. He doubted the lawyer or Bridget would say anything to the police, but it was still reckless. 'I'll talk to him, Rab.'

2

THE WOMAN WAS BLONDE. Not bright and brassy but a soft blonde, a honey blonde. Sometimes she had it tied up in a ponytail, held together by a red ribbon, but today it was long and loose and draped over her shoulders like a shawl. She wore a white t-shirt and a pair of blue denims. She wasn't thin, but there was no way you could say she was fat. She had a figure and it was eye-catching enough to make Jimsie look twice.

She emerged from the closemouth as Jimsie pulled up at the kerb and McCall started to climb out. She nodded to McCall, giving him one of her electric smiles as she passed. Jimsie watched her walk down the street, admiring her curves. 'Oh, man, would you look at that?'

She must have heard him because she stopped, looked back. Jimsie's face reddened but his Glasgow machismo did the talking for him. 'Anytime you're ready, doll. You and me. I'll show you a good time, know what I'm sayin?'

She frowned, took a few paces towards them, her eyes looking the young man over, as if she was appraising him.

'Tell you what, son,' she said. 'Next time I've got ninety seconds to spare, I might take you up on that.'

McCall felt his lips tremble as he fought a grin. Jimsie's mouth flapped open as if he had something else to say but he had nothing. She gave McCall another smile, turned and went on her way. Jimsie watched her go, then gave McCall a sideways glance. When he saw the stung look, McCall couldn't keep the smile at bay. It felt good to smile, he did it less often these days. The young man glared and his voice was subdued when he spoke, 'When'd *she* move in?'

McCall opened the back door to let Arrow out. 'A couple of months ago, the floor above me.'

Jimsie squinted across the roof of the car at McCall. 'She got a name?'

'Everyone's got a name.'

'Aye, so what's hers?'

'Donna. Donna Bernardi.'

Jimsie grinned, 'So you do notice women, eh, McCall?'

McCall frowned back at the boy, 'What's that supposed to mean?'

'You're no the cold fish we all think you are, are you? Don't get me wrong, we don't think you're gay or nothin, but we didn't think you noticed women, that's all.'

The suggestion of a fresh smile flickered at McCall's lips and he glanced back at the figure of the woman walking down the road.

'I'm taciturn, Jimsie, son,' he said. 'Not dead.'

McCall's foot tapped to the beat of 'Bizet Had His Day' by Les Brown and his Band of Renown as he shaped the drawing on the pad. He sat in what had become known as his music room – a bedroom filled with vinyl albums and CDs alongside a stereo system that had cost Joe the Tailor, Davie's old friend and mentor, a considerable sum back in the day. Joe had loved the music of the Rat Pack era and old-fashioned swing music, and young Davie had learned to appreciate it, too. His tastes had broadened in the years since Joe's death, but he still returned to the old albums. He never invited anyone in here, for this room was his fortress of solitude. This was where he could forget The Life and be himself. This was where the bad memories could be kept at bay. Most of the time, anyway.

He had started to draw in prison and continued on his release – people he'd seen that day, places he'd been or seen in photographs. There were a number of Arrow and some of his previous dog, Abe, sketched from memory. There were other drawings, sketches he hardly looked at, all tucked away between the vinyl albums. These were images of the past, faces of the dead, mostly. He didn't need to look at the drawings to remember them. They were there, in the dark recesses of his mind, always waiting to swim to the surface.

His glasses were perched halfway down his nose as he peered at the sketchpad on his lap. In two years he'd be forty, an age he'd never believed he'd see, and as Bobby had once remarked, middle age comes at the cost of eyesight and hairline and replaces them both with love handles. McCall's dark hair was not thinning but it was threaded with grey while his waistline remained trim. But he'd found his eyes needed correction two years before, just for reading and close-up work. No-one knew he wore glasses, though, partly through vanity, partly because the ageing process could be viewed as weakness.

He was working on a country scene, a small white cottage beside a loch and a mountain in the background. It was a typical Highland Scotland scene and he'd drawn it before – lots of times and from different angles – and he knew he'd draw it again. He'd never been further north than Stirling, but there was something about the scene that made him want to find it for real. Maybe some day. Maybe never.

He carefully – lovingly, even – shaded in the side of the mountain with the pencil. When he was finished, he held the pad out at arm's length and studied the drawing over the top of his glasses. It was, to him, a little piece of heaven.

A small TV flickered in the corner, the sound muted, and something on the screen caught his eye. He slipped off his glasses just as a shot of the cemetery wall with the words DAN MILLER IS A GRASS etched in white paint appeared on screen. Then the image cut away to a long shot of police standing around a stretch of wasteground that McCall recognised as the site of a disused factory near the Gallowgate. There were more cops and guys in white overalls studying what looked like a bundle of clothes in the background, but McCall knew it wasn't old togs that were attracting all this attention. Then the picture of a brown-haired man flashed up, obviously police issue because he looked like a mean bastard, as they all did in their mug shots. McCall had never seen the guy before but he didn't need to turn up the sound to find out what this particular news segment was about. He knew instinctively the body on the wasteground was that of Dan Miller. He didn't know if the man had been a grass or not, but someone obviously wanted him out of the way. McCall knew how it would've worked without even being there. Miller would've been lured out by someone he recognised, someone he trusted, and somewhere a third man would've stepped out and shot him. Chances were, the last face he saw was of the man who'd betrayed him. That's what The Life did. It destroyed friendships, it destroyed trust.

He was so very tired of it all.

Voices drifted in from the stairwell outside. He'd heard them a few minutes earlier, a man and a woman, as they passed the door of his flat on their way to the floor above but now there was an edge to them, especially the woman's. He laid his sketchpad on a small coffee table, sat his glasses on top, and stood. Arrow had been stretched out on his side in front of the stacks of albums but as soon as McCall moved he was on his feet and following him out of the room. McCall opened the front door a crack and listened. He couldn't make out the words but he recognised Donna's voice. He motioned Arrow to stay, stepped out and began to ease up the stairs, the words becoming clearer as he grew closer. He halted midway up the first flight and listened.

'No, Peter, I've told you before.' Donna's voice, thin, stretched, trying to be patient.

'You've told me what before?' The man's voice now, East Coast accent, slurred with drink but harsh and edgy. 'You've told me bugger all, darlin. You're still my wife.'

'Not for much longer…'

'You'll always be my wife, darlin. Because we were made for each other, you know that. Always and forever.'

McCall was still out of sight and could not see Donna's face, but the silence that followed the man's statement spoke volumes. Finally she spoke, her voice weary and hurt and sad. 'Go away, Peter. Go away and don't bother me again. Get it through your head – you and me are finished.'

'No, sweetheart, we're not finished. Not until I say it. Now, you going to let me in?'

'No.'

'Let me in. I'll no try nothin, honest.'

Her voice was firm. 'No, Peter.'

The man's voice hardened. 'Let me bloody well in.'

'*No!*'

McCall could tell from the strained tone and the soft rustles and grunts that events had taken a more physical turn, so he picked up his pace and took the stairs two at a time. On the landing he saw a tall, blond-haired man with his shoulder to Donna's door. Donna had wedged her body against the wood, blocking him. The man had a lopsided grin on his face and was unsteady on his feet. Then he lost patience and lashed out, his hand darting through the gap to catch Donna across the cheek. The sound of the slap shot around the landing, echoing from the china tiles on the walls. Rage splashed in Donna's eyes as she jerked open the door and flew at him, her own fists balled. The man was taken unawares and she landed a solid blow to his cheek. He swore again, took a step back, his hand darting to his already reddening face. Donna swung the other fist but he jerked out of reach and raised his own hand again.

McCall leaped across the few feet between them, grabbed the man by the shoulder and wrenched him round, placing his body between them. The man swore in surprise, sending a cloud of whisky breath wafting in McCall's direction. McCall reeled back and pushed him away to arm's length.

'Who the fuck are you?' asked the blonde man.

'Someone who's asking you to leave,' McCall replied.

'Bugger off.'

'Mister McCall...' began Donna.

The man shot an accusing glance over McCall's shoulder at Donna. 'You shagging him? That it? He your boyfriend?'

'He's a neighbour, Peter.' Her voice was sharp and cut through the air between them like a blade.

'He just being right neighbourly then? That what it is, big man? You some sort of Neighbourhood Watch?'

The door behind Peter opened a crack and he whirled round, thrusting his face at the old woman peering out. 'Fuck you lookin at?'

'It's okay, Mrs Mitchell,' McCall said gently to the old woman. 'Go back inside.'

The door swiftly closed again.

'I think you should just go, pal,' said McCall, quietly.

'Bugger off, you,' said Peter again, stepping forward. 'I'm talkin to my wife.'

McCall stepped in his way. The man stopped and McCall knew he was contemplating throwing a punch. He always knew.

'Don't do it,' McCall warned, but he saw the look bleed from Peter's eyes into his face, saw his jaw set, his teeth grit and felt electricity pulse through the air. A great calm washed over McCall and his flesh turned cold. The area around Peter – the landing, the stairway, Mrs Mitchell's door – all faded into shadow until only the man himself was clear. There was a roaring in McCall's ears, like the tide on shingle, and he knew he was ready.

When the man lunged forward, one fist swinging, McCall had already stepped aside. He grabbed Peter by the hair with his left hand while the fingers of his right bunched into a club. He jerked the man's head back and raised the fist ready to bring it crashing down in a single, nose-shattering blow.

Then he heard Donna's voice saying, 'Don't.'

Just that one word, not very loud – more than a breath but not yet a whisper – but it was enough. The roar faded, the heat returned to his flesh. McCall checked the thrust of his hand and hurled the man's body back across the landing.

'You bastard!' Peter snarled as he rubbed his scalp. 'I'll fuckin kill you!'

'Go home Peter,' Donna ordered. 'Sleep it off, for God's sake.'

'The bastard pulled my hair! He pulled my fuckin hair! What are you, some sort of poof? That it, eh? Gonnae scratch my eyes out next?'

'Listen to her, Peter,' said McCall, his voice even. 'Go home and sleep it off. You don't want to do this anymore, believe me.'

Peter's eyes narrowed, something in McCall's voice, or his stillness, warning him that this was not a man to mess with. He nodded but could not resist a final verbal volley.

'This doesn't end here, mate,' he said. 'We'll talk again, you and me, and next time it'll no end with some hair pullin.' The man didn't wait for a reply. He turned and reached out with an unsteady hand for the hand rail.

McCall shot a glance at Donna. Her eyes still shone with rage as she watched her husband descend. Her fists remained clenched and he had no doubt that she was prepared to land a couple if he turned back. Suddenly he felt self-conscious, as if he had intruded.

'I'd better make sure he doesn't fall and hurt himself,' he said quietly, but he didn't know if she heard him.

McCall kept a safe distance between them in case Peter decided to try for a rematch. He really didn't want to hurt him. It was a slow business, for the man found the mixture of drink and stone steps difficult to cope with. He cursed to himself as he finally reached the ground floor landing, stumbling on the final step before he staggered out into the evening sun. He halted again, framed in the closemouth, and looked up and down the street as if he didn't know which way to go.

'You want me to call a taxi?' McCall shouted and the man turned to peer into the gloom of the close.

'Sod off,' he said, then lurched away in that carefully haphazard way drunks have when they think they're walking in a straight line.

McCall was giving Arrow a brush when someone knocked at the door. He thought nothing of it – in his line of business, it was not unusual for him to have late-night callers. However, when he opened the door he found Donna giving him a nervous little smile. She had changed her clothes, pulled back her hair and put on some make-up. Not much, just enough to cover the redness around her eyes.

'I didn't thank you properly,' she said. 'For what you did.'

McCall didn't know what to say so he just stood there as Donna lifted her arm slightly to reveal a bottle of wine.

'I thought I'd give you this, as a way of saying thanks,' she said, but McCall shook his head slightly.

'I don't drink,' he said. 'And there's no need to thank me.'

There was an awkward pause. Finally, he remembered his manners.

'Do you want to come in for a minute?'

The smile in her eyes told him she did.

'It's the old story – married too young and to the wrong guy. Took me twelve years to realise it, though.'

She sat in one of his armchairs, her wine in a tumbler because he didn't own any proper wine glasses. Arrow had stretched out like a rug in his usual place before the gas fire, even though it wasn't on, and was snoring softly. McCall hadn't asked her about Peter, but she volunteered the information anyway. Maybe she felt she owed him an explanation. Maybe she just wanted to talk about it.

'Don't get me wrong, he was all that was wonderful at first. He was good-looking, had prospects – his dad owned a car showroom in Edinburgh, selling top-of-the-range Mercs. And he was fun to be with. He was funny, you know? Always had me laughing. Laughed me right into bed, truth be told. So we got married and everything was fine. Had a nice house in the suburbs, garden, friends, barbecues in the summer, all that stuff. But then the showroom hit a rocky patch and they lost the Mercedes franchise. The firm went bust and Peter... well, he took it hard. That was when the drinking started. He's no alcoholic, don't get me wrong, but he liked the stuff a bit too much. He got a good job with a bigger firm and I worked in a call centre for an insurance company. But when he got to drinking, it brought out another side to him. You ever seen that happen?'

McCall nodded. He knew what drink could do.

'So I put up with it for about three years before I decided one day I'd had enough. I packed my bag, quit my job and moved to Glasgow. And everything was all right for a few months. But Peter – God knows how – tracked me down. So I moved and he found me again. This is my third flat in nine months. And here he is again.'

She shook her head, drained the tumbler and reached out to the bottle lying on the floor at her feet to fill it again. McCall saw the cork bobbing up and down inside. In addition to not owning any wine glasses, he also did not possess a corkscrew, so the cork had been shoved down the neck with the handle of a spoon, which was yet another thing to be embarrassed about.

'Did he hit you?' McCall asked.

'No. He's never laid a hand on me, I'll give him that. Until today, anyway. I'd've given him what for if he had.'

McCall nodded. He had no doubt she would've given as good as she got, he'd seen that upstairs. That was one of the reasons he'd waded in. Violence takes its toll, can leave a person drained, if they're not used to it.

A shy little smile made her look down when she thought about what had happened upstairs. 'I've got three brothers and my dad didn't know what to do with a girl, so he treated me like a boy. His reasoning was that there were a lot of creeps out there and it wouldn't do me any harm to be able to throw a punch or two.'

'He taught you well.'

'Yeah,' she said, still a little ashamed. 'You should see me spit and scratch myself.' She took a sip of wine, regarded him again over the rim of the tumbler. 'What about you? You ever been married?'

'No.'

'Why not?'

McCall shifted uneasily in his chair. 'The opportunity never arose.'

'Find that hard to believe,' she said as she looked around the room. 'You've got a nice place here. You keep it very tidy.'

McCall gazed around him. He had never thought of the flat as being nice. But now, with Donna here, he saw it differently. It *was* nice. Most of it had been put in place by Vari, a woman he'd lived with for a few years. But she left because he could not give her what she wanted.

And then there were the memories.

I can't compete with a ghost.

Vari's voice, echoing down the years.

Then the flash of a knife in a man's hand and green eyes, accusing him.

You could have saved me.

Audrey's voice this time, even though she had never spoken the words. But her eyes had, as she died in his arms while the wind whipped up a grey sea to mix salt water with the blood that streamed from her throat...

'What do you do for a living, Davie?' Donna's voice banished the memories. He was thankful.

'This and that,' he replied.

'Self-employed?'

'Sort of.'

'Doing what?'

'Odd jobs, I suppose you'd call them.'

'Like a handyman?'

'Something like that.'

Another memory, another day.

A housing scheme in the East End, a ground floor flat, a dark room, his hand swinging a hammer and the sound of metal striking flesh and breaking bone and the man screaming and screaming and screaming...

'Well,' said Donna, 'if ever I need a plug fitted, I know who to call.' She glanced quickly at the clock on the wall and said, 'Listen, it's getting a bit late. I'd better head back upstairs.'

She laid the tumbler on the table beside her and walked to the front door. McCall opened the door but she paused on the doorstep.

'Thanks again for the help with Peter,' she said.

'I didn't do anything. You could've handled him.'

'True. But thanks anyway.'

He nodded acceptance but felt he had to say something else.

'I'm sorry about not having a corkscrew,' said McCall and she turned again, still smiling.

'That's okay,' she said, 'next time I'll bring a screwtop.' Then she started to climb the stairs and McCall closed the door. He leaned against the wood, listening to her footsteps climbing the stone steps to her own flat. Arrow had followed them up the hallway, probably expecting a walk because it was round about that time, and he sat before McCall, his tail wagging. McCall looked down at him.

Next time, she had said. *Next time.*

There couldn't be a next time.

Donna's flat was in darkness when she entered so she switched on a table lamp before moving to the window. She looked down at the street and saw the car parked at the opposite kerb. There was someone inside and although she couldn't make out exactly who, she knew they would be watching her closely. Donna nodded, just once, then reached up and drew the curtains together.

It was cooler in the moonlight, but that's all you could say about it. McCall walked the streets, Arrow at his side, enjoying the drop in temperature but knowing it was still too warm for sleep, knowing he'd toss and turn in bed, even with the covers thrown off. And in the night, in that strange half-world between being awake and being asleep, the memories would reign supreme and he couldn't face them. He could never face them. He enjoyed the city streets after dark, always had done, and as he walked along Duke Street he felt the stress and care of the day slide off. He passed by the café once owned by Luca Vizzini, a man who had once been a friend but who changed. It was still owned by his widow, but operated by a man who once worked for Luca.

It brought Joe Klein to mind. It always did.

Davie was fifteen when Joe Klein – Joe the Tailor, they called him – took him under his wing, became the closest thing he had to a father. He was a crook, certainly, but he'd had a sense of honour, a set of rules that he ensured Davie followed. Don't hurt women. Don't hurt children. Don't hurt civilians. Davie added his own – don't use knives or guns. He'd upheld them all, but it hadn't been easy. The Life had changed over the years, become meaner, more violent, less discriminating. Rab, under Luca's tutelage, had been at the forefront of that change and McCall struggled against the excesses, but it was a losing battle. Jimsie's antics with the lawyer were just an example of how The Life was turning ever more bloody. There had always been firearms, but in the ten years since McCall had left prison, there seemed to be more and more of them. Five years before there had been an explosion of gun violence in the city and Rab had been at its centre. He paid a hefty price for it – his wife, Bernadette, their four-year-old daughter and their unborn child. All three dead in a bomb blast.

Davie, too, had paid the price of being part of The Life. His mother, murdered by his own father, Joe the Tailor, shot to death, friends like Mouthy Grant and Kid Snot, both gunned down, although their talkative natures lived on in Jimsie.

And Audrey, of course, dying on a windswept harbour.

He walked the streets with his dog and their ghosts walked with him.

3

MCCALL LAID THE two big tins of paint on the concrete floor of the
store room and stepped into the small yard where Bobby Newman
already sat in one of two folding canvass chairs, his face tilted up
to the sun. McCall dropped into the empty chair and raised his
own head to the light, feeling its warmth. Bobby nudged his arm
and held out a can of Irn-Bru. McCall sipped the sparkling drink,
feeling the cold liquid snapping at the back of his throat. *The
nectar of the gods*, Joe used to call it.

'Thanks for that, Davie,' said Bobby, wiping his mouth with
the back of his hand and jerking his head to the tins of paint piled
beyond the open door. 'I'd've been all morning unloading that
bastard.'

McCall had arrived at the decorators' yard just as Bobby had
driven up in his white transit filled with paint and wallpaper. He'd
known Bobby since primary school and together they had
rampaged through the city streets as part of Joe the Tailor's young
team, along with Rab. But just after Davie was released from jail,
Bobby got out of The Life. He'd met a straight arrow – Connie, a
primary school teacher – and he wanted to leave it all behind. He
took over his uncle's painting and decorating store on Duke Street,
had a little girl on whom he doted, and lived the life of an honest
man. Part of Davie McCall envied his old friend. A big part.

'You hear about Choccie Barr?' McCall hadn't heard anything
but he was unsurprised that Bobby had. He may have been out of
The Life but he still had a vast array of contacts who fed him all
kinds of information. Choccie Bar had been one of Rab's guys, but
he'd sold out to a rival. McCall shook his head and Bobby continued, 'He's dead. A DIY incident – somebody left a screwdriver in
his eye. He'd surfaced again, the dick, and he must've been
spotted. Was found in a hotel car park in Kelso, of all places. What
the hell he was doing there is anyone's guess.'

Neither of them mourned the man's passing, for what he'd
done was unforgiveable, even though he'd never intended the final
outcome. He was the man who'd wired Rab's Range Rover to

explode. But it all went wrong and the blast took out Bernadette and little Lucia. McCall had been there and it was yet another memory that would never leave him.

Bobby took a sip from his can and said, 'So what's on your mind, Davie?' McCall knew Bobby would suss there was something he wanted to discuss. Old pals always knew.

'I want out, Bobby,' said McCall.

'Out The Life?'

'Aye. I've had enough.'

Bobby nodded, having expected this for some time. 'What's brought this on?'

'Been thinking about it for a while.'

'You told Rab yet?'

McCall shook his head.

'Won't be easy,' Bobby went on. 'He relies on you.'

'Too much.'

'Maybe, but he didn't force you to be one of the boys. You chose that, Davie.'

McCall nodded, knowing what Bobby said was true.

Then Bobby said, 'This about that Spencer thing?'

And McCall was back in that run down housing scheme, in that ground floor flat, in that depressing front room and the man was screaming...

'Cos you did everyone a favour there, know what I mean?' Bobby was saying. 'He was a wee scumbag. Deserved everything he got.'

'I know.'

'Then why beat yourself up about it?'

McCall had asked himself the same question hundreds of times. Spencer was not the sort of creature he should lose sleep over, but there he was, popping into his head when he least expected it, creeping into his dreams, his screams filling his thoughts. Of all the people McCall had hurt over the years, why did it have to be a little pervert like Spencer that made him feel guilty?

'Because I enjoyed it, Bobby. I always told myself that I was the kind of person I was expected to be – I'm Danny McCall's son, after all. I did what I did because I was born to it. I never took any pleasure in it; it just had to be done. That was the only way I could cope. But then I'm asked to deal with Spencer and I get this thrill when I'm doing him.'

Bobby listened to the speech and nodded in understanding, then said, 'Right, first off, take a sook of your Irn-Bru because your throat'll be dry after all that speaking. It's no used to that sort of treatment.'

McCall smiled and swallowed some of the soft drink as instructed.

'Okay,' Bobby went on, 'you're Danny McCall's boy, that's true. But that doesn't mean you have to be like him. You're your own man, Davie – you do what you want to do. Okay, maybe the violence is in the genes, but you were never really like your da. Never. You can put that aside. So you're sick of The Life. You should be. So you want to get out. Get out. Listen though – you're the only one who can get yourself out. It'll no be easy. Rab never did like people leavin him, but hey, it's no the Mafia. You're no gonnae be sleepin with the fishes if you want to leave the family.'

'It's not that easy,' said McCall, shaking his head. 'The only way I could ever be really free of it is if I left the city, went up north maybe, found myself a new life. Somewhere away from people, in the country.' He paused. 'My own wee piece of heaven.'

'So what's stopping you?'

McCall hesitated, knowing his answer was something he had never said to anyone in his life. But if he could not admit it to Bobby, who could he admit it to?

'Because I'm scared.'

'Of what?'

McCall paused, stared at the empty can in his hand. 'What if I can't change? What if this is all I can be?'

Jerry O'Neill was a big man with thick brown hair that always looked like it needed combed. No matter what he did, it looked untidy. He'd tried gel, he'd tried his wife's mousse, but it beat everything modern hair technology could throw at it. He even tried cutting it short, but all it did then was stick up like he'd had an electric shock. He was forever being told what a fine head of hair he had for a man of his age and he should be glad to have it, but to him it was a curse. It got everywhere, and his wife constantly complained about lifting long strands from the bottom of the shower or hooking clumps from the plughole.

That hair was laced with grey now. Those grey hairs hadn't been there six years before, when he went into prison, but they were there now. Every time he looked in a mirror he told himself that McClymont had given him those grey hairs. McClymont took his business away from him. McClymont took his life away from him. Six years may not seem much, but it was too long to be sitting in a prison cell when you're innocent.

He was angry as he spat these words out at McCall while they stood at the gate of the neat little terraced house in Barlanark. Jimsie sat in the car, waiting for the nod from McCall to come and do some damage. McCall had no intention of nodding.

'I know who you are, McCall,' O'Neill said. 'I know what you're capable of. But you don't scare me.'

McCall remained silent. He knew the man was a little nervous. He could tell by the way his knuckles shone white as he gripped the top of the gate and the flood of words from his mouth.

'You see this house? We don't even own it. We rent it. And my wife has to work in a bloody pub at night and a nursing home during the day to pay the rent. We used to have a nice villa in Bearsden, a garden, a garage, the lot. We lost all that when I was convicted cos we couldn't keep up the payments. Your pal McClymont took all that, him and his bent cop mate.'

Bent cop, McCall noted. Had to be Jimmy Knight. The Black Knight, they called him. They'd crossed each other more than once in the past and he'd suspected for a few years now that Big Rab had some kind of professional arrangement.

O'Neill was still talking. 'And for six years nobody listened to me. I was just another bitter crook who got caught. Well, let me tell you something, they're listening now, all right. The Criminal Case Review Commission, the police, the press. The lot of them.

And I'm gonnae bring your pal down, McCall. I don't care how many thugs like you he sends to scare me off. I'm not giving up.'

He stopped as the front door opened and a young girl, maybe ten years of age, ran down the path. Her face bore echoes of her father's. Same lustrous hair, same brown eyes.

'Dad, dad,' she said, taking O'Neill's hand and giving it a slight tug. 'Mum says you've to come in for your dinner.'

McCall looked back at the house and saw a woman staring nervously through the front window at him. She was tall and slim with deep worry lines around her eyes and mouth which made her already sharp features even more severe.

'You tell him what I've said, McCall,' O'Neill said. 'Tell him he fitted up the wrong man when he went for me.'

McCall turned back to the car. Jimsie glanced at him as he climbed into the passenger's seat, waiting for the word that never came. The younger man sighed and twisted the ignition. Back at the gate, Jerry O'Neill watched them pull away, the little girl's hand still nestling in his.

'I don't get it, Davie,' said Jimsie, wiping the condensation from the side of his beer glass with his forefinger. 'We were sent to warn the guy off and all you did was pass the time of day with him. What's that all about?'

McCall remained silent, watching the door of the pub. Jimsie had declared he was hungry so they had come in and bought a couple of pies, a pint for Jimsie and a bottle of still water for McCall. McCall had never been in this particular pub before and experience had taught him to be wary of the unknown. From where he sat he could see both the front door and a fire exit to the rear. It seemed quiet enough, with only an elderly couple in one corner and a young guy playing the fruit machine in the other. There was one other customer, a middle-aged guy in a denim jacket with a comb-over that looked like someone had taped a handful of rattails to his head. McCall didn't like the way the man stared at them as he whispered into a mobile phone.

Jimsie asked, 'So what do we tell Big Rab? He'll be pissed.'

'I'll deal with Rab.'

'Yeah, that makes me feel a whole lot better.'

McCall sipped his water as he watched the door and comb-over man sitting beside it.

'I mean, we were sent to do a job, right?' Jimsie was still rabbiting and spraying bits of food across the table in the process. 'And we didn't do it. Big Rab will be pissed, Davie, believe me. He will be *pissed*.'

The double doors opened and sunlight flooded the shadowy interior of the pub. McCall saw two men silhouetted against the glare, then the doors swung closed again. One of the newcomers was in his mid-twenties, of average height, his hands thrust into the pockets of a brown leather bomber jacket. His brown hair was long, stringy and apparently a stranger to shampoo. His eyes were narrow and decidedly shifty, while his single eyebrow grew in a straight line above a long nose. His features were sharp, his mouth seemed set in a permanent giggle and what little chin he had was pockmarked with stubble. His face was covered in acne like a dot-to-dot puzzle. McCall reckoned he was not about to win any beauty contests.

The other man was more presentable; tall and well-built, wearing a smart green Italian-cut suit, with a face that wouldn't look out of place in a TV advert for razors. It was square and tanned and framed by a carefully groomed head of short dark hair. He looked at comb-over man, who nodded in McCall's direction before hurriedly downing what was left of his pint and darting out the door.

Jimsie paid no attention to the newcomers. He looked at McCall's plate and asked, 'You gonnae eat your pie?'

McCall did not answer but fixed his eyes on the two men as they sauntered across the bar room towards them.

'Davie – are you gonnae eat your pie?'

'Jimsie,' McCall said simply, and the young man looked up as the men stopped at their table.

Italian suit man smiled broadly at them, showing a neat line of dentistry.

'Enjoying the food, lads?'

'Tasted worse,' replied Jimsie. 'What are you, the food critic from *The Herald*?'

'I can be your worst fuckin nightmare, sonny boy,' said the man, but his smile didn't falter, nor did his eyes leave McCall.

'I don't know about that,' said Jimsie. 'I've got a recurring dream about Maggie Thatcher, a French Maid's outfit and a pair of handcuffs that wakes me up screaming.'

The man dragged his eyes away from McCall long enough to study Jimsie.

'Why don't you shut the fuck up, son? Let the big folk talk, okay?'

Jimsie shrugged and settled back in his seat, aiming for a relaxed look, but McCall knew he was tense. The young man's hands rested on the tabletop but his fingers trembled slightly. McCall felt his own heart beat a little faster and his stomach begin to churn, but he forced himself to remain perfectly still as he watched the man in the suit hitch up the legs of his trousers, sit on a stool and take care in arranging the fall of the material so that the razor-sharp crease remained intact. He cleared the table of debris before placing his suited elbows on the surface and leaning forward to face them. His rat-faced friend stood to the side and a little behind, his hands still deep inside his jacket pockets. McCall wondered what he had in those pockets apart from his fingers.

Italian suit gave them a wide grin. 'You're Davie McCall, right?'

McCall stared back at him and waited. He could deny his name but it wouldn't do any good. Something was coming and he could almost smell the blood in the air. He carefully positioned his feet in readiness to spring up if he had to.

Italian suit asked, 'Do you know who I am?'

McCall kept his voice low and even, 'You mean apart from his worst nightmare?'

'My name's Joe Rafferty.'

'Congratulations.'

'Billy Rafferty was my brother. D'you remember Billy Rafferty?'

McCall made no effort to reply.

'Let me jog your memory. Eight months ago, the Blind Man pub, you cornered him in the toilet and gave him a kicking. And I don't mean a wee slapping, I mean a kicking. And d'you know what? You gave him such a kicking that he suffered brain damage. He cannae even feed himself now, no without help. Twenty-nine years of age and the boy's a turnip. You did that.'

McCall shook his head.

'Wasn't me.'

'You must have a double then.'

'That's very nice of you, make mine a Glenmorangie,' chimed in Jimsie, a big smile on his face. Rafferty, his own smile gone, turned his head slightly to gaze at the younger man.

'Don't make me tell you again, son. Shut the fuck up.'

McCall said, 'You've got the wrong guy, pal. I've never met a Billy Rafferty.'

Rafferty looked back at him. 'S'funny that, everybody said it was you that crept up behind him while he was taking a pish, hit him with an old chair leg then kicked and stamped on his head while he was down. They all say it was Davie McCall.'

'They're all wrong.'

'You expect me to believe that?'

McCall shrugged. He didn't really expect this guy to believe anything he said. Rafferty was out for blood and he wouldn't be satisfied until he got it. He stood up and smoothed the creases from his suit. 'I think maybe we should go for a wee walk. What do you say?'

'What if I said no?'

Rafferty nodded to Rat Face, who partially withdrew one hand from his jacket to reveal the dark metal of an automatic pistol.

'We would have to insist,' said Rafferty.

McCall's mind ran through all the variables. The pub was an enclosed space and controllable, but there were witnesses and that was dangerous. Sure, they could be made to button it, but all it took was one Boy Scout. McCall had never liked threatening straight arrows, although he'd done it on occasion. It always left a bad taste in his mouth. No, whatever went down had to happen outside, away from civilians.

He suspected Rafferty and his pal would take them somewhere

secluded, making either him or Jimsie drive while the other was watched closely. And once in that lonely place, they'd put one in each of their heads. That was the way it was done and, as it turned out, that would play right into McCall's hands.

He felt the chill settle on his flesh and the world around him began to slow. The pub, the patrons, the sound of the TV and the fruit machine all faded, replaced by the sound of surf. All he saw were the two men, bright against the gloom. All he heard was Rafferty's voice through the tidal roar.

'Let's go, lads,' said Rafferty. 'We'll take your motor, shall we?'

McCall almost smiled.

'What? Me too?' Asked Jimsie.

'Aye, you too.'

'What did I do? I've never met your brother.'

'Because you're a fuckin comedian, okay? And I don't like comedians.'

'No? Then why don't you put a bullet in your pal's face there, cos it's as funny as fuck.'

Rat Face stepped forward to say something, but Rafferty held up his hand, shook his head. His voice was soft as he said to Jimsie, 'Don't make this difficult, son. There's civilians here – let's not get them involved, eh?'

McCall jerked his head to Jimsie and they all stood. McCall led the way, feeling the heat blast his face as he exited, and turned right towards the alleyway. The street was empty of pedestrians, which was a good thing. The roaring in his ears had died away and he could now hear everything with crystal-clear clarity – the traffic to his left, the footsteps of the men behind, Jimsie's elevated breathing. The boy was nervous but he'd follow his lead, of that he was confident. All McCall needed was a momentary diversion and he knew he'd get that as soon as they reached the car.

The Rover was in the shadow of the pub building, the windows open. McCall reached for the door handle but was stopped by Rafferty's hand on his arm.

'Allow me, mate,' he said, agreeably. 'Wouldn't want you to reach in and pull out something nasty, eh?'

McCall shrugged and stepped back. Rafferty grinned and opened the door.

With a snarl, Arrow hit him full in the chest, sending him flying back, just as McCall knew he would. Jimsie moved immediately, throwing himself at the man as he sprawled in the dirt. McCall jerked his elbow into Rat Face's nose then whirled and clamped his left fist over his gun hand, preventing him from drawing the weapon. He kicked the man's legs from under him and followed him down, snapping three quick punches into his nose. The man squirmed on the ground, trying to free the weapon, but McCall retained his firm grip. He rammed his knee hard between Rat Face's legs. Rat Face's eyes bulged and a thin squeal escaped his lips. Another thrust with his knee and McCall felt the grip on the gun relax sufficiently for him to ease it from the man's pocket. He stood, the weapon held loosely in one hand, while the man rolled over both hands holding his aching balls. Jimsie was doing a Riverdance number on Rafferty, who had curled up like a hedge-hog to escape the kicking. Arrow had the cuff of a trouser leg in his teeth and shook it like a rat. McCall wondered if Rafferty would be more pained by the battering he was taking from Jimsie or the damage to his suit.

'Enough, Jimsie,' McCall said and Jimsie, who had been drawing his foot back for another kick, froze. Sorrowfully, he lowered his leg.

Jimsie asked, 'Did you really do that boy's brother, Davie?'

McCall stared at the young man. He looked sad.

'There's a lot of things I've done that I've never done,' he said.

4

THEY THREW RAT FACE's gun into the Clyde from a secluded wharf between Anderston and Partick and Davie told Jimsie to drop him off at the Mitchell Library. Surprisingly, Jimsie made no comment. He'd been very quiet in the car since they left the men lying in the dirt of the alleyway. Davie put his silence down to the close-quarter violence. Using the 20-gauge on the lawyer, that was remote, in a way. But getting up close and personal, feeling your opponent's skin under your hands and their breath in your face, smelling the blood mixing with their body odour, that was something different. McCall was unaffected by it. He was used to it.

He felt out of place in the huge domed building overlooking the M8. It wasn't the silence that got to him – actually, he quite liked that – it was just that he felt libraries weren't for people like him. They were for people who had an interest in the world, in history, in life. McCall read books, he didn't know anyone in The Life who didn't. Most of them picked up the habit in jail. But he felt daunted being in a place that was all about books. Not that he was there to read any. He knew he was going to have to find out more about Jerry O'Neill. He didn't know why, wouldn't have been able to explain it to young Jimsie at all, but he knew this was something he had to do.

So instead of going back to Big Rab's office and reporting in, he had the boy drop him off at the city's main reference library and made his way to the room that housed the newspaper records.

A dark-haired woman leaned over him as she showed him how to operate the microfilm screen. Her perfume was delicate and pleasing but he felt uncomfortable with her being so close. He leaned away as she threaded the cumbersome film into the viewer and showed him how to spool it on. He waited until she'd left before he self-consciously put on his glasses.

The days sped past his eyes as McCall wound the handle. Type blurred, the world whipped by in black and white and colour, until he reached the first report of the MacDougall raid. And as he read, he began to remember the case; his memory kicking in with details he thought he had forgotten. One very nasty detail made Davie both sick and angry.

In order to bring pressure on MacDougall, they raped his wife and threatened his daughter. Davie knew then that he wasn't going to let this lie.

After half an hour he sat back in his chair and stared at the screen, not really seeing the type and pictures in front of him. Something wasn't quite right about the whole thing. McCall knew fit-ups took place. Cops lied in court, evidence was planted, statements invented, witnesses coerced or bribed into speaking up for things they had never seen or heard, all to ensure the guilty were punished. One senior cop had even admitted it once, calling the lies fellow officers told 'pious perjury'. The problem was, sometimes it wasn't the guilty who were punished. The other side – Davie's side – could do the same to suit their needs – in other words, to ensure the guilty got off scot-free. Lies and half-truths were the way of the world, everyone on the streets knew that.

He had also heard the stories about Big Rab; that he was a regular grass, that he was protected by police officers who relied on him for information, that he used those same police officers to further his own business interests. That was pretty standard stuff, for there was no honour amongst thieves – they each would grass one another up without a second thought if it was to their advantage. And yet, informers were hated and dealt with harshly, as the luckless Dan Miller found to his cost. If he really was a grass, of course, because McCall didn't believe everything he read. Accusing someone of being an informer, making it the writing on the wall, didn't make it so. It could simply be that someone wanted him out of the way. Permanently. And to accuse him of grassing was one way to justify a killing. As for Rab, McCall had never fully believed all the stories he'd heard. He'd told Jimsie that there were a lot of things he'd done that he'd not actually done. Rab was the same.

He stared at the report of O'Neill's sentencing. One name had leaped out at him. A name he knew well. He wasn't surprised to see it.

'So you don't think the talk did much good?'

Jimsie shook his head as Big Rab frowned and sipped coffee from a mug that looked like part of a child's tea set in his huge mitts. The boy felt uncomfortable, not just because he was facing the big man alone, but also because he was talking about McCall. Big Rab paid the wages, but McCall was a mate – and his grand-dad always told him to protect his mates.

'I told McCall it would take more than a telling with that bastard,' said McClymont. 'Where is he now?'

'Who? O'Neill?'

'No, fuckwit – McCall. Where'd he go?'

'Dunno,' said Jimsie, keeping it vague. 'I dropped him off in the town.' He didn't know why Davie had to go the library, but he sensed it wasn't something he should tell Rab. He already felt he'd said too much. He was used to Big Rab being like a bear with a burnt arse but there was a deeper scowl than usual on his coupon today. Davie not giving that guy a slap had obviously pissed him right off.

'The town?' Rab said, his lip curling a little. 'What was he doin? Getting his Christmas shopping done early?'

Jimsie cleared his throat. He was growing more uncomfortable by the second. He didn't like being questioned and he didn't like the notion that he was somehow letting his mate down by answering those questions. 'Never said. Don't think it would've done me much good to ask. You know Davie.'

Big Rab nodded, Jimsie's answer obviously making sense. He sighed, waved his hand towards the door, his tone smoothing a little. 'Aye, right – I know Davie. I'll speak to him later. Away you go, son. I'll phone you later if I need anything else done.'

Jimsie nodded and left the office as quickly as his manly pride would allow. Big Rab sipped his coffee again and thought about McCall. He was worried about the man, worried about the way he'd been acting lately. There was a time when he would've skelped O'Neill without even thinking twice, let alone break sweat. Now he was having a conversation with the guy and then swanning off into the town on an errand.

Davie was his mate and he and Bobby Newman had both been there for him after Bernadette and his wee Lucia had been murdered. Bernadette had always liked Davie, maybe too much, Rab suspected. He'd seen the little looks, the sly glances, the touch that lasted just that little bit too long. Davie was a good looking guy. There were lots of women who wanted him, not that he ever seemed to care. Apart from that reporter lassie, Audrey. She'd got to him, got under his skin and taken root. Rab had been there when she died, throat cut by Davie's own father. That had shocked even him – and Rab had done many a thing himself. Then there was Vari. That lasted a few years and Rab thought Davie would settle down, as had Bernadette. She'd seemed genuinely pleased when Vari had moved into the Sword Street flat with Davie. But that fell apart, too. Lately, Davie had been unusually quiet; ever since the Spencer thing. Now this. There was something far from right about the whole set-up, but Rab was buggered if he knew what it was.

He picked up his mobile phone, pressed a button then waited until he heard a familiar voice answer.

'I think we have a problem,' said McClymont.

5

MCCALL SAT IN THE dark of a room that smelled of cheap whisky and damp walls listening to the soft snores of the man in the crumpled bed. He wondered if he should shake him awake but decided against it. He was enjoying the peace and quiet of this gloomy little room, even though the sound of traffic rose up in a cloud of fumes from Dumbarton Road beyond the curtained window. Arrow lay on the threadbare rug, his face on his two front paws. McCall reached down to stroke him, enjoying the silky feel of his fur, and Arrow's head lifted to look at him, then laid back down. He was used to waiting.

Eventually the man stirred and turned onto his side. His eyes opened and he saw McCall watching him from the torn armchair. He did not seem surprised or frightened, or even perturbed. One moment he was asleep, the next he was awake and reaching out to his bedside table to hook a fag from a pack of Embassy tipped. Slipping it between his lips, he sat up, picked up a box of matches and struck a light. He drew the smoke in deeply and held it in his lungs as if he didn't want to let it go before almost grudgingly breathing it out. Then he began to cough, a rasp that rattled from his chest to come to a liquid halt in his throat. McCall still waited.

'You can get lifted for breaking and entering,' said Donovan, his voice hoarse.

'Phone the police then.'

Donovan took another long draw on his cigarette. 'I would, but it's too much effort.' He waved a dismissive hand, cleared his throat. 'Take what you want.'

McCall smiled. 'You always sleep this late in the afternoon?'

'This is the crack of dawn for me. What do you want, McCall?'

'You gonnae get up? I don't like holding a conversation with a man in his jammies.'

'Just think of me like that French writer – the one that never got out of bed.'

'Porno writer, was she?'

'It was a he, braindead, and he was a great artist.'

'The only artists you know are the ones that draw the dole. Get out of bed, Donovan, and I'll make you a cup of tea.'

McCall stood up and walked from the bedroom across the hall to the living room-cum-kitchen, Arrow at his heels. Dirty dishes lay in the bottom of the deep sink in the corner and a cockroach was trying to dislodge some dried-on baked beans from a plate. The insect barely moved as McCall filled the kettle from the tap.

Donovan padded into the room wearing a frayed dressing gown and sat down at a small kitchen table, dripping ash onto the yellow and black formica. He ran his hand through his unkempt greying hair.

'You've got a bloody great cockroach in the sink,' McCall told him.

'Leave it alone, it scares away the rats.'

'Jesus, Donovan, how can you live like this?'

'You call this living?'

McCall shook his head and took a clean mug out of a cupboard above the sink. He dropped a tea bag in and, when the kettle boiled, poured the hot water over it. He found a relatively clean spoon in a drawer and stirred in some milk and sugar, then carried the mug to Donovan at the table.

'You've still not told me what you want, McCall.'

'I need to pick your brain.'

'Christ, if you pick it, it'll never get better. What about?'

'Jimmy Knight.'

Donovan looked interested for the first time. 'That bastard? What's he done now?'

'How bent is he?'

Donovan gave a rueful laugh, 'The man can tie his shoelaces without stooping.' He sipped his tea, watching McCall suspiciously. 'What's all this about, McCall? What's your interest in the Black Knight all of a sudden?'

McCall didn't answer. There was nothing sudden about his interest in Detective Inspector Jimmy Knight. The big, brutal police officer had fitted McCall up for a warehouse robbery when he was eighteen. He'd done the job, but the evidence that put him away was false. Since then their paths had crossed many times and to say there was little love lost between them was a serious under-statement.

'Okay,' said Donovan. 'Why've you come to me?'

'You know him. You don't like him.'

Donovan jerked his head to the side, conceding that point. 'So what's in it for me?'

'I thought we were friends.'

A throaty chuckle. 'You don't have any friends. Neither do I, come to that. You and Knight have been circling each other like a pair of pitbulls for years. Why now?'

McCall said, 'You heard of Jerry O'Neill? The MacDougall raid?'

'I do occasionally read more than the racing in the paper. I know he's out on interim lib pending an appeal. What's he to you?'

'Nothing. But Jimmy Knight was the arresting officer.'

Donovan sipped his tea thoughtfully. 'And you think there's something dodgy?'

McCall shrugged then repeated, 'Jimmy Knight was the arresting officer.'

Donovan conceded that point too. 'Again – why you so inter-ested?'

McCall fell silent. He couldn't answer because he wasn't sure himself why he was doing this. Donovan waited for a few moments but was not put out by McCall's lack of response. He looked down at his dressing gown as if realising for the first time that he was wearing it.

'Okay,' he said with a sigh, 'you want to walk the mean streets then you're going to need help. You asking questions about a six-year-old case is going to raise more than few eyebrows. Me, on the other hand, we can put down to having a client. What's the point of being a private detective if you don't do a bit of private detecting now and again?'

'Why would you want to do that, Frank?'

'What are friends for?'

'I thought we didn't have any friends.'

'Figure of speech, man – don't get all misty-eyed on me. I'll be billing you for my time. Now, let me get out of this Noel Coward get-up and pull on some clothes, and you can take me out for something to eat. Then we'll decide the next step.'

Like Big Rab, Jimmy Knight was a dark man. His hair was black, thick and wavy but always immaculately cut by a city-centre hairdresser who catered to media personalities and football players. His skin was tanned, although it was a natural dusky hue and not one cultivated by tanning salons or foreign holidays – he didn't like the heat, although he made sure his wife took trips abroad twice a year. It got her off his back. But it wasn't his hair or his complexion that led to him being dubbed the Black Knight. That had more to do with his personality.

The young man fidgeting at one side of the folding table in the small kitchen of the tenement flat knew all about Knight's dark temperament. He held a cigarette between shaking fingers and avoided looking into the policeman's eyes

'I don't like what I'm hearing here, Shoog,' said Knight. Shoog didn't reply but shrank back slightly in his chair. He had seen Knight like this before and the end result had not been pretty. 'I don't like it at all. I think you're comin the fuckin bandit. Am I right, Shoog? Are you comin the fuckin bandit?'

'Naw, Mister Knight, honest! This is all gen up. You know I wouldnae mess you aboot.'

Knight's eyes narrowed. 'I'm no so certain. Naw, I'm no so certain at all. See, I think you know more about that jewellers gettin done over than you're tellin me. See, the fact that the old man got slapped with the butt of the shotgun? It's what they call an MO, Shoog. A Modus Operandi, if you're a Latin scholar. And that operandi has your modus all over it, if you know what I'm saying.'

'Naw, naw, Mister Knight, it wasnae me! I was here all night last night, so I was, watchin the telly. Never went over the door.'

'Son, I see your lips movin and there are words comin out but know what I'm hearing?' Knight put his hand to his ear and he whispered, 'Shoog's a lyin wee shite, Shoog's a lyin wee shite.' Shoog opened his mouth to object but Knight waved him silent. 'You always were and always will be. I'll bet if I turned your place over right now I'd find something linking you to that job – some wee bit of evidence. A balaclava, maybe, a shotgun with bloodstains on it, maybe a ring that got nicked. What do you think, Shoog? Think I'd find anything?'

'You'd need a warrant,' said Shoog and regretted the words immediately. Knight stared at him, his face growing darker, which was never a good sign.

'A warrant, is it?' The policeman's voice was soft, which also didn't bode well for Shoog's future wellbeing. 'A warrant, by God! You been readin they law books again, ya wee bastard? You're talkin to me about a warrant?'

Knight rose in his chair and leaned over the table, pressing his face so close to Shoog's that he could smell what he'd had for breakfast.

'I don't need a fuckin warrant!' Knight roared and then slapped the boy across the face. He didn't hit him hard, didn't put his back into it, but it was forceful enough to send the young man flying out of the kitchen chair and onto the faded linoleum. Knight jumped out from the table and kicked the boy hard in the stomach.

'There's my warrant, ya wee shitehawk!'

He slammed his foot into the boy's chest.

'And there's a receipt for anything that might take my fancy!'

He booted Shoog between the legs.

'And that's for makin me lose my legendary cool!'

The boy whimpered as he tried to roll himself into a ball, but it was too late for that, Knight's temper had died as swiftly as it had ignited. The policeman took a deep breath and stepped over to the kitchen door, crooking a finger at the detective standing outside.

'Please let Mister McLeish read the warrant in your pocket then tear this pisshole apart.' He smiled then and glanced back at the young man still groaning in agony on the floor. 'When you find something – and you will, cos he's no the brightest bulb in the box – you'll remember that he went berserk and had to be restrained.'

'Aye, boss,' replied the detective, looking down at the boy on the floor and smiling, no pity for the little scroat who had left a sixty-eight-year-old man in a coma.

'I'll leave you to it then, Alec,' said Knight. 'Get the uniforms outside to give you a wee hand.'

'You got an appointment, boss?'

'I've got bigger fish to fry,' said Knight, then noticed that some of Shoog's spittle had landed on a shoe. He sighed, pulled a dishcloth from a hook beside the sink and wiped the saliva off the black leather. Then he threw the cloth onto the floor and walked out.

McCall watched Donovan shovel the final forkful of fried egg into his mouth before slurping a mouthful of tea. The man had put the plate of egg, chips and beans away like he hadn't eaten in a week, which might not have been all that far from the truth.

'Jesus, that was good,' Donovan said, wiping his face with a small paper napkin and sitting back in the plastic chair. It was late afternoon and the small café was empty apart from the two men. A young girl with green streaks threading through her brown hair stood behind the counter reading a Sunday tabloid's magazine section. Outside the grimy windows, traffic streamed along Dumbarton Road, one of the main roads west out of the city.

Donovan fished a cigarette from the pack on the table. 'Okay, so we've got the MacDougall raid. Two hundred grand snatched by a team of four, maybe five, from south of the border, at least as far as the initial reports suggested, right?'

'Right.'

'Right…' Donovan held a lit match to the end of the cigarette before waving the flame out and dropping the blackened sliver of wood into an ashtray. 'Okay, the police are well flummoxed – not that easy to do but not impossible – and leads are thin on the ground. And the investigating officer is our old pal Detective Inspector Jimmy Knight, who pulls a certain Ricky Ramage out of the hat like a bloody rabbit. Ricky's a slimy wee scroat who would've undercut Judas to fire in Jesus. Ricky drops Jerry O'Neill's name – who knew MacDougall, if I remember right – says he confessed during a drinking session, although why anyone would believe a lying little turd like Ramage is beyond me.'

'Don't forget it was corroborated by Duncan Two-Fingers.'

Donovan laughed. 'Another guardian of truth and honesty. You know how he ended up with two fingers on one hand?'

'I heard it was an accident with a chainsaw when he was working with the Forestry Commission.'

'He told me your pal Joe the Tailor had them chopped off for grassing.'

'Joe wouldn't've done that.'

'Maybe not, but my point is he was another lying toe-rag, like Ramage. Anyway, he miraculously comes out the woodwork too, says he heard O'Neill blabbing all while he was pissed. We'll need to see Ramage but if we want to talk to Duncan Two-Fingers we'd better get the Ouija board out cos he's dead.'

'He's got a son, he might know something.'

'Maybe. Anyway, a subsequent search of O'Neill's premises turns up a plan of the MacDougall house and the security code. And to cap it all, O'Neill is verballed in the back of a polis motor.'

McCall nodded. A verbal – cops will say it's a bolt-out-the-blue confession, crooks say it's a figment of the cop's imagination. Whatever it was in this case, the phrase 'I never wanted the woman harmed' was used against O'Neill.

Donovan tapped off some ash. 'Okay, O'Neill's got no record, apart from a couple of speeding tickets over the years. No big deal. He's got a good going security business – he's a Rotarian, for Christ's sake, and a regular churchgoer. Mind you, neither of them are guarantees of staying on the straight and narrow. There's no way he was at the house on the night of the raid – he was at his wife's father's birthday party – but the evidence suggested that he planned the whole thing, brought the team together and sent them off on their merry way for some rape and pillage. The bastards.'

Donovan puffed thoughtfully on his cigarette. McCall knew

that at one time the man had been one of the sharpest cops on the beat and was impressed by the way he had soaked up all this from his own brief outline of the case. He had known him for as long as he'd known Knight. A gangster had been gunned down and McCall, Rab and Joe Klein had all been hauled in for questioning. That killing had opened up a can of worms, as street killings often do, and Donovan wound up bleeding from a gunshot wound on the ground floor of Davie's building. Over the years they had developed a grudging respect for each other. Then Donovan was forced out the job on suspicion of corruption. It was never proved but bad smells linger, especially in Strathclyde Police, and he lost his job and his family. Now he worked for a former Detective Sergeant with his own private detective agency operating out of a tumbledown wooden structure off Byres Road. Word was his boss had been diagnosed with cancer. Donovan would have no luck at all if it wasn't for bad luck.

Donovan was still mulling over the details of the MacDougall case. 'And then we have Big Rab's involvement. He was looking to buy out O'Neill but Jerry was having none of it. Big Rab seems to walk away saying no problem, pal, no harm done. Then a few months later, O'Neill's fingered for the raid and has to sell the business to pay for the lawyers and the bills and God knows what else. And guess who's there with his cheque book open and pen poised?'

Donovan paused for another puff of smoke. 'Sure, it could all be one big coincidence, but where your pal Big Rab is concerned, I don't believe in coincidences.'

'You think he fitted O'Neill up?'

'I think it's on the cards. It's his style.'

'Aye, but only guys like him. He's never actually falsified evidence against someone – he's only fired them in for something they really did do.'

'Come down off cloud nine, Davie. Big Rab's planted stuff all his bloody life. Okay, he's never done a straight arrow like O'Neill before, but he's hurt plenty of them. This code of honour thing – not hurting civilians – only exists in your head. Maybe you've never damaged an innocent person, but I'll bet Stringer has – and on Big Rab's say-so.'

McCall looked away, knowing that what Donovan said was true. Donovan picked up his teacup and carried it to the counter for a refill, then came back and sat down heavily in his chair.

'Then there's Jimmy, the Black Knight. He's not averse to planting evidence. But why would he pick on O'Neill? Now, I know Jimmy and Big Rab have done business. Quite a bit of business. So was it a plan concocted between the two of them – Knight comes up with the evidence, cracks the case, gets all the attaboys, and McClymont takes over the security firm? Is that all there is to it? Is there anyone else who could gain out of the thing?'

Donovan fixed his gaze on McCall. 'Which brings me back to you, Davie boy. You've still not told me why you're doing this. What's got you so fired up about O'Neill? What's in it for you?'

McCall thought about it for a moment, and flinched as he felt the hammer in his hand and heard the man screaming with each blow. He forced the memory from his mind and gave his answer in one word.

'Redemption.'

6

DONNA STUDIED THE picture on the wall opposite her. She didn't know whether it was in oils or watercolours, but it fascinated her. She didn't even know who painted the damn thing. All she knew was that she couldn't take her eyes off it. It was a country scene and there were two people, a man and a woman, meeting by a river. They were in period costume – she guessed nineteenth century – and they were facing each other over a fallen tree while a flock of birds, crows maybe, massed around a church steeple in the middle distance. Donna wondered why the couple was meeting in that remote setting. Were they lovers? Were they committing adultery? Were they spies, criminals, what? If she looked at the card underneath she thought she'd find it was called *The Rendez-vous* or *The Assignation*, maybe even *The Tryst*. Whatever it was called, she felt part of that scene, even though she was sitting in a side room in the city's public art gallery and not in the picture's rural landscape. She, too, was there for a meeting. The difference was, she knew why she was there.

'You been waiting long?'

The voice startled her. She had been so lost in the painting that she hadn't heard the woman enter. They were the only people in this particular part of Kelvingrove Art Gallery, although Donna could hear the distant squeak of shoes against polished floors and hushed voices echoing among the high ceilings. Donna watched the woman circling the room with a guidebook in her hand, studying each of the paintings in turn. Some people have the knack of taking possession of whatever space they're in. This woman's self-confidence was evident in the way she walked, in the way she stood, in the way she spoke. As usual she was immaculately dressed – tall people have a way of carrying clothes – and her jet black hair was so perfectly coiffed that Donna had to resist the urge to pat her own into place. The woman's features were thin and severe, and Donna knew her no-nonsense manner had been known to terrify men, something Donna understood. She'd been told to call the woman by her Christian name but she could never bring herself to do it. She stopped with her back to Donna and leaned in for a closer look at a Turner watercolour.

'We need to move a bit faster,' she said without turning.

'I've just made contact,' Donna replied.

'I know. But events are gathering pace, shall we say.'

'These things can't be rushed. I told you that when we started. You can't rush it.'

'It can't be helped. We need to speed it up.'

'How?'

The woman turned then and smiled. The expression softened her features, but Donna wasn't fooled.

'Already taken care of,' the woman said.

McCall came home to find her sitting on the bottom step, leaning against the wall beside his front door. When she looked up he saw angry tears boiling in her eyes and he knew her husband had been back.

'Where is he?'

'Gone,' Donna replied. 'But he's been in my flat.'

'How do you know?'

'See for yourself…'

McCall helped her to her feet and opened his own front door, handing her Arrow's lead.

'Wait in there for me,' he said, then climbed the stairs.

The door to her flat was lying open so he pushed it wider and stepped in. He heard glass grind under his shoe and looked down to see a couple of framed photographs of the city at the turn of the century lying on the carpet. Someone had torn them from the wall and stamped on them. The living room was a mess. Furniture had been turned over and ripped with a knife. Ornaments had been destroyed. More pictures ruined. But the worst of it was the word BITCH painted in red above the fireplace, the five letters dripping down onto its polished wood.

McCall felt his body go cold and his mind slow down.

As he left the flat, the wrinkled face of the old woman across the landing watched him from behind her security chain.

'It's all right, Mrs Mitchell,' said McCall.

'I heard noises, things being smashed,' she said, her voice bearing strong traces of her native Poland. She was growing increasingly feeble but McCall did what he could for her. Joe the Tailor had once been her landlord and his will had dictated that she be allowed to stay in the flat rent-free for as long as she wished. For McCall, the old woman was a last link to his old boss. 'I should phone the polis.'

'No need for them, Mrs Mitchell. Everything's okay. Go back inside.'

'Did that man come back?'

'Aye. But I'll not let him harm you, you know that. Go back inside. Don't worry about it.'

'Okay, Davie, if you say so.'

'Everything's fine. I'll come up later and check you're all right, okay?'

'You're a good man, Davie McCall. A good man.'

McCall watched as she closed the door and listened as the lock was turned. A good man. He wished he were.

Donna waited at his front door and he led her back inside.

'I suppose he didn't like the way I laid out my furniture,' she said, her light tone forced, her anger palpable. His first thought was to ask where her ex-husband lived, but he dismissed it. She wouldn't tell him and she didn't need him to fight her battles. She just needed a friend.

'I'll make some tea,' he said. 'Make yourself comfortable.'

Donna was stroking Arrow's head and he was loving it when McCall came back into his sitting room from the kitchen with a tray bearing two cups and saucers, a tea pot, milk jug and a bowl with sugar.

'I don't have any biscuits, I'm afraid.'

'That's okay. I'm not a big biscuit eater.' Donna dropped her hand but Arrow was not having that. He edged closer and laid his head on her lap. She smiled and rubbed his ears. She looked at the tray and her smile broadened.

'What?' McCall asked.

'It's nothing,' she said, still smiling. 'It's just that I didn't see you as a cup and saucer man.'

McCall felt embarrassment flush his face. The cups and saucers had been another of Vari's little touches, but he didn't think he'd had them out since she left. He'd even had to give them a wash to clear a thin layer of dust before he brought them through.

'Well,' he began. 'I don't get much company...'

'Davie,' she said, reaching out and touching his hand. 'I'm only teasing.'

McCall busied himself with pouring the tea and she took her hand away. But as he poured he could still feel her touch, cool and soft, against his skin. *Jesus, Davie, behave yourself.*

Donna leaned back and glanced at the bundle of drawings on the floor beside her. She picked up a pad and began to leaf through it. McCall tried not to look shame-faced again. He'd forgotten he'd left that pad there.

'These are good,' she said. 'Did you draw them?'

'Yes.'

'These are *very* good.'

'They're okay.'

'No, they're more than that. I don't know art, but I know what I like, as they say, and I'd say these are really something.'

She stopped at the series of pictures of the highland cottage, each one from a different angle. 'Where's this?' McCall glanced at the drawings and shrugged. A little piece of heaven, he thought, but he'd never say that to anyone but Bobby. 'Somewhere. Anywhere.'

'You made it up? All this detail? The mountain and the loch? And the apple trees in the garden? And the different views?'

McCall looked away. He was uncomfortable with this talk. His drawings were something he did for himself only. They were personal. He had never before allowed anyone else to see them, let alone talk about them. Part of him wanted to reach out and take the sketchpad out of her hands, but another part wanted her to look at them. That part of him liked the way she appreciated his drawings, liked the way she was looking at him as if she had found something new in him. That part of him had to be ignored. *Don't let this woman in*, he warned himself. *No good will come of it.*

Donna leafed through the remainder of the sketches silently. Then she closed the pad and laid it back down on the floor where she had found it and looked across at him.

'They really are good, Davie. Honestly. You've got real talent.'

'Ach,' he said, embarrassed. 'It passes the time.'

She seemed to sense he was on edge for she laid her cup down and stood. 'I'd better start tidying upstairs.'

'I'll help.' The words were out before McCall realised it. He wondered where they came from.

She smiled. 'Okay. But I pay for a carry-out afterwards.'

'Deal,' he said. But he thought, *Davie – what the hell are you getting yourself into?*

Sammy squeezed a thin line of adhesive onto the edge of the plastic wing and inserted it carefully into its correct position on the fuselage of the Flying Fortress. All around them in the tidy front room of the top floor tenement flat were examples of the old man's work – fighter planes and bombers mostly, a couple of aircraft carriers and one sailing ship which he had abandoned halfway through because he found the rigging too bloody fiddly.

Jimsie's eyes briefly turned to the soap opera on the screen, where a burly looking cockney geezer was talking to a sharp-faced blonde girl. Jimsie knew the guy was hard because he talked in a hoarse whisper. All the hard characters on this soap talked in hoarse whispers. It didn't make them hard. It made them sound like they needed a bloody throat lozenge. Losing interest in the dialogue, he looked back as the old man gently laid the almost completed bomber down on the tabletop. The boy took a deep breath and began his confession.

'I think I might've done something stupid today, Granda,'

Sammy peered over his glasses at his son. 'What'd you do?'

'I might've dropped Davie McCall right in it…'

Jimsie told him about Jerry O'Neill and his own subsequent conversation with Big Rab. When he was finished, his grandfather remained silent as he picked up a piece of the second wing from the tabletop. He fingered the edge, feeling it rough, and reached for a small piece of sandpaper. He began to rub away at the blobs of plastic while Jimsie waited for his verdict on his transgression. He knew his grandfather had never wanted him in The Life. It had never done him much good – he'd spent decades inside for his part in the death of a man during a robbery. Jimsie's older brother Marty was now banged up for life for a murder he didn't actually commit. Sammy had tried to stop Jimsie from getting involved, but for some people the die is cast.

Finally, the old man said, 'You spoken to Davie yet?'

'No, I've no seen him.'

'Then let him know Big Rab was asking about O'Neill. It's only fair that Davie knows.'

'So should I have kept my mouth shut, or what?'

'No point in lyin to the man. He might've found out already from someone else – might even have known before he asked you and was wantin to see how you answered. You never can tell with a man like Big Rab. He's so devious, even his left hand doesn't know what his left hand's doin. And it's only got worse since his wife was killed.'

'Will Davie be pissed off at me, d'you think?'

Sammy put the piece of wing and the sandpaper down again. 'Davie knows what Big Rab's like and he'll be fine with it.'

'That's okay then,' said Jimsie, reassured.

'You like Davie, then?'

'He's okay. Don't know if he likes me much.'

'What makes you think that?'

'Never says much, does he? It's like pullin teeth tryin to get a word out of him.'

'That's just Davie. But you stick with him – if he's willing to go on the streets with you then he likes you well enough. You listen to him and you learn from him. He'll keep you right.' Jimsie knew

that the old man had long ago given up trying to keep him out of
The Life. His Being with Davie seemed to satisfy him, somehow.

'He told me the other day not to enjoy the work so much.'

'Were you?'

'Was I what?'

'Enjoying it too much?'

The boy looked away, feeling shame. 'Maybe. But the bastard
had it coming.'

'Bastards have always got it coming and sometimes you've got
to dish it out. But Davie's right – don't take pleasure in it. Once
you do that, you're lost.'

The tops of the trees swaying gently in the breeze were little more
than dark shadows against the faded blue of the night sky. Knight
leaned on the bonnet of his car, watching them wave back and
forth and feeling the warm air against his face. He puffed on his
cigarillo as he waited.

Wide-beamed headlights swung into view at the far end of the
road that wound through Pollok Country Park and Knight
straightened as a Landrover Discovery approached. He knew
McClymont would be alone, that his minders would have been left
at the park gates. Sure enough, when the vehicle stopped Big Rab
peered through the driver's window. Knight's eyes flicked admir-
ingly over the vehicle. It was an expensive piece of kit, made even
more costly by Rab's personalisation – bullet proof windows,
specially strengthened bodywork. Christ, for all Knight knew
there was a rocket launcher and an ejector seat in there, too. The
life of a Glasgow Godfather. Knight was glad he was a law-abiding
citizen. Okay, maybe not, but he did not need to take such precau-
tions to protect life and limb. No-one would come after a cop.

'It's about bloody time, Rab,' he said. 'I've got better things to
do than hang around parks waiting for you. I felt like a fuckin
pervert here.'

'We've got trouble,' said McClymont, ignoring the cop's anger.
He wasn't scared of Knight. They were both big and powerful and
he had too much on the man to be frightened.

'Aye, you said. So what's up?'

'O'Neill.'

Knight took a draw on his smoke and half smiled. 'Mind that Y2K virus scare? The one that said every computer was going to crash come the new century? Turned out to be a lot of worry over bugger all. That's O'Neill – nothing but a Y2K virus on legs.'

'I'm not so certain. I sent one of my boys to deliver a wee message.'

'I told you to stay away from him. You turning heavy-handed will only give him ammunition.'

'So what was I supposed to do? Sit on my arse and let him accuse me of grassing him up?'

'That's exactly what you were supposed to do.'

'When I'm threatened, I fight back. You know that.'

'Jesus Christ!' Knight threw what was left of his cigar into the darkness. 'What did your boy do to the man?'

'Nothing.'

'What do you mean nothing?'

'I mean all he did was talk to him.'

'Talk to him?'

'Talk to him.'

Knight frowned. 'I don't get it.'

'Aye, it beats the hell out of me, too.'

'Who'd you send?'

'Davie McCall.'

Knight paused to take this in. 'And all he did was talk?'

'How many times you want me to say it?'

'Jesus…'

'Aye.'

'I didn't know that guy *could* talk.'

'Well, he's learned. I don't mind telling you, Jimmy – that worries me more than O'Neill. Davie's been acting strange lately.'

'In what way?'

'Difficult to say. It's no something you can just put your finger on. I've known him for years but lately he's been… different, know what I'm sayin?'

'Maybe he's reached the end of his shelf life.'

Big Rab fell silent, knowing that Knight had put into words something that had been niggling him for some time. He didn't want to believe it, though.

'It happens,' Knight went on. 'Guy gets older, slows down, doesn't have the heart for things he used to. Man like McCall, without the ambition or the brain to be anything other than what he is, well, he can outlive his usefulness. Time to be put out to pasture, maybe.'

McClymont remained silent, considering Knight's words, then shook his head. 'Davie's all right. He's just going through something just now.'

Knight stared at the man through the window. 'Fair enough, but I'd keep an eye on him anyway. You never can tell with people. You know?'

McClymont nodded and started the Discovery again. 'I'm not sitting back and letting O'Neill badmouth me, Jimmy. You better understand that. Davie might have chickened out, for whatever reason, but I've got other boys who won't. If that bastard keeps shooting his mouth off, I'm gonnae shut it for him.'

'That'd be the worst thing you could ever do.'

'We'll see. But if you don't do something about him, I'll have to.' He gave Knight a pointed look. 'I mean it.'

Knight watched McClymont perform a three-point turn and drive off, his taillights finally merging with the trees. The policeman took out his packet of small cigars and lit up a fresh one. He thought about McClymont, about O'Neill and about McCall. The first he could handle – he had as much on McClymont as he had on him. The second was a minor irritation, but the third... well, McCall was an unknown factor. An enigma. And Knight did not trust what he could not understand.

'Tell me about the drawings.'

McCall sat on the settee in Donna's flat and thought about what to say. Together they had tidied the place up as best they could until only the word scrawled above the fireplace remained. It would be difficult to remove, so Donna said she would buy a pot of paint and simply cover it over. She ordered Indian take away from a restaurant on Duke Street and they made small talk while they ate. In truth, Donna made the small talk, McCall not being adept in the delicate art. It wasn't that he didn't have opinions on current affairs, books, TV and films, it was simply that he wasn't in the habit of sharing them. He was also still puzzled over why he had inserted himself into her life. He blamed himself for what had happened to Audrey. He had taken the decision not to reconnect with Vari, although it had been a close call. He saw himself as bad news for women and yet, here he was, against his better judgement, with someone new. Something was happening here that was outwith his control and it made him uneasy.

He said, 'What about them?'

'When did you start?'

McCall hesitated. The drawings were personal, they were something born deep inside him and were untouched by the world outside his front door. Now Donna was asking him about them and, as usual, part of him wanted to shrink away from the scrutiny. But that other part of him, the part he suspected was gathering strength, wanted to tell her.

'Didn't know I could do it until I was...' He hesitated, about to mention his time in Barlinnie Prison. Too soon for that. '...until I was older. Never did it as a boy. Not sure my father would've approved.'

'Not the arty type, your dad?'

Davie's lips tightened into a grim little smile. 'You could say that.'

'Do you still see much of him?'

Images flashed through Davie's mind, unbidden, unwanted.

Danny McCall, floating on seawater that was alive with current, his hand wafting back and forth as if he was waving.

'He's dead,' said Davie.

Donna's voice was soft, sympathetic. 'I'm sorry, Davie. I didn't know that. Were you close?'

Close? An ironic laugh echoed in his mind. He looked at the

woman sitting opposite him but saw Audrey being held by his father, a blade at her throat.

Then there was blood, lots of blood and Audrey was in his arms but she was dying.

And she became Vari, beaten and bloody.

And then the final transformation. His mother, dead on the floor of a small flat.

Then, last of all, his father's face, smiling at him as bullets tore into his chest to send him tumbling into foaming water.

'No,' he said, 'we weren't close.'

7

THE MORNING WAS bright and warm and the city was still coming to life when Donovan emerged from Hillhead underground station and crossed Byres Road, which was already busy with the stop and start of traffic. It had been a long time since he had been sober at this time of the morning. It had been a long time since he had seen this time in the morning.

He worked out of an old wooden building situated on a cobbled lane that jutted off the busy road. To say it had seen better days was an understatement. It leaned like a drunk against the rear of the tenement that fronted onto Byres Road. Donovan knew how it felt. The small wooden sign on the doorway read Premier Investigations, but one look at the building would tell anyone that the firm was hardly in the premier league of anything, unless there was a premier league of under-achievers.

Jack Bannatyne stood outside the office. As usual, he was dressed to perfection and he made the old place look even more shabby.

Donovan hurried down the cobbled lane. 'Been waiting long?'

'Just got here,' said Bannatyne.

Donovan gave his old boss the once over as he inserted the key in the lock. 'Jesus, Jack – you're retired now. You can look sloppy, you know.'

'You should never drop your standards, Frank.'

Donovan opened the door and looked down at his own clothes. He was wearing scuffed brown slip-on shoes, an old brown jacket that had once formed part of a three-piece suit, a white shirt frayed at the collar and a pair of tan trousers that hadn't been threatened with an iron in living memory. Bannatyne smiled, knowing what he was thinking. 'Don't worry, Frank – you never had any standards to let slip.'

Donovan grimaced but declined to defend his sartorial choices and motioned Bannatyne ahead of him. Bannatyne looked around at the mess, taking in the piles of old newspapers, brown folders curling at the edges, the two old filing cabinets in the corner, the desk littered with bits of paper and more folders and smiled. 'Business is booming, I see.'

Donovan felt shamed. 'Yeah, well. Most of the clients prefer John working their cases.'

Bannatyne's smile dropped from his lips as he thought of John Docherty, the agency's owner. 'How is he?'

Donovan shrugged. 'Hanging in there, for now.'

Bannatyne's face remained impassive but Donovan knew the news was painful. They had both worked with John Docherty. Bannatyne looked around him, moved a pile of old newspapers from the chair in front of the desk and sat down. 'So, why do you need to see me?'

Donovan didn't think it was right for him to place the desk between them so he perched on the corner. 'You remember a case from a few years ago, 1994 – the raid on that bookie, MacDougall?'

Bannatyne pursed his lips before saying, 'Why you asking, Frank?'

'Got a client.' In his own mind Donovan wasn't lying. He said he'd bill McCall and it would serve him right if he did just that.

'If I ask you who that client was, you wouldn't tell me, right?'

Donovan raised his hands in apology. 'You know how it is, boss.'

'It's a hot potato down at Pitt Street at the moment.' Bannatyne may have retired the year before, but he still kept himself current. He'd headed up the Serious Crime Squad and had more contacts than Specsavers. 'Some task force is looking into it. Jerry O'Neill's been granted an appeal on some technicality or other – I think the judge made some mistake. O'Neill's got himself a sharp lawyer who spotted it, threw it at the Scottish Criminal Cases Review Commission, who've referred it back to the Appeal Court. But the Job's conducting its own inquiry.'

'Why's the Job investigating if it's a legal matter?'

'You know Pitt Street, you can never tell what these things might throw up and they want to be ready.'

'You know much about it?'

Bannatyne twisted his hand back and forth to show he knew a little. 'Nasty business.'

'Jimmy Knight was on the case, wasn't he?'

Bannatyne's lips pursed again as he stared at Donovan. He knew all about the history he shared with the Black Knight. 'He was with C Division at the time. Cracked the whole thing wide open with that statement from Ricky Ramage.'

'How well did he know MacDougall?'

'Jimmy? Don't think he did, not before the case anyway. Naturally, MacDougall was suspected at first, husbands always are, but Knight cleared him when Ramage came forward.'

'Aye, what about that? Did Ramage contact Knight or did Knight seek him out, d'you know?'

Bannatyne thought about this for a moment. 'Can't really remember. He was banged up on remand for a newsagent blag, I know that. Knight was sent up to the big house to trawl for information – you know what C Hall is like up there. There's always someone knows something about a case and is ready to trade it. I think Knight just kind of stumbled on Ramage, who was looking to make some sort of deal.'

'But Duncan Two-Fingers said he'd heard O'Neill confess, too.'

Bannatyne's head inclined in agreement. 'Knight found him as well, come to think of it. You know what Duncan was like, not a face as such, more a hanger-on. I wouldn't believe a word that came out of him, but then, that's just me. Had a boy in the jail at the time, if memory serves.' Bannatyne looked at Donovan sideways. 'You really think there's something not right about the case?'

Donovan shrugged. 'What about O'Neill, what do you remember about him?'

'He was just a security specialist, far as I know. You know, glorified night watchmen. "Have uniform, will guard" kind of thing. He mixed with some dubious company, but anyone seeing me here today would say that about me too. Again, he wasn't a player, but a hanger-on. They say that's how he pulled the gang together, knowing a guy who knows a guy. He denied it all, of course.'

'He knew the MacDougalls?'

'Friendly with them. He lived a few streets over. He and his wife were often over there for dinner. The theory is that one or other of the MacDougalls let the alarm code slip somehow and O'Neill passed it on to the gang.'

'And what about MacDougall himself?'

'Dorrell Simeon MacDougall – there's a name, eh? Dorrell's an old Scottish name, I think. His dad was a nut on Celtic history, passed it on to his son. He inherited the bookie business, built it up to quite a size. I think at the time he had fifteen shops across the city, a couple in Aberdeen and another three in Edinburgh. I'm sure you've spent a pound or two in one or other of his shops.'

Donovan couldn't argue. He'd been in more than one of MacDougall's betting parlours.

Bannatyne said, 'He also owned a chain of sports shops, if I remember rightly. He's worth quite a bit.'

'How did he meet O'Neill?'

'Rotary Club, I think. Or Round Table. Or some businessman's breakfast club or other. Anyway, they became friends.'

Donovan thought about this. 'And Mrs MacDougall?'

'Aline? Quite a beauty, although I never saw her face-to-face. Her picture was in the paper, of course. The daughter took after her. She had another strange name I always remember, the girl. Morrigan. It's Celtic, too, I think. God knows what it means.'

'They still living in the same house?'

'MacDougall is. They divorced a few months after the trial. Can't blame the wife really. In her eyes, he let it happen. You know what happened to her?'

Donovan nodded. Like McCall, the rape angle sickened him. 'Where's she staying?'

'Not a clue.'

'But you could find out?'

Bannatyne sighed.

Knight scowled as he unfolded his mobile phone, glanced at the LCD display and recognised the number immediately. This was not good, he thought. He stepped away from his wife, who had her eyes on the changing room doorway as she waited for their daughter to reappear. She barely noticed he was on the phone, so used was she to him receiving calls at all hours of the day and night.

'Knight,' he said.

'It's me.' Rab's voice. 'We have problems.'

'The whole world's got problems.'

'I don't care about the world. It's the O'Neill problem I'm worried about.'

'I've told you not to worry about that.'

'You told me it would go away.'

'And it will, trust me.'

'Then why have I had a visit?'

'From who?'

'Cops. Two of them. Some task force or other. Asking me about the case.'

Knight fell silent, thinking, *cops – what's that all about?*

Sarcasm oozed down the line as Rab said, 'So much for your Y2K shite, eh?'

Knight asked, 'Did you get names?'

'Some young guy called Simms, didn't catch the other one's name.'

Knight knew young Simms. 'What did you tell them?'

'I told them they had me bang to rights and they should slap the bracelets on me. What do you think I told them?'

Knight tried to sound casual. 'Routine. O'Neill's mentioned you so they need to interview you. It'll blow over.'

'I'm not so sure.'

'Look, have I let you down before?' There was a pause on the line and Knight continued, 'The word you're looking for is "no". This is nothing. They have nothing. It'll blow over. Trust me.'

'It had better be. Because if this thing goes pear-shaped, I'm not going down alone. Trust me.'

Knight found himself listening to a dead line. Thoughtfully, he snapped the phone shut and thrust it into his pocket. He had heard inquiries were being made, but he hadn't realised how thorough

they were going to be. Time, he decided, to make a few inquiries
of his own.

He looked up as his daughter emerged from the changing room
in a top that showed off her bare midriff and cut deep across her
burgeoning cleavage. The trousers were tight enough to have been
sprayed on.

'Jesus Christ, Doreen,' he whispered to his wife, 'I've seen
bloody strippers wear more than that at the end of their act.'

Jimsie dropped the leather sports bag on the tabletop and unzipped
it. He looked expectantly at the carrot-topped youth standing
opposite him. Jimsie read the guy's expression and his own face
hardened. 'Don't say it, Bru,' he warned. They called him Bru,
short for Irn-Bru, Jimsie had explained earlier. *Because he's got
ginger hair, get it?* McCall got it, the term 'ginger' being common
parlance for soft drinks in the city.

Bru shrugged and a nervous smile jerked at his mouth. 'Havnae
got it, Jimsie.'

'That's a month, Bru.'

'I know.'

'You know Big Rab doesnae like waitin that long.'

'I know, but what can I tell you?'

Jimsie sighed and glanced at McCall, who remained impassive,
though he knew what was coming. Bru had accepted some brown
from Big Rab on a sale or return basis, only this city being what it
was, there wasn't much chance of it being returned. Bru had not
yet come up with the cash. Both Jimsie and McCall knew that Bru
had stretched McClymont's goodwill as far as it could stretch.
Time now for something to snap.

'Bru, Bru, Bru,' said Jimsie, shaking his head. 'The big man's
waiting for his money. He's been more than fair with you.'

'I know, I know – but, see, I'm still waitin for my guys to bring
it in to me. You know how it is – cannae get the staff.'

The red-headed youth, no older than Jimsie, smiled at them,
hoping for a smile in return. He was disappointed.

Jimsie stepped around the table. 'All he wants is what's his, Bru, you know that.'

'Aye, but...'

'Twenty grand, that's what you owe.'

'I know, but...'

'I'll tell you what, though, as we're pals, I'll talk to the big man for you, square it with him for now. He listens to me.'

Relief flooded across Bru's face. 'Aw, Jimsie mate – see if you could, I'd appreciate it. I'll have the scratch by next week, honest.'

'You'd better, son, cos I cannae keep doin this. Pals or no, next week is the final deadline, know what I'm sayin?'

'I'll see you right, Jimsie. Honest.'

Jimsie nodded and zipped the bag again. He made a gun out of his hand and forefinger, pointed it at Bru and thumbed a make believe hammer. The warning was clear. McCall stared hard at the young man until the colour drained from his face, before he followed Jimsie out of the room.

Bru operated out of a council flat on the tenth floor of a high-rise block towering over a sprawling housing scheme. McCall was surprised they were leaving without anything physical, but was happy to walk away. Jimsie said nothing in the lift or as they walked past the concierge station on the ground floor. He kept his silence as they continued to the car park and climbed into the blue Rover. Jimsie started the car and pulled away, his face set hard as he performed a series of right turns and parked at the mouth of a street facing the block of flats. From here they could see both sets of doors, front and back.

'Bru was always a waster,' Jimsie said, finally. McCall unlocked his seat belt and sat back, wondering what was going on in the young man's head. Arrow sat up in the back seat, tongue lolling, watching the world go by. Jimsie glanced at McCall, then resumed his angry stare through the windshield. 'You spoken to Big Rab this morning?'

'No.'

The young man paused, thinking about what he had to say next. 'I had to tell him about you and that guy O'Neill.'

'What about me and that guy O'Neill?'

'Well… that you just talked to him. I think Rab was expecting a wee bit more, know what I'm sayin?'

McCall knew what he was saying. 'I can handle Big Rab.'

'So you're no angry at me telling him?'

'Did you have a choice?'

'I could've lied.'

'And said what?'

Jimsie thought about it. 'I don't know,' he conceded eventually.

'You did the right thing, Jimsie, son. Don't worry about Rab, I'll sort him.'

'As long as we're okay.'

'Aye, we're okay.'

'That's okay, then.'

His conscience eased, Jimsie relaxed in his seat. Nothing was said between the two of them for a full minute, but McCall knew it couldn't last.

'Davie, see if you had a choice, what would you rather be – a drawing pin or a piece of Blue Tac?'

McCall turned his head slowly to face the young man and saw that he was serious. 'What sort of question is that?'

'No, listen – it's a wee exercise in logic.'

'Logic?'

'Logic. Think about it, what are they things used for? To pin things up, right? So what would you rather be, a drawing pin or a dod of Blue Tac?'

McCall shook his head, wondering where the boy came up with this stuff.

Jimsie said, 'Me, I'd rather be a drawing pin.' McCall waited for the inevitable explanation. 'Think about it, they're used to hang things on walls, posters and stuff. So what if it was a Britney Spears poster, or that Elizabeth Hurley bird? I sure as fuck don't want to be a bit of Blue Tac on the back of the thing, I want to be a drawing pin on the front so I can scope them out, know what I mean?'

McCall smiled. 'Do you sit up nights thinking up all this?'

'This is important stuff, man. A guy's got to think of these things. Anyway, it passes the time.' He sat forward suddenly and reached for the ignition key. 'Here we go. Time for some fun.'

McCall clipped on his seat belt as the ginger-haired youth left the block of flats and walked in the opposite direction from where they sat. Jimsie let him move a fair distance away before he edged the car in his wake. Bru sauntered along the road in a long-legged style. He was cocky, so sure of himself. McCall watched as the boy nodded to people he knew, stopping once for a brief chat with two young girls, laughing with them, then moving on. Jimsie trailed him slowly, keeping the car a respectable distance away from the young man.

'Come on, ya dozy bastard,' he muttered. McCall knew he was playing with the dealer. He sighed, but Jimsie paid him no heed as he kept his eyes on Bru, who still had not spotted the car. He strutted on, his shoulders back, his long hair flowing behind him, completely oblivious to his wheeled shadow. He stopped again, this time for a quick word with an edgy looking young man with a beard and the pale-faced, hollow-eyed look of a user. The newcomer handed Bru something and he slipped his hand in his pocket. Even from this distance, McCall knew there was a tenner bag in Bru's hand when it reappeared. He palmed it into the junkie's grasp and glanced around.

And that was when he saw them.

At first he tried to be nonchalant. He patted the user on the back and went on his way, but McCall detected a change in the body language. The cocky walk was gone and the step was brisk; his shoulders were hunched and his head was down, both hands shoved into his jacket pockets. Jimsie pressed the accelerator gently. Bru picked up the pace, looking neither right nor left, and McCall knew he was on the verge of flight.

'Any minute now,' Jimsie murmured, and it was as if he had given some sort of signal, for suddenly Bru was off and running, breaking across the road in front of them, heading for a stretch of open ground and a line of empty tenements beyond. Jimsie smiled, gunned the engine and spun the wheel after the fleeing dealer.

McCall held onto the handle above the passenger window with one hand and braced the other on the dashboard as the tyres bounced onto the pavement and then onto the rough ground.

'Look at that bastard go!' Jimsie shouted. Bru was really flying now, his legs pounding under him, his arms pumping at his sides, and he might have made it if he was being chased on foot, but McCall knew there were damn few people who can outrun a two litre engine, and certainly not a backstreet dealer from this city. Jimsie drew level, grinning out of the side window at the running man, then surged ahead before suddenly spinning the wheel to the right, the tyres kicking up a cloud of dust from the parched ground as the car veered directly into the fleeing youth's path and before he knew it Bru had rammed into the motor's side wing and tumbled over the bonnet, arse over tit, to land in a jumble of legs and arms on the other side. Jimsie braked sharply and leaped out of the car.

'You think you're a fly man, ya bastard?' He screamed as he walked around the front of the car.

Bru rolled onto his back and tried to push himself away but his legs weren't working properly. He propped himself up one arm and stretched the other out to ward off any blows. 'Naw, Jimsie, honest...'

Jimsie was leaning over him now, his face taut with rage. 'You think you can play me for a fuckin dildo, that it?'

'Naw, Jimsie!'

'Then what, Bru? What makes you think you can get away without payin for your gear, eh?'

Jimsie kicked the man's arm away from under him and Bru fell back into the dirt.

'Four weeks it's been, Bru. You got the gear, you sold the gear, now you don't want to pay for the gear. What is it? You been smoking too much of it yourself, or jagging it into your own arms? That it?'

'Naw, I don't use that stuff.'

'My arse! You were a fuckin junkie when we were weans and you're still a fuckin junkie.'

'I'm off it, Jimsie, on my mother's life, I'm off it.'

'You never had a mother, ya low-life shitehawk. Some bitch whore squeezed you out up a back alley and then went off and shagged some fat loser up a close.'

Jimsie grabbed the young man by the hair and hauled him to his feet, then rammed a knee deep into his groin. Bru's face crumpled and a moan slid from his lips as he tried to double over, but Jimsie wouldn't let him. He held him steady and nutted the boy on the nose. Even a few feet away, standing beside the car, McCall heard the bone crunching. Bru screamed and Jimsie pushed him away to let him stumble backwards onto the earth again. Jimsie pulled his foot back and booted him hard on the chest, once, twice, three times. Each time Bru groaned and tried to roll into a ball. By the third kick he didn't have the strength to move. He just lay there on his side, blood pumping from his nostrils, one hand cupped between his legs, the other lying outstretched towards Jimsie, who stood panting over him.

'That's just a wee warning,' said Jimsie, breathing deeply. 'You have the cash ready for us next week, or by God I'll cut your balls off and feed them to you. You understand me?'

Bru groaned.

Jimsie leaned in closer and screamed, '*Do you understand me?*'

Bru nodded once and waved his free hand weakly. Jimsie hawked and spat a glob of phlegm at him before walking back to the car. McCall quickly scanned the waste ground and the street beyond to ensure they had not been observed while Jimsie paused at the wing and fingered a deep indentation.

'Fucker dented the motor,' he said.

McCall climbed back into the passenger's seat and buckled up again.

'Think the bastard got the message?' Jimsie asked and McCall glanced out the window at the young man curled up in the dirt before shrugging. He felt no pity for the dealer, for a lesson had to be learned, but Jimsie's theatricality could've been avoided. McCall knew then that his advice had been wasted. Big Rab had wanted a message sent and Jimsie had done as he was told, having some fun at the same time, and that saddened McCall.

He felt a weariness bear down on him. He was tired of The Life. He was tired of scroats and scumbags. He was tired of the ever-present threat of violence. He couldn't stop Jimsie being sucked in, just as he couldn't help himself all those years before. He didn't want to do this anymore.

But he didn't know how he could get out. And the fear he had expressed to Bobby was real. In the end, was this all he was?

'Fuckin bawbag better've got the message,' Jimsie said, his voice soft as the adrenaline ebbed, and started the ignition. 'Be a big pay day that day – we're pickin up Fat Boy McQueen's payment next week, too.'

8

MCCALL KNEW THAT Bobby meeting Donna was a bad idea, albeit accidental. He'd known Bobby was coming round that night but he hadn't planned on Donna stopping by after her shift at the supermarket. McCall saw his pal's face light up as he turned questioning eyes towards him. McCall knew he was about to be shamed.

'So you live upstairs, eh, Donna?' Bobby asked, his face innocent but his tone bloated with mischief, and before she could answer he turned to McCall. 'You never mentioned Donna, Davie. Why did you never mention Donna?'

McCall threw him a glare but Bobby ignored him, turned his Robert Redford grin back to Donna. 'Davie's not very talkative.'

Donna smiled back. 'I've noticed.'

'Has he mentioned me at all? Bobby Newman?'

'Once or twice.'

'Once or twice? As much as that? I'm honoured, so I am.'

McCall decided it was time to say something. 'Yeah, right.' It wasn't much but it was all he could think of.

'Sit down, Donna,' said Bobby, waving to the six pack of Budwieser on the coffee table. 'Have a beer.'

'I only popped in to say hello to Davie, that's all. It's been a long, hard day and all I want to do is get into a hot bath. But maybe another time?'

'Another time it is.' Bobby stared at McCall, 'It's a date.'

McCall saw Donna back up the hall, opened the door.

'Sorry, I didn't mean to intrude.'

'You didn't.'

'Bobby seems nice.'

'Yeah,' he said, dryly. He knew he was in for some ribbing when he got back to the living room. She smiled and headed up to her own flat.

Bobby said nothing when McCall came back. He sat on the

settee, sipping his beer from the bottle, watching a red-haired newsreader outline the Scottish news on the telly. He remained silent as McCall settled himself in the armchair. He took another slug of his beer. McCall waited. Bobby's eyes flitted in his direction, just once, but he saw the amusement gathering strength.

Finally, he said, 'You sly old dog.' Arrow looked up and Bobby said, 'Not you, pal, your master.'

'She's just a neighbour, Bobby.'

'Just a neighbour, right. I don't see old Mrs Mitchell popping in on her way back from the shops, though. Or is it just the good-looking ones you encourage?'

'I don't encourage her.'

'Don't know why not. And you do seem pretty chummy. She calls you Davie. No woman's called you by your first name since Vari. What's that all about, eh?'

'It's not what you think. She's just a friend.'

Bobby cocked his head. 'You sure?'

McCall said, 'I'm sure.'

Bobby's grin was proof that he didn't believe him. The problem was, neither did McCall.

Knight knocked once on the office door before walking in. Detective Chief Inspector Forbes Morton looked up from his paperwork and raised his bushy eyebrows.

'Thought this was your day off, Jimmy,' he observed, settling back in his chair and dropping his pen, grateful for the chance to break away from the endless round of reports, memos and forms he had to complete to satisfy the ever-increasing bureaucratic nonsense that emanated from headquarters. He was a country-boy-turned-thief-taker who preferred feeling collars to filling forms.

'A good copper's never off,' said Knight, smiling.

'Aye,' the superior officer smiled back. 'What's up?'

'The O'Neill Case.'

'What about it?'

'You tell me, boss.'

Morton's brow furrowed and he reached out to turn the fan

that oscillated silently on his desk towards him. Knight knew the man was avoiding eye contact. 'Don't get you, Jimmy.'

'There's someone sniffing around it, I hear. But no-one's spoken to me. Makes me nervous, boss. Makes me think there's something someone's not telling me.'

'It's not me.'

'Didn't think it was. But you know who it is, right? And if you know who, you must know why.'

The DCI self-consciously shuffled the paperwork, still not looking directly at him. 'It's nothing to get your y-fronts bunched up about, Jimmy. It's routine.'

'Routine? A case being reinvestigated six years after someone is sent down for it? That's not part of any routine I've ever known.'

'Okay, first, it's not being reinvestigated. The Commission has referred O'Neill's case back to the Appeal Court.'

'On a technicality.'

'True, but these things can snowball. The feeling is that the sentence could be quashed because of the judge's misdirection and O'Neill knows this. He's talking to some bastard journalist about his case and the Job just wants to make sure that we're fireproof on it, that's all.'

'So why the sneaking around, talking to people? Why not come straight to the arresting officer?'

Morton looked straight up now as he spread his hands in front of him. 'Can't help you there, Jimmy. This is all being dealt with at Pitt Street. A special squad.'

'A special squad? For a routine job? I don't bloody think so, boss.'

'What do you want me to tell you, Jimmy? The word handed down is that this is just a quick look at the case by officers from outwith the Force, just to make sure there're no loopholes as far as we're concerned.'

'Who's in charge?'

'A DCI Vincent from Lothian and Borders. Come on, Jimmy, you know that's the routine. It's all for appearances.'

'The whole thing stinks like a fishwife's finger, if you ask me.'

'Maybe so, but I don't think it's anything to worry about.'

Knight's jaw tightened. 'Aye, but is it all right if I worry about it anyway?'

'Is there something for you to worry about?'

'No. As you say, these things can snowball. These guys get gung-ho about stuff. First they're just taking a look at a case, next you're up on a disciplinary because you forgot to call some scroat "Mister".'

Morton smiled. 'You'll be fine, Jimmy. Believe me, it'll all blow over in a few days.'

Knight looked at his boss and tried to read anything in his broad farmer's face, but all he saw was a yearning for retirement. He unclamped his jaw and smiled back.

'If you say so, boss,' he said and wondered if it sounded as insincere to Morton as it did to him.

'I'm worried about you, Davie.'

McClymont had pasted a concerned expression across his face, but McCall kept his own impassive – an easy for thing for him to do – and let the other man continue to talk.

'You've no been yourself these past coupla months,' Big Rab continued, drumming his fingers on his desktop. 'What's got into you?'

'Why don't you tell me exactly what the problem is, Rab.'

'You know what the problem is, Davie. O'Neill's the problem. You've still no sorted it like I asked you.'

'I spoke to the man.'

'I sent you to put the fear of death in him.'

'Has he been saying anything more about you these past coupla days?'

'No, but...'

'Then how do you know I didn't put the fear of death into him?'

Rab sighed. 'I wanted him warned off, Davie.'

'No, you wanted him hurt.'

'Exactly.'

'I didn't think it was necessary.'

McClymont couldn't believe his ears.

'You didnae think it was necessary? *You* didn't think? Who the fuck told you you could think?' McCall's eyes flashed and McClymont curbed his anger. 'Look, Davie, I said I was worried about you and I am. Time was I would've sent you out to see to O'Neill and you'd bring me back his ears, know what I'm sayin? What's got into you these days?'

McCall thought about Spencer. He thought about swinging the hammer and hearing the bones shatter and the man's screams reaching a crescendo. And he felt the guilt stabbing at him with each blow.

'Nothing,' he said.

'Then are you gonnae do your job?'

'O'Neill's no danger to you.'

'So you say.'

'I mean it, Rab. He's just a bitter man blowing off steam.'

'What d'you know about it? I mean, what the fuck d'you know about it?'

'Did you fit the man up, Rab?'

'What sort of question is that?'

'Did you?'

'Course I didnae! He was a straight arrow, far as I knew. Why would I want to fit him up, especially with a job like that? What happened to that woman was bang out of order.'

'He says to get his business.'

'Christ, Davie – I'd've got his business out of him eventually. You know that. I didnae need to go to the bother of fittin him up. I could play the waiting game.'

McCall thought about this. He knew Big Rab's methods. By playing the waiting game – which was another name for a campaign of firebombing, intimidation and robberies – he would've forced O'Neill to sell. McCall also could not believe his old friend would sanction the rape of a woman. Rab had some scruples – especially back then, when Bernadette was still around.

'I'll talk to him again,' said McCall.

'It'll take more than talk, Davie. You know it and I know it.

Sooner or later he's gonnae need to be taught a lesson and the more contact you have with the bastard, the more vulnerable you are. Get it over with, Davie. You know it's coming.'

'I'll talk to him, Rab.'

McClymont stared at McCall again, trying hard to read the man, but after twenty-odd years of what passed for friendship, he was no closer to understanding him than the day they met.

He exhaled deeply. 'Okay, Davie, do it your own way.'

McCall nodded, got up from the seat and left McClymont's office. In the waiting room outside, Stringer sat at a low table looking at the pictures in a movie magazine. He raised his head as McCall passed, but McCall didn't acknowledge his presence. Stringer looked back to the office door and saw Big Rab giving him a thoughtful stare before he reached some sort of conclusion and motioned Stringer inside.

9

THE MacDOUGALL HOUSE was a big mock Tudor affair on the northern outskirts of the city. Set back from a road that was never too busy, it nestled amid mature hardwood trees and well-kept lawns. The nearest neighbour was about two-hundred yards away through a dense line of bushes and on the other side of a high stone wall. Behind the house was nothing but fields and small woods. Donovan decided this was the nearest thing to living in the country without actually scraping the cow shit off your shoes every day.

His battered blue E-Reg Metro City looked decidedly out of place on the gravel driveway. He felt incongruous himself in a baggy blue suit that was so out of fashion it was almost back in, and a shirt that had once been white but was now looking as grey and old as its owner. He had worn a tie especially for the occasion, a nondescript cotton job from C&A, and had unearthed his old leather briefcase. He'd thrust a few old newspapers and a couple of beige file covers inside to make it look full. He was about to impersonate a Government officer and he wanted to look the part.

The doorbell jangled somewhere deep inside the house and he waited on the step, pulling at his jacket sleeve to conceal the worn shirt cuffs. A ghostly figure began to materialise on the other side of the frosted glass panels and the door opened to reveal a tall man, good looking in a patrician sort of way, sporting a thick head of well-groomed white hair and a face that, despite its lines, any ageing soap star would kill for. His pastel Pringle sweater and the open-necked shirt underneath were expensively casual and a faint trace of over-priced cologne wafted across the doorway. The man held a copy of that day's *Scotsman* in one hand, a pair of rimless glasses in the other and he gazed at Donovan as if he was a bad smell.

'Mister MacDougall?' Donovan asked.

'Yes.'

'Mister Dorrell MacDougall?'

'Yes. Who are you?'

'The name's John McCarthy,' said Donovan, proffering a business card. 'I'm with the Scottish Criminal Cases Review Commission.'

MacDougall took the card and studied the printing. It looked official enough, though Donovan had printed it up at a railway station only half an hour before. MacDougall transferred his attention to Donovan, studying him as if he was something the cat had just thrown up on the parquet flooring. Donovan suddenly wished he'd polished his shoes.

MacDougall handed him the card back. 'What can I do for you?'

'We're conducting some inquiries into the robbery. I thought I'd ask you a few questions.'

'I've already been questioned about this. Twice. It was my understanding that Mister O'Neill's case would now go to the Court of Appeal.'

'Yes, but there are always loose ends to tie up. We're very thorough at the Commission. It's standard procedure to send an investigator out at this stage just to go over everything again, a fresh eye, if you like. Didn't the previous investigator explain this?'

'No. Neither did the police officers who were here the other day.'

Donovan kept his face straight. So the inquiry team had already been. They were fast. 'Well, they're doing their own thing, Mister MacDougall. I'm sure you can understand that their agenda is not ours. All we want is to get to the truth of the matter.'

MacDougall stared at him and Donovan had the horrible sensation the man was not buying his story. He waited, feeling that to say anything more would simply dig him a deeper hole. Finally, MacDougall nodded and stepped aside.

'You'd better come in.'

Donovan smiled and stepped past him into a spacious hallway featuring a wide, square-shaped stairway of wood so highly polished it could have been used as a mirror. The wooden floors were also buffed to a high gleam, but covered with an Oriental rug that looked expensive enough to be used as a down payment on a house. MacDougall motioned him towards a room to the left and Donovan stepped through an open door into a bright, comfortable sitting room where four large bay windows looked out onto a lawn as big as a golf course and just as well maintained. A large open fire took up one wall, the empty grate obscured by a foldout willow pattern screen. The fire surround, high and wide and made of sturdy dark wood, was decorated with pictures of what Donovan assumed were family members. One showed Dorrell standing beside a teenage girl with sad, dark eyes. Above the mantle hung a large painting of a statuesque woman, a warrior, with a tangle of long, curling black hair and clad in black feathers. The landscape behind her was dark and blasted and the woman herself was surrounded by a flock of ravens. It was a striking picture and Donovan found himself staring at it.

'That's the Morrigan,' said MacDougall behind him. 'The Celtic goddess, the phantom queen. Sometimes known as the Goddess of Death or even the Guardian of the Dead.'

Donovan looked back at the photograph and noted the similarities between the girl in the snap and the woman in the painting. 'Morrigan – that's your daughter's name, isn't it?'

'Yes. My wife and I were both devotees of Celtic culture. Dorrel means King's Doorkeeper.'

Donovan wondered why a man would name his daughter after a Goddess of Death.

'Please take a seat,' said MacDougall, his hand indicating a pair of long leather Chesterfields facing each other across a chunky, low, square coffee table made, like the fireplace, of thick dark wood. Donovan reckoned the delivery man who brought it went home with a hernia.

Donovan settled himself into one of the settees, which was so comfortable it was like sitting on a cloud, and faced MacDougall, who had sat down opposite him. The man laid his newspaper and glasses on the large coffee table and sat back.

'What do you want to know, Mister McCarthy?'

Donovan snapped open his briefcase and took out a large pad and a pen. 'Basically, if you don't mind, I'd like to talk about the robbery, go over it again.'

MacDougall made a small noise of exasperation. 'I've been

through this dozens of times already. Surely you have access to my previous statements?'

'A fresh eye, remember, Mister MacDougall?'

MacDougall scowled. 'Very well. My wife, my daughter and I had been dining at the home of Sir Kenneth Grant...'

'The QC?'

'Yes. We returned here at about eleven. I found the alarm had been switched off – not cut, but switched off properly with the security code. Before I could do or say anything, we found ourselves surrounded by four men in dark clothing and ski masks. One had a pistol, the others knives and what looked like baseball bats, but they could have been pick-axe handles. They forced us into my study...'

'Which is where, exactly?'

'At the rear of the house.'

Donovan nodded. 'I'm sorry, go on.'

'They wanted me to give them the combination of the safe. They had already removed the large picture that covered it and had obviously been awaiting our return home.'

'But you refused to give it to them?'

'Yes.'

'Can you describe any of the men at all?'

'I told you, they all wore dark clothing and ski masks.'

'Were they tall? Were they fat, thin? Anything?'

'The leader was quite tall and slim. I call him the leader because he was the only one who spoke. I know now, of course, that Jerry O'Neill was the real leader.'

Donovan let that one pass. 'What about his voice?'

'He was English. London or the south, anyway. He was very calm about it all. Even when he instructed one of his men to...' MacDougall stopped, his mouth working as he looked for a way to describe what happened. 'To do what they did to my wife.'

'I'm sorry, Mister MacDougall, but I must ask you about that. While your wife was being raped...' Donovan looked up to see how the man reacted but there was no show of emotion. 'What did the other men do?'

'One was holding me – the one with the pistol. Another was holding my daughter, a knife at her throat. The leader simply stared at me, asking me for the combination, over and over again. They had taken my wife into another room ...'

Considerate of the bastards, Donovan thought.

'...but I... we... my daughter and I... could still hear it all.'

'Why didn't you give up the combination?'

'I really didn't believe they would do it at first. And when they did, I couldn't believe what was happening. My mind went blank, I'm afraid. I couldn't think. I couldn't move.'

'And then they threatened your daughter?'

'Yes – that was when my senses returned and I finally gave them what they wanted. They bundled the money into a large plastic shopping bag and left. They had a van waiting in the roadway. I hadn't noticed it when I drove up.'

'And you phoned the police right away?'

'Yes... well, no – I saw to my wife first and then I had to run to the house next door because they had cut the lines into here. Approximately five minutes passed before I alerted the authorities.'

Donovan nodded. 'Yes, that ties in with the records,' he lied, not knowing whether it did or not. 'And they took two hundred grand, that right?'

'Yes.'

'Why so much cash in the house?'

'It was destined for a couple of my shops. By necessity we're a cash-based business, do you understand?' Donovan understood all too well. 'It was due to be delivered the following day to the shops.'

'Was that a common practice?'

'Not common, but it wasn't unknown. I'd have the cash here for only a day, two at the most, before it was taken elsewhere. In this case, I wanted to keep the money in my control until it was needed. Employees are not always trustworthy.'

'So who knew the money was there on this particular day?'

'Just me.'

'Your wife? Daughter?'

'Of course.'

'No-one else?'

'The managers of the shops, of course. And the security firm who were due to uplift the following day.'

So not just him, Donovan thought. He was surprised he hadn't advertised it in the newspapers, too. 'So – about Mister O'Neill. You knew him, didn't you?'

'Yes, he lived a couple of streets away at the time. We often dined there, and he and his wife just as often came here.' Disgust crinkled his face. 'When I think about all the times I've shown that man hospitality. God knows how long he'd been planning this outrage.'

'How did you meet?'

'We are... *were*... in the same Rotary Club. He's no longer a member, of course.'

'Were you surprised when he was charged in connection with the robbery?'

'Stunned, I think is the word. He didn't seem the type. Oh, he wasn't like the others around here. Most of us are old money, apart from a few who used to be called yuppies. But O'Neill had built up his security firm single-handedly. He'd done well.' The shadow of a smile crossed his lips. 'Clearly not well enough.'

Donovan nodded, seemingly staring at his notes, before asking, 'You and your wife are separated now, I understand?'

MacDougall shifted slightly in his seat. 'Divorced.'

'May I ask if it was related to this incident?'

'No, you may not.'

Donovan looked up and met a suddenly hostile stare from the man. 'I'm sorry, I didn't mean to pry...'

'Yes, you did. Exactly why my wife and I have split up is none of your concern.'

'Of course not,' said Donovan quickly, wondering why the man was so touchy about it. He got to his feet. 'Well, thank you, Mister MacDougall, for the time.'

MacDougall rose but remained silent. Donovan followed him out into the hall and to the front door.

'One thing, though,' said Donovan. 'Your daughter...'

'My daughter has suffered enough,' the man replied, his tone cold enough to freeze meat. 'I don't want this impinging on her life any more than it has.'

'No, I was only going to ask if she was hurt in any way during the raid?'

'No, not physically.'

'It was just your wife?'

'Yes.'

Donovan nodded thoughtfully. 'Well, thanks again, Mister MacDougall. I won't need to trouble you again.'

MacDougall opened the front door. 'Good.'

Jerry O'Neill entered the park with his daughter and spotted McCall immediately, which was just the way McCall had planned it. He had followed them from their home, watching O'Neill hold the youngster's hand as they walked and occasionally stooping slightly to say something. When O'Neill saw him, just after they passed through a set of large cast-iron gates, he knelt down by his daughter's side, pressed some money into her hand and nodded towards an ice cream van parked nearby. The girl ran towards the van and stared at the illustrated selection of frozen goodies on offer. O'Neill sat on a bench and waited.

'I thought I told you to leave me alone,' he said as McCall sat down beside him.

'I'm here to help.'

O'Neill's laugh was short and derisive. 'Aye – one of McClymont's boys is going to help me, right enough.'

'I am. At least I'm trying.'

'Why?'

McCall watched O'Neill's daughter pointing to a picture of an ice lolly. 'My own reasons.'

O'Neill stared at him. 'You think I did the MacDougall thing?'

McCall shook his head, still watching the girl.

'You think McClymont fitted me up?'

McCall shook his head again.

'But you could be wrong, right?'

'I could be wrong,' McCall conceded. 'But I need you to keep quiet for now. If you keep shouting, you'll be dubbed a grass, your name'll be spray-painted on some wall and the next thing you know you're lying dead with a bullet in your head. And nobody'll care, because everyone will believe you're an informant.'

'What is this? Some sort of threat?'

'No, no threat. It's the way it's done.'

O'Neill was beginning to rankle now. 'I'm not so sure. I think you're still working for McClymont, trying to shut me up. I told you I've heard about you, what you're capable of. But let me tell you – I'm no frightened.'

'Listen to me, O'Neill,' McCall said, softly, turning to face the man. 'There's only so long I can put McClymont off and you shooting your mouth off doesn't help. I'm asking you to keep your head down and let McClymont think you've given up. If you do that, then I think I can keep him off your back and maybe we can find out what really happened that night.'

O'Neill frowned. 'I don't get you, McCall.'

'You don't need to get me. You've already missed six years of your kid's life. Do you want to miss the rest?'

O'Neill glanced at the girl as she moved towards them from the ice cream van, a huge lolly in her hand.

He sighed. 'Okay, I'll try it your way. But if you're pissing me about, McCall, believe me – I'll bring your boss, and you, down.'

McCall nodded and stood up. The young girl gazed up at him, the lolly in her mouth, recognising him immediately. She looked at her father for reassurance. O'Neill reached out and ruffled her hair affectionately. 'Could you not have got a bigger one, hen?'

The father took the girl's hand and together they walked down the path. O'Neill paid no more attention to McCall, acting as if he wasn't even there. But the girl knew he was there and glanced back at him, fear wide in her eyes. She was young, but knew instinctively that this man was trouble. McCall wanted to tell her everything was fine, wanted to reach out and reassure her. But he couldn't. He stood by the bench, alone amid the crowds of people out to enjoy the summer sun, and watched the man and child head towards the pond, the daughter sucking the frozen treat and looking over her shoulder at him, the father facing defiantly ahead, his shoulders set firm.

Not far off, in the shade of some trees, Stringer watched all three.

10

THAT NIGHT, MCCALL and Donna were in his living room, Benny Goodman on the small CD player, dirty plates with the remains of take-away Chinese meals on the floor, Arrow fast asleep in his usual place in front of the cold fire. She'd popped in again after her shift, suggested they share a meal and he'd agreed. He hadn't meant to but the word 'yes' was out of his mouth before his brain was in gear.

Now he was drawing her.

He hadn't wanted to do it – he'd only ever drawn Vari from life, everything else was from memory – but she'd talked him into it. Granted, he didn't take much convincing, which both puzzled and terrified him. She sat in an armchair near the window, with the evening sun filtering through the blinds, while he settled in the other armchair and nervously slipped on his glasses, glancing over at her as he did so, though she made no comment. Then he began to sketch, hesitantly at first but gradually gathering confidence. Then...

'Davie,' she said, 'who's Rab McClymont?'

McCall's pencil froze just as he was describing the curve of her nose. He didn't answer. He didn't know how.

'Davie?'

'He's just a guy.'

'A guy you work for?'

'Aye. Where did you hear his name?'

'A woman in the shop. She saw me talking to you one day and she told me to steer clear of you, that you work for Big Rab McClymont.'

McCall finished off her nose and went to work on her lips.

'Davie?'

'Does it matter who he is? He's just a guy and I work for him.'

'She said he's a gangster. She said you're a gangster.'

McCall continued drawing.

She said, 'Is it true?'

McCall was having trouble with her mouth, a problem in getting the fullness of the bottom lip just right.

She said, 'You don't want to talk about it, is that it?'

He just couldn't get that bottom lip right. It was either too thick or too thin and he wanted it to be perfect. He knew she was staring at him intently but he refused to look at her and focussed on the image he was creating.

'She said you were evil.'

McCall's pencil hung above the pad, her words hitting home. He knew people thought that of him, he was used to them avoiding him, used to the tension in rooms as soon as he walked in, but to hear the words coming from her was like being stabbed.

'I don't feel evil,' he said quietly, still working at her lips, still not looking at her.

'Are you a crook, Davie?'

'Would it make a difference if I was?'

'I don't know. Do you steal from people?'

'I don't steal.' *Not anymore, anyway,* he thought.

'What do you do?'

He hesitated, knowing she deserved an answer but not sure how to word it.

'I... hurt people.'

'Innocent people?'

'No-one's ever that innocent.'

'That's not an answer, Davie.'

McCall sighed and laid the pad and pencil on the floor beside his chair then pulled off his glasses. On the CD player, Goodman switched to the Tommy Dorsey Band and Frank Sinatra's rich vocals filled the room.

'That's the only answer I can give you, Donna. I am what I am. Am I proud of what I do? No. Would I like to change? Yes. But I'm still Davie McCall and nothing will ever change that. I am what I am.'

Donna did not move from the chair. She stared across the room at McCall and he stared back at her, not knowing what she was going to say, expecting her to get up and walk out, or burst into tears, or be outraged that such a monster had come anywhere near her. But she didn't do any of those things. She just sat there with the side of her face bathed in the soft golden glow of the setting sun and stared at him.

'I was told you were the best,' the woman said. They were back in their side room at the art galleries. Sunlight slanted through a large window, bathing the bench in light. Donna squinted against it, held the woman's steady gaze as best she could. She had just expressed the view that what they were doing was a waste of time. She had come to know Davie McCall a little over the past few days and felt he was not the man for the job.

'I am the best,' said Donna.

'Doesn't seem like it to me.'

'Why? Because I'm questioning this whole set-up?'

'A true professional gets the job done, no questions asked.'

'That's not a professional, that's a robot.'

The woman looked at her, her face hard. 'Remember to whom you are speaking,' she said, her voice soft but still sharp.

Donna looked away from her to the painting on the wall. Now, more than ever, she wished she were one of the figures beside the river. She would rather be there than in this art gallery, talking to this woman.

The woman exhaled deeply and sat down beside her. She looked from the side room into the main gallery, ensuring no-one was nearby. 'What's the real problem?'

'There is no problem – I just think we're wasting our time.'

'I think there is a problem. I think you're developing feelings for this individual.'

Donna looked back at her, her smile dismissive. 'That's ridiculous.'

'I'm not so sure. And let me tell you – that would be a big mistake.'

'I know that. I know what I'm doing.'

The woman's eyebrow raised. 'Do you? He's not someone who deserves anyone's tender feelings, you know that. He's a violent man, maybe even a killer. He's hurt innocent people.'

'We don't know that for sure.'

'I know that for sure. You know about Spencer...'

'No-one could prove he did that.'

'Proof? Proof is something for the court. We *know*, Donna. He took that man and he systematically broke every bone in his arms and legs. With a hammer, Donna. Think about that. He took that man, God knows why, and he took a hammer and he did his arms and hands and then his legs and feet. Do you know how many bones there are in the hands and feet, Donna? Do you? Every one of them was shattered. Every. Single. One.' She said the words slowly, her emphasis heavy on each of them. 'Think about that, Donna. Think about the kind of man who is capable of doing that to another human being.'

Donna knew about the Spencer incident, knew that it was horrible, brutal, senseless. But she also knew she had heard only one side. At one time that would have been enough but now she had seen something else in Davie McCall, something not in the file or in the stories she'd been told. She hadn't wanted to see it but she had. She resolved to find out more about Spencer the first chance she got.

'He's not going to turn,' she insisted.

'Everyone turns, given the proper inducement.'

'He won't.'

'He will. He has a weakness and it's women. He's never hurt one yet and he sees himself as some great protector. That was why I sent Peter to you, and it worked. Although it would've been better if you hadn't shown yourself to be quite so self-reliant.'

'Peter shouldn't have hit me.' She hadn't been expecting it and had reacted instinctively. What she'd told McCall was true, her father had taught her to look after herself and it was a skill she found vital in her line of work.

'He was in the moment, as they say.'

'He's lucky he's not in the hospital.'

A slight smile then. 'Nevertheless, the little scene worked, that's the main thing. It brought McCall out and now you have to continue to work on him, get him to open up to you.'

Donna shook her head. 'He won't turn.'

'He'll turn. You can make him turn.'

Donna knew this was true, she'd done it before, but she couldn't help thinking, *What if I don't want him to?*

Knight sat back in his chair, one of his cigarillos clenched between his teeth and his hands behind his head as he stared at the ceiling. The plaster was cracked and there was a dark stain where water had dripped through after some stupid bastard upstairs had left a tap running, but he didn't see any of it. The interior decoration of a crappy old police station was the furthest thing from his mind. He was thinking about the investigation.

He had a strong sense of self-preservation. He knew when there was a threat in the air and right then he was picking something up on the wind. They were after him. Him. They weren't covering the Force's back. They weren't just going through the motions. This was no routine inquiry. They didn't give a tinker's about MacDougall or Jerry O'Neill. They wanted him, DI Jimmy Knight. Okay, he could deal with that. He was smarter than any of those bastards anyway. What puzzled him – no, what *worried* him – was why. What had put them on to him in the first place? Who had they been talking to? And who had been talking to them?

There was a sharp knock at the door and DS Alec Calvert poked his head into the room. 'Got a minute, boss?'

'Come in, Alec. I'm just thinking about the state of the world. What's up?'

'Shoog MacLeish.'

'What's that wee shite done now? Gone on hunger strike in the jail? Got himself shagged in the shower? What?'

'He's got himself bail, boss.'

Knight was stunned. He slowly removed the cigarillo from his mouth and stared at the burly Detective Sergeant. 'Bail?'

'Aye, boss.'

'How the hell did he manage that? He's been out of the jail for what? Three months? Then he does that jeweller's – we find evidence in his flat, for God's sake! – and he gets bail! So just how did he manage that?'

Alec shrugged. 'Beats me – and I was there. His lawyer applied for bail pending trial and the sheriff agreed. It was as simple as that. I'm telling you, boss, my jaw dropped so fast it clicked.'

'And what was the deputy DS doing all this time? Playing with his briefs?'

'It was a female and she never said a word. Not one word.'

'So Shoog MacLeish is out on the streets again?'

'As we speak.'

Knight jammed the cigarillo back in his mouth and sat back in his chair again. His gut told him this was no coincidence. There were wheels in motion here. Somehow, Shoog MacLeish was mixed up in the investigation.

'Something funny, boss?'

Knight looked back at Alec. 'How d'you mean, Alec?'

'You're smiling.'

'I'm showing my teeth – there's a difference,' said Knight, but he had been smiling and he knew it. Because now he had somewhere to start. Now he had something to work on. And that something was Shoog MacLeish.

11

Once an idea took root in Bobby Newman's head, it was difficult to blast it out. And the latest notion was a couples' night with McCall and Donna. His reasoning was that the girl deserved to know that McCall had normal friends. In fact, the idea was to show that McCall had friends, period. McCall, being McCall, hesitated. A night out with another couple was a big step, one he was unsure he should take, but Bobby wouldn't let him off the hook. He warned that if he didn't ask Donna, then he would do it himself, after all, he knew where she lived. McCall knew this was no idle threat so he broached the subject with her. He hoped she'd say no, he hoped she'd say yes. So that Friday night, with Bobby and his wife Connie's five-year-old daughter in the capable hands of his mother-in-law, they had a meal in a city centre Indian restaurant before finding themselves in a nearby bar that promised live music every night.

To McCall's horror, the live music that night was karaoke.

He should have known. Bobby was a karaoke fiend who thought he could sing like Robert Palmer. Every chance he got he grabbed the microphone and launched into 'Addicted to Love' or 'Bad Case of Loving You'. McCall had been roped into many a karaoke expedition by his pal, but he still cringed with embarrassment every time Bobby started. Connie loved it; not because she agreed her husband was the new Robert Palmer, but because she thought the whole thing was incredibly funny. Better than *Shooting Stars*, she once told McCall.

McCall covered his face with one hand and tried to shrink into the seat as Bobby bowed to the polite applause, and walked beaming back to the table.

'So how was I?'

'Brilliant as ever, doll,' said Connie, without a trace of irony.

Donna glanced at McCall, who rolled his eyes. 'It was an experience,' she replied. 'If Robert Palmer was here tonight, we'd never be able to tell you apart.'

'Very true,' said McCall, 'apart from the fact that Robert Palmer can actually hold a tune.'

Bobby glared at his old friend. 'Don't mind him. He wouldn't know decent music if it came up and bit him on the arse. I'll maybe do a couple of Sinatra numbers later to keep him happy.'

'A bite on the arse might be preferable,' replied McCall. Joe the Tailor, a huge Sinatra fan, would be doing cartwheels in his grave.

'Don't you listen to him, doll,' said Connie. 'If you want to sing, you sing. Self-expression is an important thing.'

'Aye – see? Self-expression. I'm maybe no a great singer, but I'm a stylist.'

McCall laughed.

'Ignore him,' said Connie, soothingly. 'And nip up to the bar and get us all another drink. I don't know what was in that curry, but I've got a mouth like Gandhi's flip-flop.'

'Same again for everybody?'

Donna nodded and Bobby picked up the empty glasses. McCall said he'd give him a hand and left the two women alone as they made their way to the crowded bar.

'So,' said Connie, 'how you getting on with our Davie?'

'Well, you know Davie. He's not an easy man to get along with.'

'Aye, he's a deep one, right enough.'

'He's very fond of Bobby and you.'

'Well, Bobby's the only real friend he's got, you know? I used to worry about that, Davie being what he is... I take it you know about him? What he does for a living?'

Donna nodded. 'He won't talk to me about it, though.'

'He doesn't talk to anyone about it, except Bobby. Does it bother you?'

'A bit.'

'Aye, used to bother me, and more than a bit. I never liked Bobby having anything to do with him, to tell you the truth. I still don't, to an extent. I like Davie, don't get me wrong, but he scares me. He can be so cold, so distant. He's friendly enough, pleasant enough – you saw him here tonight – but he never lets me in. I never see any warmth in those eyes. Bobby sees it, even if no-one else does. But over the years I've seen one thing and that's what makes me feel relaxed about Bobby and him being mates.'

Donna said, softly, 'Honesty.'

Connie tilted her head and studied Donna anew. 'You see it too?'

Donna held Connie's gaze with steady eyes. 'There's more honesty in Davie than a lot of straight people I know. I'd trust him before I trusted a lot of them.' This was no act, no pose. She really believed that. But now, saying it out loud, she was surprised at herself. She was a professional and she kept her distance but something else was happening here. She knew about Davie McCall, knew what he'd done, what he was capable of, but she genuinely liked him.

Connie said, 'Aye. It took me a long time to learn that, despite my reservations. You've seen it faster than most. In fact, most people never see it. All they hear are the stories.'

'Like the man he supposedly took the hammer to?'

'You've heard that one already?'

Donna nodded. 'Woman in the shop told me. She said he broke every bone in his arms and legs.'

'Did she say why?'

'She said the guy had never done anything to harm Davie, that's all.'

Connie snorted then. 'That's the truth. He'd not done anything against Davie personally, but he'd hurt someone else. A wee lassie, ten years old.'

'Hurt her how?'

Connie paused, and Donna sensed she was considering how much she should tell. Then she saw her shrug slightly, little more than a twitch and jerk of an eyebrow, and she said, 'Spencer was a paedophile.'

Donna hid her surprise. That had not been in the file she'd been shown.

'I'd seen him a couple of times,' Connie said. 'He was fat and he was soft and he waddled when he walked, you know the type? Anyway, couple of weeks before Christmas last year he lured a wee lassie who lived upstairs into his house and he molested her.'

Donna shifted in her seat. None of this had been in the file.

Connie continued, 'He didn't rape her as such, but he violated her, forced her to do things she didn't really understand but knew were wrong. And before he let her go, he threatened her. The usual stuff from these sickos.'

Donna closed her eyes and she could hear a thin, reedy little voice in her head.

Don't say a word.

Don't tell a soul.

It's all your fault.

Donna asked, 'Did they report him?'

'Aye, fat lot of good that did. No-one had seen the girl go in the flat, or come out. She couldn't describe the interior or even be certain what he'd used to molest her. A doctor examined the girl and said that although something had penetrated her, it wasn't enough to cause any physical damage so it was always possible she had been experimenting with sex with another boy.'

Donna sad, 'She was only ten!'

Connie nodded. 'He let the police search his flat. They found nothing, no kiddie porn, nothing. So he got away with it.'

Donna said, 'And that's where Davie came in.'

Connie nodded in agreement. 'The mother knew him slightly. She was a friend of Bobby's – everyone knows Bobby – and had met Davie once or twice in his company. She wanted justice for her lassie. Davie said what would happen wasn't justice, it was revenge. He's always one for calling a spade a bloody shovel.'

'And that's when Davie took the hammer to him?'

'Yes. He broke into the flat and tore the place apart, pulled up floorboards, found a box with disgusting pictures and magazines inside. When Spencer came home Davie was waiting for him with a claw hammer.'

Donna saw the scene in that dark little living room, as the sun died and the street lights outside flickered into life, hearing people moving in the close outside, delivering Christmas presents maybe, talking, laughing, living. And then she saw the man on the floor, Davie standing above him, the hammer in his hand, his blue eyes cold and distant.

And then, through the din of the bar, she could hear the man's screams, echoing, echoing. 'Didn't the neighbours hear anything?'

Connie gave her a rueful little smile. 'They heard but they ignored it. Justice was being served. There's nobody in that close, or in that street, who would say what happened was wrong. Spencer was an evil pervert who got what he deserved and if the law couldn't do it, then Davie McCall did.'

'And what happened to Spencer?'

'The police were told eventually and when they arrived they found him unconscious in the living room, with the photographs of the kids laid all around him. He was taken to hospital and later charged with possession of child pornography and for assaulting the wee lassie.'

'Did they know it was Davie who hurt him?'

'Rumours, of course. But they never really tried to find the man who did it. Spencer had paid the price. But so did Davie.'

'How do you mean?'

Connie shook her head. 'It's funny. Of all the people Davie should eat himself up over, it's strange that it was Spencer. He's hurt a lot of people, has Davie, and he's seen a lot of people being hurt. People close to him. Spencer really deserved what he got, if you ask me. But Davie can't get him out of his mind, so Bobby says.'

'Why's that?'

Debbie glanced over at the bar, where Bobby and McCall were picking up the drinks and beginning to head back to the table and said, 'Because for the first time, he found himself enjoying it…'

Later, at her door, Donna almost asked McCall about Spencer but held back. She sensed he had enjoyed his night out – more, that he had too few such evenings – and truth be told, she had enjoyed it too. For the first time since she'd met him, McCall had seemed relaxed. Not completely, because that would be too much to hope for, but just enough. He had smiled and he had laughed and she had caught a glimpse of a different person.

He saw her to the door of her flat, where they lingered for a moment, both unsure what to say. If this had been a real date they would've kissed, but Donna had to avoid that. She reminded herself this was business. She knew he would not make the first move in that way. He wasn't the type.

He shook his head, as if to clear it. 'Well,' he said, 'I'll see you tomorrow.'

'Yes.'

He hesitated and for a moment she thought he was going to kiss her. She wondered what she would do if he did. But he smiled weakly and then turned towards the stairs. She watched him go, then stepped into her flat.

Once inside, Donna leaned against the door. She realised with no small measure of surprise that she was nervous. Her heart thumped, her fingers trembled. What the hell was that all about? She had done jobs like this in the past. Get close to the subject, manoeuvre the subject to reach the objective, then get out. Each time she had managed to retain her objectivity, to keep her distance. But somehow, this was different. Not only did she feel strongly that they were wasting their time, for Davie McCall would never turn, she was also coming to understand that he wasn't the man she had been led to believe he was. Not quite, anyway.

McCall reached his flat to find Donovan waiting at the door, a small smile on his face. 'Good-looking woman, McCall. What does she see in you?'

'Sod off,' said McCall, but there was no rancour in his voice.

'Obviously it's not your witty banter.'

Donovan grinned and McCall felt his own smile widen. 'To what do I owe the pleasure anyway?'

'I need to talk to Ricky Ramage and somehow I don't think he'll open up to me. However, if I had a man with your particular talents along with me, his tongue might loosen.'

'Scare the hell out of him, you mean?'

'That's the idea, yes.'

'Didn't you once tell me you didn't need that kind of help from me?'

'That was then, this is now. Different problems call for different solutions.'

McCall nodded. 'When do you want to do it?'

'The night is yet young. And our friend Ricky is a creature of the night.'

McCall nodded again, dropped his front door keys back into the pocket of his coat and the two of them walked towards the street.

'So, this lady friend,' Donovan said as they neared the opening to the close, 'is it charity work she does, or what?'

'Sod off.'

12

RICKY RAMAGE LIVED in a Parkhead street where at certain points the pavement had been extended into the roadway to slow traffic to protect children. It didn't do much to stop the boy racers, though, they treated it like a chicane. At just after midnight there were no children playing in the street and as yet no boy racers, but a knot of teenagers hung around the corner, trying to look casual and surly at the same time. Donovan parked his car in one of the specially created parking bays outside Ramage's close and glanced at the would-be street gang.

'Think it's safe to leave the car here?' He asked as he locked the door.

McCall glanced at the pale blue Metro. One of the front wings had been replaced with a red-coloured spare found in scrap yard, there were rusty holes on the passenger door and the aerial was a wire coat hanger held in place with brown parcel tape.

'Somehow I think it's safe enough,' McCall deadpanned.

The controlled entry system was broken, which was a bonus, so they pushed open the heavy black door and began to climb the stairs. White and black tiles decorated the walls and the whole close smelled like bleach. Donovan was panting when they reached the fourth floor landing and he paused, leaning on the banister to catch his breath.

'You gonnae have a heart attack?' McCall asked.

'You gonnae give me the kiss of life if I do?'

'I don't know where you've been.'

'You could phone your lady friend, then. I'm sure she'd bring me back to life.'

'She's fussy, no fusty.'

'All evidence to the contrary...'

Donovan pressed the buzzer on Ramage's door and waited but there was no sound from inside.

'Are you sure he's in?' McCall asked.

'No.'

McCall glared at him. 'So we might've come out here for nothing?'

Donovan shrugged, then they heard a faint movement on the other side of the door and a voice called out, 'Who is it?'

'Need to see you, Ricky,' said Donovan.

Ramage said, 'D'you know what time it is?'

'How? Is your watch burst?'

'It's late, man. Who is it anyway?'

'Open the door, Ricky. We've got business.'

McCall heard a sigh through the door and Donovan grinned at him, obviously enjoying himself. A lock turned, then another and finally, a third. The door opened a crack, a thin silver security chain offering some measure of safety, and Ramage's face peered out, a cigarette dangling from the corner of his mouth. He squinted at Donovan, not seeing McCall at the side.

'Who the fuck are you?' Ramage asked and that was when McCall stepped into his view. The man's jaw dropped, the cigarette staying in place through a mixture of saliva and good luck.

'I didnae see you there, neither I did,' he stammered, fingers scrabbling to free the chain. He would know that the flimsy precaution wouldn't be enough to keep McCall out if he was intent on getting in. 'I didnae know it was you, like.'

Donovan stepped past Ramage, giving him a broad grin. McCall kept his face straight and followed.

The flat was a revelation. They both saw Ramage as an obnoxious wee scroat, but he was a tidy obnoxious wee scroat. McCall kept his place clean, but Ramage's flat positively sparkled. The man himself paced around the room, the gravity-defying fag tucked in the corner of his mouth as he nervously moved things around. He plumped up a cushion on the incredibly comfortable-looking settee; he shifted a tasteful little ornament on the mantelpiece; he straightened a magazine that somehow had the audacity to sit slightly askew on the glass-topped coffee table.

'I wasnae expecting company, neither I was,' he said as he flitted about. 'No at this time of night. I mean, you don't, do you? Expect people at this time of night? Know what I'm saying?'

'Ricky,' said Donovan, 'do me a favour and sit down, will you? You're making me nervous.'

'I'm makin *you* nervous?' Ramage almost smiled but he caught himself in time and went back to looking shifty. 'I'm shittin bricks here, man, know what I'm sayin?'

'Why?'

'Well, I don't know who you are but I know your man there…' Ramage bobbed his head in McCall's direction, 'and I know he's no here for a nightcap, know what I'm sayin?'

He looked towards McCall as if he expected some kind of explanation for his presence. McCall stared back. This only served to increase the little man's tension. 'What have I done? Can you tell me that? Have I pissed Big Rab off somehow? Just tell me what I've done, I'll make it right.'

'Ricky, Ricky,' said Donovan, soothingly, 'calm down. We're only here to ask you a few questions, that's all.'

'Questions? What sort of questions?'

'About Jerry O'Neill.'

Ramage paused then, one trembling hand rising to pluck the cigarette from his mouth. A tiny blizzard of silver ash flaked off and snowed on the carpet. He looked down at it mournfully and Donovan got the impression he was contemplating fetching the vacuum cleaner. Ramage looked back at Donovan, deliberately kept his eyes away from McCall, and then sat down in an armchair, perching on the edge as if he didn't plan to settle for long. Which he probably didn't.

'What about Jerry O'Neill?' He asked, his knee jiggling up and down as if he was listening to a particularly frantic dance tune.

'Oh, I don't know,' said Donovan, sounding vague. 'How about, who got you to fire him in for the MacDougall thing?'

'Don't know what you're talking about.'

'No?'

'No.'

Donovan squinted. 'You sure?

'Just said so, didn't I?'

'Well, I think you do know what I'm talking about, Ricky. I think you came up with the story to get yourself out the jail.'

'No, I never.'

'Or someone fed it you in the jail.'

'No.'

'I don't think you ever had a drink with that man in your life.'

'I did.'

'Where'd you two first meet then?'

'In the pub.'

'Which one?'

'I cannae remember.'

'Try.'

'Jesus, we're talkin years ago here, man. Who can remember pubs?'

Donovan let that go. 'Okay – so how'd you get to know him?'

'You know how it is, guys get to talkin at the bar and that. Fitba, that sort of thing.'

'You two just got talking?'

'Aye.'

'At the bar?'

'Aye.'

'And this was a regular thing?'

'Depends what you mean by regular.'

'Was it weekly, monthly, what?'

'No, no, every now and again, that's all.'

'An occasional thing, then?'

'Aye. Occasional, that's right.'

'And it was during one of these occasional talks at the bar, about fitba and the like, that he blurted out that he knew something about the MacDougall thing?'

'Well, I don't know about blurted, but he said it all right.'

'So how did he say it?'

'It was on the news, on the telly, about the polis investigation. He'd had a couple of pints by then, know what I'm sayin, and he said the polis would never catch they boys because they was long gone.'

'And what else did he tell you?'

'You know what else he told me.'

'I like the sound of your voice. Humour me.'

Ramage sighed and his eyes flickered towards McCall, who was sitting back in the settee, his impassive gaze never leaving Ricky's face. Ramage swallowed and then looked back at Donovan.

'He said there was five of them – four in the house, one outside – and that they shoved the money into one of they Marks and Spencer's bags – the big ones that take clothes – then they got away in a Ford Transit motor.'

Donovan waited.

'So, basically that was it,' Ramage went on. 'There was things there that hadnae been in the papers and that showed I was telling the truth.'

'The truth's a foreign language to you, Ricky. If he told you all this, you two must've been good pals.'

'Drinking pals, that's all.'

'Drinking pals? But he more or less confesses everything to you? A drinking pal?'

'I cannae explain it, but he did. What can I say?'

'Did he tell you other things about himself?'

'Like what?'

'Well,' said Donovan, appearing to think, 'personal stuff. He told you all about the raid, but did he tell you about his life? That he was married?'

'Aye, I knew that.'

'About his business – the security firm?'

'Aye.'

'Did he say he lived only a few streets away from the MacDougalls?'

'Aye, I think he might've mentioned that.'

'That he knew MacDougall?'

'Aye.'

'And his kids – two of them, a boy and a girl.'

'Aye, he talked about them all the time.'

Donovan stopped. His eyes flicked to McCall, who was scratching his ear.

'Uh-oh,' said Donovan and Ramage stiffened.

'What?'

'That's not a good sign.'

'What's not a good sign?'

'My pal here, scratching his ear. See, he's got this gift, a talent, call it what you will, but he's got it. It's called a bullshit-o-meter. He can sense when someone's lying, Ricky, and when he senses it his ear starts to itch. And his ear's itching like buggery, isn't it, Davie?'

McCall didn't answer but his hand slowly moved to his ear again and began to rub it. Ramage watched him and his already pale face turned whiter.

'I'm no lyin,' he said, but his voice was hoarse and he didn't sound very convincing.

'Please, Ricky, don't insult our intelligence – or his ear. You've told more stories tonight than the Arabian Nights. You never drank with Jerry O'Neill in your puff. He never told you anything about the MacDougall raid. He never told you about his life.'

'He did! I knew all about his security company, and that Big Rab wanted to buy it, and that he wouldnae sell. I knew all that!'

'And you knew about his wife.'

'Aye, he talked about her all the time.'

'And the kids?'

'Aye, he doted on they weans, so he did! Doted! He…'

'Ricky,' Donovan spoke very softly and Ramage stopped in mid-sentence. 'Ricky – O'Neill's only got one wean. Just one. No two. One.'

Ramage got up then and walked over to the window. He reached out and touched the heavy curtain that was drawn across it, obviously thinking about pulling it back. But he was on the top floor and he couldn't escape that way and even if he screamed for help, who would come? He knew what he was – a thief and a grass. If he was the only entry in a popularity contest he'd still lose. He dropped his hand again.

'So I made a mistake. So what? Doesn't prove nothing.'

'You made a mistake, son, and it proves everything. To my pal's ear and me, at any rate. The question now is do you want to compound that mistake and keep telling us porkies, or do you want to tell us what actually happened?'

'I've told you what actually happened.'

'You lied about it all.'

'I didnae!'

'What happened about the charge you were on remand for?'

Ramage had the decency to look ashamed. 'It got no pro'd.' No Pro'd. Short for No Further Proceedings. It went away.

Donovan said, 'Convenient, that.'

'They had nothing on me.'

Donovan sighed and looked at McCall. 'You were right, Davie,' he said. 'We'll need to do it your way. I'll wait outside and make sure no-one disturbs you. I'll switch on the radio before I go, shall I? Drown any noise?'

Ramage turned round just in time to see McCall nod and get to his feet. Donovan walked over to the hi-fi sitting on a coffee table in the corner of the room and bent down to study the controls. McCall made a great show of taking off his jacket and flexing his arms, as if loosening the muscles up for some work. Ramage swallowed hard, his eyes darting from Donovan to McCall and back again.

'I cannae tell yous nothin,' he said and Donovan straightened up. 'You don't understand, these is evil bastards we're dealing with here. I mean fuckin evil.'

'Who are they, Ricky?'

'Are you no listenin to me? I cannae tell you that! I'd be murdered!'

'They won't know you've told us, Ricky.'

'They'd know! He'd know!'

'Who? Big Rab?'

Ramage smiled then, which struck Donovan as strange. 'Jesus, is he the worst you can come up with? Big Rab? He's a pussycat compared to this guy.'

'I can protect you from whoever it is,' said McCall and Ramage turned to face him, his voice catching him by surprise. Then he shook his head.

'No,' said Ricky, almost sadly, 'you cannae. No-one can. Not from him.'

'Give us a name, Ricky,' Donovan urged. 'We promise there'll be no comeback on you. We're not making official inquiries. You'll not be mentioned.'

'No way, man.'

'Just tell us, Ricky. We just need to hear his name.'

'You'll no hear his name from me. You can do what you like to me, but it'll be nothin compared to what he'd do if he found out I'd grassed him. So go ahead – do me some damage. Cripple me. But you'll no get the name out of me, I promise you that.'

Something in the man's tone and the defiant way he held himself told them both that he was telling the truth. Ramage would never say the name.

'Okay, Ricky,' said Donovan, 'relax. We'll not hurt you.'

McCall pulled his jacket back on and followed Donovan into the small hallway and to the front door. Ramage moved behind him.

'But remember this,' said Donovan, his hand on the knob of the Yale lock. 'We weren't here. If we hear even a whisper about our visit, we'll be back. Understand?'

Ramage nodded and watched them step out onto the landing. He shut the door quickly behind them and they heard the security chain being slid into place and the locks clicking. Donovan motioned McCall down the stairs but didn't speak until they reached the door leading to the street.

'So at least we know for certain that Ramage lied, that O'Neill was telling the truth,' said Donovan, his voice low. 'And there's only one guy we know who's involved in all this that can generate that level of fear.'

'The Black Knight,' said McCall.

'The very same,' said Donovan. 'The question is, who was he doing it for? Big Rab? Or is there another player in this wee game we don't know about yet?'

Jimmy Knight's thoughts were also on Ricky Ramage, but for another reason.

He had spent all evening looking for MacLeish. Naturally, the man's flat was empty. He knew that because he had broken in. You don't spend twenty-five years on the Job without picking up a trick or two. He checked out his favourite pubs, the local cafés, even a drop-in centre in a nearby church, but there was no sign of the wee scroat. It was as if he'd been abducted by aliens. When Knight found him, he'd wish he had been.

Before setting out, Knight had checked MacLeish's record and discovered one or two things about him. He hadn't bothered to look into the wee shit's previous before hoovering him up for the jeweller's job because he had only been involved as a favour to Alec Calvert, who was handling the investigation. Knight had paid no more attention to the matter until Alec told him about the court shenanigans. He knew MacLeish had only been free for a few months, but he hadn't realised that the bastard had served eighteen months in Durham Jail, having been sentenced to seven years for a theft in Newcastle. That came as a surprise because he didn't know MacLeish had ever been outside the city in his life. He was out on license, parole being granted unexpectedly just three months before. The parole was unexpected because MacLeish was an habitual offender and a far from model prisoner. Knight knew what that meant – a deal had been struck. MacLeish had information to offer and had been granted freedom in return. His conviction hadn't been quashed, not yet. That would only happen following the successful completion of the probe into Knight. Of course, whoever struck the bargain didn't reckon on the stupid sod being picked up for another robbery back home, so more strings had to be pulled. The question was, what did MacLeish have to offer that was deemed so important that it bought him freedom twice over? And where was he now?

Knight thought about this as he lay in bed, listening to the soft breathing of the girl sleeping beside him. She was on her side, her naked back towards him, the corner of the duvet clutched to her chest and one delicately tanned leg poking out to lie on the top.

He reached out and almost absently caressed her smooth thigh. He'd been seeing her for years, on and off, and they had a mutually beneficial arrangement – he kept her supplied with controlled substances and she did things to him that would make the Happy Hooker blush. She was a very, very energetic girl and tonight she had outdone herself. Of course, the top quality coke he had confiscated from a dealer earlier that evening helped stimulate her libido considerably.

As he lay there feeling the silkiness of her flesh, Knight decided he would have to employ other methods to find MacLeish. The wee bastard was lying low somewhere, but no-one can just disappear, aliens or no bloody aliens. He was a user and users have to have their fix. He'd surface somewhere; but Knight couldn't be everywhere at once. He needed eyes – watchful eyes, greedy eyes. And there was no shortage of them in this city.

Ricky Ramage was his first thought.

13

IN 1994 DUNCAN Two-Fingers had already been on his last legs. A heart condition and a sixty-fag-a-day habit had conspired to help him shuffle off this mortal coil in 1998. His son, Howard, had been a small-time dealer and Bannatyne had told Donovan that at the time of the MacDougall thing he was banged up on remand for possession of some blaw. As soon as Two-Fingers had given his statement, young Howard was given bail on the cannabis charge. As with Ramage, the charge miraculously evaporated like smoke from a joint after O'Neill's conviction. To both Donovan and McCall, it smelled suspiciously like a deal.

The address Bannatyne had provided was a bottom floor flat in an East End scheme built in the early-sixties, when the city was in the full thrust of its outward expansion. The first tenants were delighted to get these two-bedroomed flats, but that was then. Now the scheme was a run-down wasteland just waiting for the demolition crews and the tenants were either dreaming of getting out or wondering how the hell they got there in the first place.

Metal sheeting blocked off the door to the ground floor flat once occupied by Howard Lindsay, so it was obvious the boy was no longer resident. A wraith of a girl appeared on the stairway as they wondered where to try next. She was of medium height but so pale and thin she almost wasn't there. She looked at them with the eyes of someone who has no past, no future and isn't too sure about the present.

'Excuse me, hen,' said Donovan, 'you lived here long?'

She stopped and stared at them, peering at them through the gloom. 'Don't live here. My sister does. Up the stair.'

'Did you know Howard Lindsay? Used to live in this flat?'

She looked from Donovan to the metal barrier. 'Howie? Aye, I knew him. Doesn't live here anymore.'

No shit, thought McCall, then he saw her claw at her left arm and he knew without even seeing the track marks that she was a user.

'He moved,' she continued.

Donovan asked, 'D'you know where to?'

She scraped at her arm with her thumbnail as her face screwed up with suspicion. 'You polis?'

'No.'

'Why you want Howie then?'

'We need to talk, that's all.'

She stepped closer to get a better view. 'Don't know if I should tell you.'

'He your dealer, hen?'

'What makes you think I use?'

Donovan smiled. 'Just a wild guess. Look, hen, we're no after Howie for anything. We just need a wee word, okay? So how about givin us his new address, eh?'

The girl stared at McCall's face and he saw the first flicker of recognition in her dull eyes. 'I ken you, don't I? I've seen you around here.'

'Now and then,' said McCall.

'You're no polis, right enough. I ken you.' She looked back at Donovan. 'I don't ken you, though.'

'He's with me,' said McCall.

She looked from one to the other then nodded slowly, as if the effort of the conversation was proving too much for her. When she spoke again there was a weariness in her voice. 'They new flats up the road there. Howie lives in the first block.'

Donovan said, 'Can you show us, hen?'

She sighed and her body began to sag a bit but she nodded. 'You got a fag?'

Donovan took out his packet of cigarettes and offered her one. She took it with an unsteady hand and slipped it between her thin lips. Donovan struck a match and lit the cigarette for her. In the glow of the tiny flame, McCall saw that she was only about sixteen. But the drugs and the hopelessness of her life had taken its toll and left a shell of a girl. He felt a stab of guilt because it was Rab McClymont, and others like him, who had helped cause that. And it was men like him who had helped the McClymonts of the world.

She stepped past them into the night, walking quickly with her shoulders hunched and her arms folded across her chest. Occasionally she sucked on the cigarette, her wasted cheeks drawing thinner as she inhaled the smoke. Nothing was said between them as she led them up the street towards a set of newly-built flats. She stopped at the concrete path leading to the first block of four and nodded at the front door.

'Ground floor left in there,' she said.

'Thanks, hen,' said Donovan but the girl just shrugged.

She asked, 'You got another fag, pal?'

Donovan took the packet out and handed it to her. She looked up at his face, nodded her thanks and was about to head back the way they had come when a short, fit-looking bloke with black hair and wearing what looked like a jogging suit came out of a flat on the other side of the road. The girl stopped when she saw him and turned back to them.

'That's Howie there,' she said and turned away. The man paused on the pavement under a streetlight, one foot on the road in front of him, a set of house keys in his hand. He looked at Donovan, then at McCall. Something flash in his eyes, something McCall had seen many times before in neds who knew that his presence would be harmful to their health. Donovan must've recognised it, too, for he murmured, 'He's going to run.'

And run he did. Howie skittered off down the road like a jackrabbit, vaulting a low metal railing around a primary school like it wasn't even there. McCall took off after him, the folds of his thin coat flapping around his legs as he ran.

McCall used one hand to lever himself over the railing and saw the figure sprinting across the playground towards the fence on the other side. He ran across the concrete, keeping his eye on Lindsay as he leaped over the second fence like Aldiniti heading for Grand National glory. God, the boy was fit. He reached the same point seconds later and pulled himself over as Howie pounded across a stretch of sun-baked grass, heading for a part of the scheme that McCall knew as The Warren. The houses crowded close together there, separated by narrow roads and lanes and hidden pathways that had proved a Godsend to many a young villain legging it from the law. If Lindsay got in there McCall knew he would never find him so he spurred himself on, his feet thudding on the hard earth beneath him. But the boy was an agile wee bastard and he was already at the edge of the grass and about to cross the first road, his eyes fixed on an opening directly in front of him.

Lindsay didn't see the car swerving into the road but he heard the motor gunning towards him. He stopped in his tracks as the headlights picked him out, looking very much the way a frightened deer looks when caught on a country lane. Donovan spun the wheel and bumped the car up on the pavement, blocking the opening. Howie crouched in the road, darting a glance over his shoulder to see how close McCall was, ready to take flight again. Donovan threw open the car door and climbed out.

'We're not here to hurt you, Howie,' Donovan said, his hands outstretched.

Howie looked back at him, his chest rising and falling. 'Aye – right,' he said.

McCall slowed down and stood a few feet away from them, his breath ragged. Howie faced him again. 'Big Rab sent you, didn't he? He wants his money. He'll get it, don't worry...'

Donovan said, 'We're not here for Big Rab.'

'What you want then?'

'We want to talk about your dad.'

Howie's eyes narrowed as he looked back at Donovan. 'My dad? What about him?'

'He gave evidence in the case against Jerry O'Neill.'

'Aye, so?'

'That's what we want to talk about.'

Howie straightened a little bit then. 'You're no here about the money?'

'I'd never heard of you before tonight,' said McCall. 'I don't know anything about any money.'

The man's head swivelled between the two of them and then he nodded.

'I moved out of that flat about six months ago,' Howie said, laying two mugs of tea down in front of them. 'Too many junkies in that block. I'd find them jaggin up in the stairwell.'

His flat was a neat little place, nicely decorated in blue, the three-piece suite comfortable but inexpensive, the only sign of extravagance being the widescreen TV and DVD player in the black unit in the corner.

'They no your clients, then?" Donovan asked, dunking a digestive biscuit in his tea.

'Gave that up years ago, man,' said Howie, dropping into the only free armchair. 'Mug's game, that.'

'How come you think Big Rab's after you, then?'

'He does more than supply drugs, man,' Howie said and jerked his head towards McCall. 'Ask your mate here.'

'He's a moneylender, too,' explained McCall.

'Aye, when I saw him I thought I was in for a couple of broken bones. I'm a wee bit overdue.'

Donovan had owed money before to the wrong people and he knew what that fear was like. He asked, 'How much overdue?'

'Coupla weeks. No big deal. I'll get it, no worries on that score.'

'So,' said Donovan, 'your dad...'

'Aye,' said Howie.

'He gave evidence against Jerry O'Neill, right?'

'Aye.'

'You were in the jail at the time...'

'Well, no when the trial was on. I was out by then.'

'But you were in the jail when your dad spoke to the police about it for the first time.'

'Aye.'

'Then you were let out, right?'

'Aye.'

'Did that surprise you?'

'How do you mean?'

'Well, getting out. You'd already been refused bail, then suddenly you were out and the charges against you dropped. Must've caught you by surprise.'

Howie sat back in the chair and lifted the mug to his lips. He sipped at the liquid thoughtfully, never taking his eyes off Donovan. Then he leaned forward and laid the mug on the small table at his side.

'Look, I really didn't know what was going on, okay? All I know was that my dad said he was gonnae fix things and then he did.'

'Fix things?'

'Aye, with the charges and that, you know? Fix things. He said he was speaking to someone and the charges would go away, no worries.'

'Did he say who he was speaking to?'

'No, just someone in the know. He didnae say nothing else. Next thing, I'm readin about that robbery and then a wee while after that I'm out.'

Donovan leaned forward. 'Wait a minute. You said you read about the robbery *after* your dad told you he was going to fix things?'

'Aye.'

'Not before?'

'No, my dad saw me in the jail and then I read about the robbery, then I got out.'

Donovan glanced at McCall then said, 'And when were the charges dropped against you?'

'Wasn't till after my dad spoke in court. That was part of the deal.'

'Do you know a cop called Jimmy Knight?'

Howie's face wrinkled. 'Christ, aye.'

'Was he the guy who lifted you originally?'

'No, an older guy.'

'Did your dad know Knight?'

'Aye – Knight lifted him a coupla times.'

'Could it have been Jimmy Knight who was speaking to your dad?'

'Could've been Kojak, for all I knew. My dad never told me, just said I was better off not knowing.'

Donovan looked at McCall over the rim of his mug as he drank from it. He wondered if he was thinking the same thing.

Jimmy Knight. Had to be.

The following morning, Donna chapped on McCall's door and immediately clocked how tired he looked.

'God, you look rough.'

He smiled. 'I had a long night,' he said.

He saw interest in her eyes. 'What were you up to?'

'I went out again after I left you,' he said. 'Business.'

'Oh,' she said, then waited, as if she expected him to explain where he'd been.

'I can't tell you about it,' he said.

'I know. I understand.'

'No, you don't. You can never understand and I don't expect you to.' He paused, trying to find the words that would somehow reassure her. He wanted to tell her that he was trying to change but he couldn't bring himself to say anything further. He willed her to understand that he was sincere. There were things in his life he could not talk about, but he needed her to know that he wished to put those things in the past, where they belonged. He'd wanted to change since he was eighteen years old – even then he could see where his life was heading. But life, as John Lennon once said, is what happens while you're making other plans. The Spencer thing was just the latest in a long line of acts about which he was not proud. For some reason it was important that she understood this.

'Okay,' she said. 'I'd better get off to work.' He led her to the front door. He was right behind her when she turned suddenly and kissed him. He was surprised at first but then he responded, pulling her tightly against him. He could smell the fabric softener in her clothes and the apples in her hair. Her hand was round the nape of his neck, her fingers threaded in his hair. Then she broke away and wiped his lips with her thumb, a playful smile on her face.

'Lipstick,' she said. 'That wouldn't do, would it?

And then she was gone.

It took him a full ten minutes to realise he was grinning.

Even before she stepped into the street, Donna knew she'd made a mistake, a big one. Her pace was brisk but she resisted the impulse to break into a run, even though she wanted to distance herself from that mistake. She didn't know why she'd done it, it just seemed like the right thing. At the time, anyway. Her mind raced as she sought justification for the kiss. He was the subject. He needed to trust her. He was easily manipulated by women, that was why she had been placed close to him. She knew all about his mother and that girl who died. She knew about his self-imposed rules – never hurt women, children or animals. Don't involve civilians. That's what made him vulnerable. So, really a kiss was necessary, just to keep the momentum going, until the time came to use him. She nodded as she walked. Yes, that's it. It was nothing, just a logical progression in the process. Nothing to worry about.

Nothing to worry about, she repeated to herself. Absolutely nothing.

So why was she so worried?

14

THE FIRST THING Knight noticed when Ramage opened the door was his pyjamas. They were striped. Blue stripes. Knight hadn't seen anything like them since he'd visited an elderly uncle in hospital twenty years before. The old man had been dying of cancer and Knight's most vivid memory was of his parchment flesh, wheezing breath and those bloody striped pyjamas.

'Wicked PJs, Ricky,' he said as he brushed past Ramage into the hallway.

'Mister Knight,' said Ramage and immediately Knight knew that the man was far from pleased to see him. He waited in the pristine living room until Ramage locked his door and followed him in.

'What's on your mind, Ricky?' Knight asked.

'Nothing, Mister Knight.' But he kept his eyes on the carpet as if he was looking for a stray dust bunny – which was always possible, given his passion for neatness.

'Come on, son – I know you. There's something up.'

'Honest, Mister Knight, there's nothing.'

'Aye,' said Knight 'I'd be depressed too if I had to wear those jammies.'

Ramage managed a weak smile, but still didn't look Knight in the eye. The wee bastard was hiding something and Knight knew it. He now had two options; he could ignore it or he could beat it out of him. Giving Ramage a slap or two might brighten up his morning but he was on the clock here, so he decided to put the matter on hold and get down to business.

'Shoog MacLeish,' he said. 'I want him.'

'I'd heard you'd already lifted him.'

'He got bail. Naturally, that hacks me off more than a little so him and me need to discuss it.'

'Haven't heard nothing, Mister Knight. But I'll keep my ears open.'

'You do that.' Knight sat down in an armchair and saw Ramage's face sag. Obviously the little man had been hoping he would leave. Knight wanted to get to force headquarters in the city centre but he also knew he couldn't leave until he found out what was bothering Ramage.

'So, Ricky, old son – how's tricks?'

'Ticking over, Mister Knight. Just trying to keep my nose clean, you know?'

'Aye, right,' said Knight, sarcasm dripping from the two words. Ramage couldn't keep his nose clean with all the Kleenex in the world. 'You had a visit yet from anyone about the MacDougall business?'

Ramage looked up then, his face a picture of shock that set warning bells rang in Knight's head again.

'I take it you have,' he said. 'Who was it? The Commission? Police officers?'

'I spoke to the guy from the Commission yonks ago. Polis havnae been anywhere near me.'

'So why the fear, Ricky?'

'What fear?'

'I can smell it off you, son.' Knight stood up again and walked around the little man, inhaling theatrically. 'It's oozing out of every pore. Pure fear. Something's got to you, Ricky, something's got you shitting yourself. Now, it can't be me. We're pals, you and me. *Compadres*. So what can it be? You say no other officers have been to see you, so it's not that. And the Commission isn't in the business of putting the fear of death into the likes of you. So what is it? Who is it? Tell me, Ricky, before my curiosity gets the better of my restraint.'

'No-one, Mister Knight, and that's gen up. I've only spoken to the guy from the Commission thing.'

'You're lying, Ricky. You know I can always tell when you're lying.' Knight snatched Ricky's right hand and stroked his palm with his fingertip, feeling a sheen of moisture. 'You're sweating like a pig in an apple sauce factory. I think you'd better come clean, son...'

'I don't know what you're talking about...AAAH!'

Ramage's face contorted as Knight squeezed his fingers together.

'Confess, my son,' said Knight, tightening his grip. Ramage sank to his knees, trying to pull his hand free. 'Confess. It's good for the soul.'

'I...don't...know!' Ramage groaned, the excruciating pain shooting up his arm. Knight was a powerful man; he abhorred fat and even in middle-age his physique was well-toned by visits to a city centre gym, so Ramage felt as if his hand was in a vice, the fingers welding together, the bones compacting. And the little man was powerless to do anything about it. He wasn't a hard man. He couldn't fight back. All he could do was take it.

'I can keep this up all day,' said Knight, his fingers clenching even further. 'I can do worse, you know I can.'

'Honest!'

Knight let go and Ramage jerked his hand away, thrusting it under his other arm as if that could make the agony disappear.

'It's a funny thing, fear,' said Knight. 'There are different degrees. Now, I know you're frightened of me – and with good reason, for my wrath is terrible and my punishment awesome. But you're just as frightened of whoever has been to see you as you are of me. And that impresses the fuck out of me, it really does.' Knight gazed at the back of Ramage's head as he knelt at his feet like a faithful servant before a king. 'Make no mistake, Ricky, I'll find out who it is. And when I do, I'll be back to see you. Things won't be quite so pleasant next time. You know that, don't you?'

At his feet, Ramage nodded and whimpered.

'Just so long as we understand each other,' said Knight, stepping around the man's body and pausing again at the living room door. 'And don't forget Shoog MacLeish.' He waited for a response but was not surprised when he didn't get one. 'Don't get up. I'll see myself out.'

Donovan peered at the buttons on the security entry system and pressed the one marked 2/1. The flat in the up-market mansion block off Great Western Road was the most recent address

Bannatyne had been able to find for Aline MacDougall. Donovan hoped she still lived there, otherwise he'd have to work for a living. He heard a click on the intercom and a woman's voice crackled from the speaker.

'Yes?'

He leaned in closer to the metal panel. 'Mrs MacDougall?'

'Yes?'

'My name is John McCarthy. I'm with the Criminal Cases Review Commission. I'd like to ask you a few questions.'

'I've already been interviewed.'

'I know, but there are always other questions, Mrs MacDougall.' Donovan kept to the line he'd peddled to her ex-husband. Consistency was the name of the game in passing off a lie, because you never who was talking to who. 'It's important, Mrs MacDougall. I wouldn't bother you if it wasn't.'

There was a pause and then a sigh and the door clicked open.

'Thank you,' he said as he pushed open the door but he had the impression she'd already switched the intercom off.

She was waiting for him at the door of her second-floor flat. Donovan had heard she was an attractive woman, but he was unprepared for just how beautiful she was. She had dark eyes that seemed to take his measure immediately, perfect olive skin and black hair that curled down to her neck. She was wearing a dark trouser suit and a white shirt with a small silver Celtic cross nestling on a chain at her throat. He felt underdressed again, and hoped the sweat that was plastering his shirt to his back was not seeping through his jacket.

'I'm sorry, were you just going out?' He asked.

'Just coming in,' she explained, her voice cultured, with the faint trace of a Highland accent adding a musical quality. 'Who did you say you were?'

'John McCarthy,' Donovan said, handing her another of his phony cards. 'Scottish Criminal Cases Review Commission.'

She took the card and studied it, then glanced back at him.

'No,' she said and Donovan knew right away that he'd been rumbled.

'I'm sorry?'

'You're not from the Criminal Case Commission,' she said, her voice more curious than angry. She held the card out to him between two fingers. 'This is clearly something you've printed up yourself. Like you, it's not genuine.'

Donovan took the card from her and glanced it, wondering how the hell she knew that.

She said, 'So, why not tell me who you really are and what it is you want?'

Donovan decided to tell the truth. 'My name is Frank Donovan and I'm a private investigator. I'm looking into the case for a client.'

'And who is your client?'

'I can't say.'

'Is it Jerry?'

'Jerry?'

'O'Neill. Surely you know Jerry O'Neill?'

'Yes, I just didn't… well, I didn't expect you to be so familiar regarding the man who…'

'Had me raped?'

'Well, yes.' Donovan was taken aback. Her attitude was not what he expected from a woman who had been brutally assaulted in her home while her husband and teenage daughter watched. He didn't expect her to be so calm about mentioning it. She looked at him, something working behind her dark eyes. She was sizing him up, taking in his crumpled suit, scuffed shoes and face that had seen better days.

'You had better come in,' she said, stepping back then leading him into a large sitting room that was so clean and tidy that Donovan felt he was soiling it just by breathing. There were three vases with fresh flowers, two on tall plinths at either side of the bay window and a third on a long coffee table in the centre of the room. The walls were painted in delicate pastel shades and the high mantelpiece surrounded an enclosed coal fire. Tiny glass cats rested on top of the mantelpiece between two framed photographs of her daughter, Morrigan. These were more recent than the framed shot he'd spotted in MacDougall's home and she'd grown into almost a carbon copy of her mother. Apart from the eyes, for something sad and lonely cast a shadow across them.

An antique, French-polished bureau stood to the side of the fireplace, the door down to reveal neat piles of envelopes and writing paper. An address book lay open beside a telephone on top of the bureau. The furniture was tastefully eclectic. No three-piece suites for her, no manly leather Chesterfields like her ex-husband. A two-seater settee sat in the bay window and three other armchairs were ranged around a long coffee table. The chairs were delicate affairs and when the woman gestured to one Donovan was afraid to sit in it in case he broke it. He settled himself in carefully and watched as she opened a small box on the coffee table and held it out to him.

'Cigarette?' She asked.

'No, thank you,' he said.

'But you do smoke?'

'Yes,' he said.

'I thought so. All private eyes smoke, I'm sure. You call yourself private eyes, yes?'

'Not really.'

'I'm disappointed. But you do have a hat and a trench coat and a blonde secretary who loves you madly but you keep things purely professional, don't you?'

'I've got an old Crombie coat, I don't suit hats and I definitely don't have a secretary.'

'You'll be drummed out of the union.'

'I left when they wanted me to work to rule. I told them I wasn't speeding up for anybody.'

She smiled and lit her own cigarette. She had seated herself on the two-seater settee and now she leaned back, one arm stretched along the back, her legs crossed.

'Mrs MacDougall…' he began and saw irritation flash across her eyes.

'I prefer Moncrieff these days,' she said. 'It's my family name. I reverted to it a couple of years ago. I didn't want to be known as MacDougall any longer.'

'Your family is from Wester Ross, right?' Bannatyne had told him that much, but had omitted to mention the name change. Maybe he didn't know. Something Gentleman Jack didn't know – wonders will never cease.

'Yes, we have an estate up there.'

'But you didn't return there after the divorce?'

She shrugged. 'There was nothing for me there. I have lived in Glasgow for twenty years, Mister Donovan. It's my home now. And my daughter never took to the Highlands. She much prefers the city.'

'Does your daughter live with you?'

'No. She's grown up now. She makes her own way.' She drew on her cigarette and then asked, 'You'll not tell me who you work for, Mister Donovan?'

'I don't have many redeeming qualities. I don't even have many morals, come to that. But I never, *never*, break a confidence.'

'No matter what?'

'No matter what.'

'That is very laudable.'

'Thank you.'

'Will you tell me who it's not?'

'How do you mean?'

'If I ask you if my ex-husband hired you, will you tell me?'

'I can tell you it was not Mister MacDougall who hired me.'

'Good.' She leaned her head back and breathed smoke towards the ceiling. 'What do you want from me, Mister Donovan?'

He decided to get right down to it. 'Do you think Jerry O'Neill had anything to do with what happened that night?'

'No.' She didn't hesitate, didn't consider her reply. The word was spoken matter-of-factly, as if she were refusing a cucumber sandwich.

'Have you told the police that?'

'I told them at the time. I told the officers who came recently to see me. I told the real man from the Commission.'

'Exactly who did you tell at the time?' Donovan asked, knowing the answer before she even answered.

'An Inspector Knight. But he obviously didn't believe me.'

'Well, the evidence he found does seem to point to Mister O'Neill being involved.'

'Jerry was not involved.'

'How can you be so sure?'

'Because I am sure. I knew him.'

'Yes, I know you and your husband were friendly with the O'Neills but...'

'No, Mister Donovan, I *knew* him. I knew him very well.'

She held Donovan's gaze steadily as she let this sink in.

He said, 'By that I take it you...?'

'We were having an affair, yes.'

'And did Inspector Knight know this, too?'

'I saw no reason to hide it.'

'And your husband?'

'My ex-husband also knew. That's why he had Jerry framed. Is that the correct word? Framed?'

'It'll do,' said Donovan, feeling something fluttering in his guts. He was on the verge of some sort of breakthrough here, but he wasn't quite sure what it was. 'Can you prove that, Ms Moncrieff?'

'If I could then Jerry wouldn't have served six years for something he did not do.'

'Have you told anyone else this?'

'Of course – the other police officers who came to see me a few days ago and the gentleman from the Commission.'

'But you told no-one else prior to that? At the time?'

'I tried to tell that inspector, but again, he didn't seem interested.'

'And you're certain Mr O'Neill had nothing to do with it.'

'As certain as I can be.'

'But you could be wrong.'

'Of course I could be wrong. I'm certain Jerry did not have anything to do with what happened to me. *But I could be wrong.*'

Donovan understood. He'd once been certain he had a career in the police and a long and happy life ahead of him. He'd been dead wrong. 'Do you still see Mister O'Neill?'

'No. I've not spoken to him since the night it happened.'

Donovan nodded. 'So let me see if I've got this right. You were having an affair with Jerry O'Neill and you think when your husband found out he arranged the whole thing – why?'

'That's simple. To punish me. Have you met him?'

'Yes.'

'But you don't know Dorrell MacDougall as I do. He doesn't like to lose, Mister Donovan. He flies into rages if a punter backs an outsider and wins. He doesn't like it. And when he found out about Jerry and me, he flew into a rage. He hit me, Mister Donovan, but that wasn't enough. Not for him.'

Donovan knew that would not go down well with McCall and hoped he'd be able to keep him in check. The last thing they needed right now was McCall paying MacDougall a visit. 'So what about the evidence against Mister O'Neill? How do you account for that?'

She shrugged. 'My husband knows many people. Lawyers, artists, businessmen, even crooks. He knew some very unpleasant people, Mister Donovan.'

As she spoke, Donovan heard Ramage's voice whispering, 'These is evil bastards we're dealin with here.'

'There was no physical evidence – no fingerprints or DNA or whatever,' the woman went on. 'The man Ramage could have been paid to say what he said, those other men also. The map planted somehow. Who can say? Money can buy anything.'

'But you have no firm evidence to back all this up?'

'None at all.'

'Then how can you be so sure?'

She sat forward then and her eyes burned. 'I was raped, Mister Donovan. You will never understand what that is like. It was a dreadful, disgusting experience and it's something I've had to live with every day since. I refuse to let it dictate my life but it's still there, the memory, the terror, the humiliation, the rage. It was a personal violation, it was brutal. Jerry would not have ordered that.'

Donovan saw the strength in this woman. There was an underlying vulnerability that he had to look hard to find but it was there. What had happened to her was unforgiveable, but through sheer power of will she kept the trauma in check. Her defences, though, had been built brick by brick and held together by sheer grit and determination not become a victim, not let the bastards grind her down, but the memories would always be there, just beyond that wall, perhaps incomplete but waiting all the same. He had no doubt that in the quiet of the night those memories would breach that wall she had carefully erected and he wondered how she dealt with it. He wondered if he should say something, sympathise somehow, but he decided against it. She was right, he'd never know what it was like, would never fully understand. Any words he could form would sound hollow. He had a job to do and he was best to remain professional.

He said, 'Perhaps Mr O'Neill didn't order it. Perhaps the crew he recruited improvised.'

She shook her head. 'You weren't there. This was planned, the entire thing. You didn't see the look on Dorrell's face while I was taken from the room. Dorrell was enjoying it. This was my punishment for betraying him.'

Donovan hadn't taken to MacDougall, but was he capable of directing such a terrible thing, just to punish his wife and her lover? Donovan recalled his superior manner and lack of emotion when discussing the raid. Maybe, just maybe…

'What about the money?'

She dismissed it with a wave of her hand. 'Who knows? Dorrell always had some sort of scheme going, maybe that money was part of it. Maybe there was no money, I certainly didn't see it. He told us it was there, there had been hefty sums in the safe before, but I didn't lay eyes on it.'

He told us it was there. *Us.* Donovan's mind turned to Morrigan. He said, 'Your daughter…?'

Her body tensed and her voice sharpened. 'You will leave my daughter out of this.'

'I don't know if that'll be possible…'

'*You will not talk to my daughter.* I will not permit it. She suffered enough at Dorrell's hands even before this. I won't have her living through it all again. She can't take it.'

'How did she suffer at his hands, Ms Moncrieff?'

'That doesn't matter.'

'I think it does.'

'You're very assertive for a man who lied his way into my home.'

'But you let me in, knowing I wasn't what I said I was. You want to tell me all this because you're not certain the police and the Commission will act on it. Is that right?'

He knew he was correct. He could see it in her eyes. 'Perhaps.'

'So, how did your daughter suffer at his hands? Physical abuse?'

She nodded.

'Mental abuse?'

She nodded.

Donovan took a deep breath before saying, 'Sexual abuse?'

She stared at him, tears glistening, and he realised she could talk of her own suffering but not that of her daughter. She was incredibly self-controlled, but this was the chink in an armour she had carefully crafted for six years. He didn't want to press this. He wanted to sit beside her and tell her it was unimportant, that she didn't need to answer, but all his instincts – old instincts he thought had drowned long before in an ocean of bitterness and booze – told him this was important. He knew he had to keep pressing.

'Ms Moncrieff, do you believe your husband sexually abused your daughter?'

She held his gaze for a moment then nodded, a single tear forming in the corner of one eye, hanging there before bursting through to trickle down her cheek.

Donovan asked, 'Did you tell anyone else about this?'

She shook her head. 'They didn't ask.'

Donovan wasn't surprised. Knight certainly wouldn't ask, he was too intent on fitting up O'Neil, by the sounds of it thanks to Dorrell MacDougall. The Commission would only be looking at the original evidence while the current police investigation was interested only in how the matter might impact on the Job. No-one was really trying to find out who committed the crime. He glanced at the photographs on the mantelpiece. Now the young woman's smile looked forced and her eyes even more haunted.

He took a deep breath, knowing how his next words would be received. 'I need to speak to your daughter...'

'No.' Just the single word, and it hung between them like an exclamation mark.

'Ms Moncrieff...'

'No! I won't have these memories brought back to the surface! She's getting on with her life. Leave her alone.'

'Ms Moncrieff, you must understand...'

'I said no, Mister Donovan.' She wiped a tear from her face with her long, tapered fingers and looked around the room for a tissue. She got up and moved to a box of multi-coloured paper hankies on top of the bureau, but it was empty.

'Excuse me,' she said and left the room. Donovan wasted no time. He got up and walked to the bureau to flick through the pages of the address book.

15

KNIGHT WAS SURPRISED and that didn't happen very often. He knew the officer in charge of inquiry, the visitor from Lothian and Borders, was a DCI Vincent. What he didn't know was that DCI Vincent was a woman. She emerged from the lift at Pitt Street headquarters with young Donald Simms, a DS from the South Side who was also the son of an old mate. That disappointed Knight, to know that Charlie Simms' boy was a Rubberheel and was turning against his own. It more than disappointed him. It pissed him off.

The woman was tall and slim, too thin for Knight's taste. She also had a superior look about her – typical bloody Lothian and Borders if you asked him. *They think their shit don't stink.* There was another look in those eyes, though, one that Knight knew all too well. She was tough and she was smart, something that some of her male counterparts lacked. He was of the opinion that most women won their promotion by shagging their way up the ladder. Not that he had a problem with that, everyone had to get ahead. He knew a couple of men who had used their masonic ties to further their career. Another had married well. It didn't make them good coppers and one had been shunted to the side when he showed he couldn't produce the goods. No, everyone had to use what they had to make their way and he didn't have anything against women bosses, just as long as they left him alone. But this Edinburgh bitch wasn't leaving him alone.

'Don't much like the company you're keeping these days, Donnie,' said Knight as they approached him. He was leaning against the wall outside the office his contact had told him was being used by Vincent and her task force. Christ, a bloody task force! And he was their task. Well, he'd show them he wasn't going to be easy.

Donnie looked surprised to see him but Vincent kept her cool and despite his automatic dislike of some east coast cow digging around in his patch, Knight was impressed. As old Rudyard Kipling said, if you can keep your head while all about you are losing theirs, you'll be taller than every other bastard in the room.

'We've never met,' Knight went on, 'but maybe it's time we did. I'm DI Jimmy Knight.'

'I know,' said Vincent, completely unfazed. Her voice was low, cultured. He could imagine her laughing with the Chief Constable over cocktails. Or something.

'I hear you've been talking a lot about me. Thought I'd come by and let you say some of the things to my face.'

Vincent said nothing as she unlocked the office door and threw it open. 'Why not come in, then? We'll get acquainted.'

It wasn't a very big office. Just enough room for three desks and a couple of filing cabinets. Each of the desks had a computer but only two were switched on. Vincent dropped the folder she'd been carrying into a tray and perched herself on the corner of a desk, her arms folded. On a shelf behind her was a variety of books, most dealing with police corruption. Donald Simms wheeled a chair towards Knight before moving behind one of the other desks. Knight sat down and pulled his packet of cigarillos from his coat pocket.

'I'd rather you didn't smoke in here,' said Vincent. 'It's not good for the computers.'

'Frightened they'll get cancer?' Knight said, but put his smokes away.

Vincent didn't smile. 'What can I do for you, DI Knight?'

'Tell me what the hell is going on.'

'In relation to what?'

'In relation to this investigation you're heading. Into me.'

'We're investigating the circumstances surrounding the O'Neill case, that's all. It's not an investigation into you *per se*.'

'Don't shit a shitter, hen! You and I both know you've got me in your crosshairs for some reason. I just want to know why. Why you turning on your own kind?'

Vincent paused and stared at Knight for what seemed like a long time. Knight knew the woman was making a decision on how much she could say. Then, without taking her eyes off him, she said, 'Donald – could you give us a few minutes?'

The young man looked grateful to leave. Now there were no witnesses to what was said in that room. The gloves were off.

'Okay, first off,' Vincent said as soon as the door was closed, 'you're not my kind. Let's get that straight from the outset, right? You're the worst kind of copper imaginable.'

'And you're a good one, are you, darlin?'

'Some people think so. That's why your bosses called me in to head this probe. And I am not, and never will be, your darling.'

'Oh, a probe, is it? I'll bet you like that word. Probe.' Knight savoured the word, rolling the 'r', lengthening the 'o'. 'Sounds kinky. Sounds like just the sort of thing they'd like down at Fettes. But you're no in Edinburgh anymore, darlin. We don't turn on our own here.'

Her eyes flared at his use of the word 'darling' again but she didn't comment. 'And that's been the problem. There aren't many coppers like you in this city, but even a couple is too many. Too many loose cannons who feather their own nest whenever possible.'

'I'm a good cop. You look at my arrest record.'

'I've looked at your arrest record. I've also looked at the number of complaints that have been made against you.'

'By scroats! What are we doing now? Listening to scroats instead of brother officers?'

'There's no smoke without fire, DI Knight, and we've got a big bloody blaze on our hands. Your methods are atrocious, man! We've got beatings, coercion, allegations of evidence tampering. Jesus, there's even a suggestion of murder!'

'Then why don't you arrest me?'

'I will, eventually. But we're a small team and we have to work slowly, methodically. We'll get there though, don't you worry. The public want and deserve police officers they can trust.'

Knight laughed. 'The public! Let me tell you what the public wants. They want their soap operas every night of the week, the fitba on a Saturday and the hope they'll strike it lucky in the lottery. They want to get on with their lives without worrying about some wee scroat ripping them off. That's what they want. They don't care how they get those things just as long as they get them.'

Vincent listened to the speech without comment, then said, quietly, 'We'll get you, Knight – and your pal McClymont.'

'He's not my pal.'

'He's a registered informant of yours.'

'That makes him a tout, no a pal.'

'He pulls your strings, Knight.'

Knight leaned forward and his voice coarsened. 'No-one pulls my strings, you understand? No-one. I'm *his* handler. I'm *his* controller.'

Vincent didn't even flinch. 'Well, see, that's the trouble, isn't it? I've heard all this before, from other coppers like you. They're in control, they say. But they're not. It's the crook who's in control. It's the crook who's using the copper, not the other way about. You're no different. You're not running McClymont – he's running you. And he's got you infected with the same kind of disease that runs through his veins. Nietzsche was right when he said "if you gaze for long into an abyss, the abyss gazes also into you".'

Knight forced a smile onto his face, sat back and pulled out his cigarillos again. He slowly lit one up and puffed a mouthful of smoke into the air. 'Who the fuck's Nietzsche when he's at home?'

Vincent appeared to be struggling with her temper and sighed. 'He's the barman down at the The Phoenix.'

Knight shook his head and stood up, deliberately flicking ash onto the carpet. He walked to the door and opened it, then paused.

'Bit flowery for a barman,' he said and walked out. Vincent stared at the open door for a few seconds, her feigned anger gone. Donald Simms, who had been waiting outside, stepped in and closed the door.

'I take it there was a full and frank exchange of views?'

'There was,' said Vincent, moving round behind his desk.

'So now he knows you're after him?'

'He knew beforehand. I just told him he was more or less right. But he doesn't know what we've got, or what else we're doing, that's the important thing at this stage.'

'He might do a runner.'

'No, not him. Not DI Jimmy Knight.'

'How can you be so sure?'

'Because he's smarter than us, or so he believes. And he's not going to run from an Edinburgh tart and her lackeys. Not the Black Knight. No, so far he's reacted according to the profile – and he'll continue to do so. And as long as he only learns what we want him to learn, we'll get him.'

'Why didn't you tell someone you were having an affair with Aline MacDougall?'

O'Neill, shovelling earth in his front garden, looked up at McCall as McCall leaned over the fence. He had waited in Donovan's battered blue Metro further down the street until he saw Mrs O'Neill and the little girl leave the house. What he was about to discuss was not for their ears.

'Nothing to do with you, that's why,' O'Neill said and drove the blade of the shovel into the ground. McCall sighed and looked away. Some kids had opened a water main and were leaping in and out the impromptu fountain as it jetted into the air, enjoying the cool water on the sweltering day. The sun beams diffused through the prism of the spray into a rainbow splash. An old woman stood on the balcony of a nearby flat and yelled at them, her words floating through the droplets, telling the kids that she'd bring the law on them, that they shouldn't be doing that.

McCall looked back at O'Neill as he sweated over the shovel. 'Did you tell your solicitor?'

'No.'

'Why not?'

'Nothing to do with him, either.'

'Did you not think it would've helped you?'

'Tell me how, Perry Mason?' O'Neill paused and leaned on the handle of the shovel. 'The prosecution would just have said I was using her to get information on the alarm system.'

'And did you?'

'No. Christ, for all I knew she didn't even know the bloody code.'

'She could've been used as a witness for the defence. The victim, speaking up for the accused.'

'It wouldn't have changed the situation. It wouldn't have changed Ramage, or that other lying bastard, or the police evidence, or the map. Nothing.' O'Neill wiped the beads of perspiration from his forehead with the back of his hand. It was another hot day but across to the west a band of cloud was slowly moving in. The air around them was stifling and carried with it the threat of thunder.

O'Neill asked. 'Did you speak to her?'

'No. A friend of mine.'

O'Neill glanced towards the Metro parked in the shade of a stand of trees. 'The guy in the car?'

McCall nodded.

O'Neill said, 'Did he say how she'd looked?'

'He said she looked fine. More than fine. He said she was beautiful.'

'She was. Is. What about the girl? Did he see her?'

'No, she lives on her own now.'

O'Neill shook his head. 'That was one screwed up wee lassie, you know? I mean seriously screwed up.'

'We know about MacDougall and her.'

O'Neill gaped at him. 'Aline told your pal about that?'

McCall shrugged. 'It's what he does.' He was being casual about it but when Donovan told him about MacDougall abusing his wife and daughter, his first instinct had been to head out to Bearsden and have a word. It took every shred of Donovan's persuasive powers to stop him but McCall knew that when all this was over, MacDougall was due a visit. 'What did you know about it?'

O'Neill sighed, looking up at the blue sky, shielding his eyes from the sun. 'Only that Aline thought MacDougall was doing things to the girl. She never saw anything, could never prove anything. But wee Morrigan went from being an out-going, kind, smart youngster to a withdrawn, stroppy wee bitch, got herself into all kinds of trouble. We're talking when she was about thirteen, fourteen, something like that. Then one day she broke down and said her dad had touched her, had crept into her bed and... well, you know.'

The image of Spencer once again leaped into McCall's mind, only this time he was holding a little girl down on a bed. He tightened his jaw. 'Did she report it?'

'Aline tried but Morrigan refused to say anything. Then she really went off the rails, staying out all night, running with the wrong people. There were boys and drugs, stuff like that. I mean, this had been a really clever wee lassie and suddenly she was in trouble with the law. Nothing serious, nothing that got to court – her dad saw to that. Then came the robbery and I don't know what happened to her after that. I had my own problems.'

Yes, you did, thought McCall. 'Aline said she believes her ex-husband had you fitted up.'

'No, not him. He knew about our affair and he didn't give a shit. He told me as much, one day down at the sports club. As long as she didn't try to divorce him and take away his daughter, he didn't care what she did with her body. He was done with it. That's what he said – he was done with it, like she was a piece of furniture.'

'Was she going to divorce him?'

'No. Well, not over me. What was between us was physical, just sex, that's it. We liked each other, she's a remarkable person, but this wasn't a big love affair. I mean, as your pal said, she was a good-looking woman and me and my wife were going through a wee bad patch, arguing, you know the sort of thing. I wasn't a threat to MacDougall and his wee world. The only person who wanted me out the way was your pal McClymont and it's about time you understood that.'

McCall shook his head and walked away, hearing the chop-chop of O'Neill's spade cutting through the dirt again. The man had been framed, he knew that, but he still could not accept Rab had anything to do with it. He had profited from it, certainly, but that was a by-product of the exercise, not the aim. Knight, though – he was in it up to his neck. McCall just didn't know why.

Donovan stared at him as he climbed into the car, waiting to hear O'Neill's response. Arrow stood up in the back seat to welcome him, tail wagging. McCall rubbed his head and stared through the windscreen at O'Neill, hacking away at the square of earth the council called a front garden. For some reason, the image of a man digging a grave sprung into his mind.

'So?' Donovan said, finally.

'He doesn't think MacDougall was involved. Still thinks Big Rab did it.'

'Christ, talk about a dog with a bone.'

'Can't blame him. As he said, Rab was the only person to benefit from his conviction. Why would MacDougall go to all that trouble?'

'To punish his wife, that's what she thinks anyway. And then to get back at O'Neill for the affair.'

'O'Neill says it wasn't much of an affair. Sex, that's all. He says MacDougall knew about it and didn't care.'

'Aye – so he says. But MacDougall wasn't the sort to let anything slip through his fingers. And have you ever thought that O'Neill's no being exactly Mister Upfront with you, Davie? Remember – he doesn't know why you're doing this. He doesn't understand.'

McCall turned to look at Donovan. 'Why are *you* doing this, Frank?'

'You asked me.'

'So if I asked you to drive your car into a brick wall, you'd do that, too?'

Now it was Donovan's turn to gaze at O'Neill. Then the youngsters leaping in and out of the spray caught his eye and he watched them for a moment. 'I never did that when I was a boy. Did you?'

McCall looked at the kids and shook his head. 'Used to wonder what it was like though. I'd see it on American telly programmes but I'd no idea how to go about it here.'

'In our day we couldn't do it. The firemen don't like it – it lowers the water pressure if there's a fire. So I hear anyway.'

'You've not answered my question, Frank,' insisted McCall. 'You know why I'm doing this – why are you?'

'Revenge,' Donovan said, finally.

McCall waited, knowing Donovan would expand. 'You know about my trouble with the Job, the cash problems?'

McCall nodded.

'It was hellish,' Donovan went on. 'Mortgage. Credit cards. Bills. Money was tight. I was over extended, as they say. All because I gambled – horses, dogs, cards, casinos, you name it, I'd punt it. I covered it up for as long as I could but that wasn't long enough. They started cutting off the power, lawyer's letters started coming. I was desperate, really desperate. Bank wouldn't talk to me, I couldn't go to friends. So I hit a moneylender. I thought I could handle it but the debt got bigger and bigger.'

Donovan paused, waited for McCall to say something. He should've known better.

He sighed. 'Anyway, I was well screwed. Then my debt was bought over – by the Jarvises. I was on the verge of proving that Scrapper Jarvis had killed that boy Himes, remember that?'

McCall remembered. The war between the Jarvis Clan and McClymont had proved costly for both sides.

Donovan said, 'Somebody fed my problem to the Job and the rubber heels came in. And that was me, my tea was out and my pie was cold.'

'That someone was Knight?'

Donovan nodded. 'He was being paid off by the Jarvis Clan. They needed me out the way. So he told the Job and the rest is history. I lost everything – my career, my home, my family. Marie had suspected things were bad, but when it all came out, and I took to drinking too much, she couldn't take it. I left the house soon after it broke, never went back. I don't think she missed me. Maybe if I'd talked about it, we'd've salvaged something, but I was too messed up, too wrapped up in self-pity to open up. I was a dickhead and I paid the price for being a dickhead. But Jimmy Knight? He's a cancer and it's time he was cut out.'

Donovan paused, looking down at his hands on his lap, then went on, 'Is there something between you and that girl upstairs?'

McCall shifted slightly in his seat before saying, 'Something. I don't know what.'

Donovan said, 'Then talk to her. Tell her what's going on with you. Don't shut her out – you've done that before, I hear, and I did it with my wife. Open up, man, or you'll regret it.'

McCall looked out of the window as O'Neill straightened from his labours to face his wife and child who had arrived at the gate. The woman carried two plastic bags filled with groceries and O'Neill smiled as he unlatched the lock to let them in, ruffling the little girl's hair as she passed him. The child smiled up at him and wriggled away from him. The woman looked at the turned-over earth, said something and laughed. O'Neill looked at her with mock seriousness and raised a dirty hand to her face. His wife laughed again and stepped away from him. McCall heard the little girl scream with delight as her father chased her mother to the front door threatening to smear her face with muck. Family life, he thought. He'd never really known it, while Donovan had let it slip through his fingers.

When he turned back he saw a light burning in Donovan's eyes.

'Happy families, Davie. Maybe it's not for the likes of you and me. But Knight's not going to ruin this one, not again. He's up to his neck in this thing and I want to bring him down. Revenge, Davie. McCall and Donovan. Redemption and revenge. We're a regular fucking dynamic duo.'

McCall smiled and nodded.

'So,' said Donovan, turning on the ignition, 'fancy a wee trip up the West End, see if we can talk to the MacDougall lassie?'

'I thought the mother refused to give you her address?'

'She did. But I did what every self-respecting detective would do. I snooped. You up for it?'

McCall nodded to Donovan, who jerked the car into gear and pulled away from the kerb just as a dark cloud rolled over the sun, casting a shadow over the street.

16

The woman was in her late fifties, walking her West Highland Terrier but dressed for an afternoon social at her local church. She glanced at Donovan's car and McCall saw her look of disdain turn to one of suspicion. It was out of place in the Gardens, incongruous against the terraced houses that stretched up the incline towards deepest Hyndland. Glasgow's West End, an admirable mix of incomes, races and backgrounds, yet McCall still felt like a stranger in a strange land. The woman looked them both up and down, no doubt wondering if they were casing a joint for a break-in, then carried on towards Byres Road. Arrow, sitting up in the back seat of the Metro City, pressed his face against the glass and watched the little dog go.

Morrigan MacDougall's flat was on the second floor facing the private gardens across the road. Donovan had found out the young woman worked for a public relations agency in the city centre, so he guessed daddy must have put up some cash to buy her this place. She was only twenty-two and there was no way she was earning the kind of scratch needed for a flat round here, even in the over-priced world of PR. Unless it was rented, of course, but even then it wouldn't be cheap. Huntly Gardens was not obviously fashionable, boasting some townhouses on either side of the gardens that reveled in the term shabby chic, but it was still a pricey postcode.

By the time they'd made their way from O'Neill's home to the West End, it was after seven. Certainly it was a Friday and the chances were a young woman like Morrigan would be out on the town with her friends but they took a gamble that it was too early for her to be hitting the streets. The narrow twin roads split by the gardens themselves were lined with cars but they found a space near the top of the hill and walked back down. The ubiquitous controlled entry system met them at the large stained-glass front door and they heard her voice answering their buzz.

'Miss MacDougall?' Donovan said, leaning closer to the microphone.

'Yes?'

'Sorry to bother you, but I wonder if I might have a few minutes of your time?'

'Who are you?'

'My name is Frank Donovan, I'm a private investigator.' Donovan had abandoned his Commission investigator ruse. He'd told McCall that he didn't believe Aline would have warned her daughter – she was insistent she be kept out of it – but if this girl was anything like her mother, she'd see through it. When all else fails, honesty is the best policy.

'What do you want to talk about?'

'Jerry O'Neill.'

There was a pause and McCall shrugged when Donovan glanced back at him. He was standing on the steps leading from the pavement and he looked up at the second floor window but all he could see was the reflection of the sky and some swiftly forming dark clouds. For a second he thought Donovan had blown it, but then there was a buzz then a click and the door snapped open.

The roomy ground-floor entrance hall boasted a high ceiling and was decorated in a shade that the tin and Bobby Newman would've described as honey white, but to McCall it was just cream. A wide stairway stood to the left, curving gently to the right up to the next landing. They climbed the stairs past a series of oils showing scenes from the Scottish countryside. In one, McCall spotted kilted ghillies holding dead fowl while tweedy aristocrats stood nearby drinking whisky. In another, more aristos, resplendent in tartan, were attending some sort of ball in a large gothic room. His artist's eye liked the way the light had been caught in the paintings – the evening sun in the first reflected in the faces of the living and the feathers of the dead; the candlelight in the second glowing in the eyes of the dancers and the silverware on the large tables at the side. One day he'd try something in oils, he decided. One day...

The girl waited for them on the polished dark wooden landing.

McCall saw a very attractive, olive-skinned girl with the largest, darkest eyes he had ever seen. She had thick black hair curling down to her shoulders and was wearing a loose fitting t-shirt advertising T IN THE PARK and a pair of tight black leggings. From what Donovan had described, she was a younger version of her mother.

Donovan asked, 'Miss MacDougall?'

The girl nodded and looked towards McCall. 'This is my associate, Mister McCall,' Donovan continued. 'May we come in?'

She stepped aside to let them pass into her flat. The door took them directly into a spacious room looking out towards the gardens. The walls were painted a pale blue, the woodwork on the skirting boards and around a built-in cupboard stripped and varnished. A black mini music system sat on one of the shelves in the cupboard and the voice of Robbie Williams fell from speakers placed on brackets high up on the ceiling. The floor was also bare, the highly polished wood gleaming a warm dark brown. One rug, of an Oriental design similar to the one in her father's house, covered a square of floor in front of the ornamental gas fire.

Morrigan gestured for them to sit on the long four-seat sofa facing the fire while she dropped into a large, soft armchair in front of the cupboard. She tucked her legs under her, one hand gripping her ankles, the other arm propped against the back of the chair with her hand buried under her hair, cupping her neck. She looked at the two of them and waited for one of them to speak.

'Thanks very much for seeing us, Miss MacDougall,' said Donovan.

'You said you're here about Jerry O'Neill,' she said, her voice steady, curious even, and McCall suddenly realised that this girl was not the nervous creature they had been led to expect. He wondered if Donovan had sussed that too.

'Yes,' Donovan went on. 'We've been hired to investigate the case.' He paused, and McCall expected her to ask by whom. But the girl just continued to watch them, her eyes almost amused. 'We wondered if we might ask you a few questions. Would that be all right?'

'Why wouldn't it be all right?'

'Well, you've probably been over it a few times of late.'

'Yes. Twice. Once with the police and once with the man from the Scottish Criminal Review thing.'

'And you don't mind going over it again?'

'Why should I mind?'

Donovan moved slightly in his seat and McCall sensed his friend knew something wasn't quite right here.

Donovan began, 'Your mother...'

The girl's eyes flashed, the amusement McCall thought he saw earlier burning out. 'You spoke to my mother?'

'Yes. And your father.'

Her eyes went dead then. Or maybe both men just imagined it. 'My father. Really. I take it one or the other of them told you where to find me?'

Donovan smiled like a little boy. 'Well, actually, no. But we have resources, you know.'

'Resources? Yes, I'm sure you have.' The smile was back in her eyes but her face remained serious. 'So what do you want to know?'

'What do you remember about the night of the robbery?'

'Very little. I think I've blanked a lot of it, you know? Wiped the memory banks.'

'What do you remember?'

She looked away, as if trying to recall, 'I remember coming home and the men in the house. I remember one of them holding me, a knife at my throat. I remember them grabbing my mother. That's all.'

'Nothing more?'

'I was sixteen. It... wasn't pretty. The mind has its own defences.'

McCall wished his mind would blank out certain things. Donovan said, 'Did you know Jerry O'Neill?'

'He'd been at the house. He was a friend of my father's.'

'Not your mother?'

A pause then. A beat. Nothing more. 'Hers too.'

She knows about the affair, McCall thought. She bloody knows.

Donovan continued, 'Did you receive counselling after the robbery, Miss MacDougall?'

'Counselling? Is that a polite way of asking if I went mental?'

'It was a traumatic experience and it would be understandable if it had... erm... repercussions. Did you receive counselling?'

'Of course I did.' She stood up, slid a cigarette from a pack on the mantlepiece, lit it up. She blew a long cloud of smoke out and turned back to face them. Her voice was strained and her face taut when she spoke again. 'I don't remember what happened but I've been told. They raped my mother, Mister Donovan. Raped her while someone pressed a knife to my throat. And I don't remember any of it. So yes, I received counselling. I still do, for all the good it's doing.'

'Do you blame Jerry O'Neill for it?'

She drew a deep lungful of smoke in as she stared at Donovan. 'Of course I do. He organised it, didn't he?'

'You believe that?'

'He was found guilty. What else is there to believe?'

Donovan nodded, deciding to change tack slightly. 'You live here on your own, Miss MacDougall?'

'Yes.'

'No flatmates? Live-in boyfriend?'

'No.'

'But you're seeing someone, right?'

'Why?' She smiled then, a bright smile, her dark mood gone in an instant. 'You want to ask me out?'

Donovan smiled and shook his head regretfully. 'If I was twenty-five years younger, then I'd be first in line.'

'Age doesn't mean anything,' she said and McCall knew she was flirting. 'Age is nothing. I like my men older.'

'There's older and there's decrepit. But there is a boyfriend, right?'

'No-one special. There's someone I see but it's not serious.'

'How long have you known him?'

She shrugged. 'A while.'

'And he's older than you, right?'

She smiled, even licked her lips. 'I told you, I like my men older. They've got nothing to prove.'

McCall knew that was a load of bollocks, as did Donovan, judging by the rueful little smile. 'When did you leave home, Miss MacDougall?'

'You mean to come here?'

'Yes.'

'About two years ago.'

'When you'd be, what? Nineteen, twenty?'

'About that. I was going to college.'

'Did your father buy you this place?'

'Yes.'

'It's very nice.'

'Thank you.'

'Not cheap, though.'

'He can afford it.'

'I'm sure he can. But still, it's quite a place for a first time buy. He must love you quite a bit.'

She stubbed the cigarette out in an ashtray, even though it was only half-smoked. McCall had only seen that in movies.

'He's my father, of course he loves me,' she said, guarded.

'The divorce must have hit you hard, though,' said Donovan. 'I mean, the robbery, then your parents split up. That couldn't have helped you much, could it?'

'I coped. Divorce isn't such a big thing. Christ, I think all my friends come from broken marriages. It's the way of the world now, isn't it?'

'Does your boyfriend know about it all?'

'What does that matter?'

'Well, what I mean is can you talk about it to other people? Sometimes people bottle things up, keep things in, you know what I mean? That's not good for you. You've got to let it out.'

She gave him a quizzical look. 'You sound as if you know what you're talking about.'

'Believe me, Miss MacDougall, both Mister McCall and I know what we're talking about.'

Her dark eyes moved to McCall. 'Your friend doesn't say much, does he?'

'Get him on the subject of model trains and he'll talk your ears off.'

She smiled, this time straight at McCall. Christ, he thought, now she's flirting with me. Or was it just male wish fulfillment, that a beautiful young woman would be interested in him? 'He doesn't look like a model train kind of guy.'

'Believe me, he's got a wardrobe full of anoraks at home.'

She moved closer to McCall. 'Do you talk?'

'When I've got something to say,' said McCall.

'Which isn't often, right?'

McCall jerked a shoulder.

'But you listen, don't you?' She was standing right in front of him now, her legs almost touching his knee. 'You listen a lot, don't you?'

He looked up at her face. She was staring down at him, a small smile on her face. She was playing with him, he knew it now. She liked her men older, she'd said. She'd been flirting with Donovan and now it was his turn. This was what she did, flirted to get her own way, to get herself out of tricky situations, to divert attention. Is this what her father had done to her?

'Miss MacDougall,' said Donovan, quietly, 'did you know your mother was having an affair with Jerry O'Neill?'

The girl stepped away from McCall as if she'd been stung. She whirled around, back to the fireplace, her hand clawing at the cigarette packet.

'Did you?'

She lit the fresh cigarette, her back to them but McCall saw her body had tensed again. She exhaled smoke and turned back. 'Of course.'

'Before or after the robbery?'

She hesitated, sucking on the end of the cigarette. 'After. A long time after.'

'How did you feel about it?'

'How do you think I felt about it? I was angry. Who wouldn't be?'

'Are you still angry?'

'No,' she said but the way she gripped the cigarette, the way she tossed her head back to get strands of her from her eyes, the way she stood with her left arm across her chest, her hand gripping the upper part of her right arm told the men she was far from happy about it all.

'I think you'd better leave,' she said. 'I think I've said enough.'

She walked purposefully to the door and opened it. Donovan shrugged at McCall and they both rose.

'Thanks for the time,' said Donovan as they walked past her but she slammed the door behind them without a word.

As they moved down the handsome staircase, McCall said, 'That girl's got issues.'

'Don't we all?' Said Donovan.

Big Rab was pissed off. He had whirled his chair round behind the desk and was staring through the window of reinforced glass behind him. There wasn't much of a view; just a young mechanic bent over the open bonnet of a taxi, Radio Clyde blaring from a transistor radio, and beyond that a wire fence and a nest of squat industrial units. From where he sat the sky was a deep, unbroken blue but he could hear the top of the hour news and the newsreader was warning the city that the spell of good weather was about to break.

'How many times has he met with O'Neill?' Big Rab asked.

'Twice that I've seen,' said Stringer, his voice like a brick bouncing around a tin bucket.

'And they seemed like the best of friends?'

'They chatted away good style both times,' said Stringer, really enjoying this. This was a day he thought he'd never see – when McCall let McClymont down so much the big man seemed about to cry. The friendship between the two men stuck in Stringer's craw. He hated McCall – for no other reason than the man thought he was better than the rest of them. He didn't mix with the other lads, apart from Jimsie. Stringer wasn't one to pal around with others, but McCall made him look like a social butterfly. And that wasn't the only thing that irritated Stringer. It was McCall's attitude to him personally. McCall looked at him as if he was something slimy that had crawled out from under the toilet bowl. Anything that decreased McCall's standing in Big Rab's eyes was something to be capitalised on.

Big Rab said, 'And O'Neill's still bad-mouthing me?'

'I've spoken to people he's spoken to,' lied Stringer. 'They say the bastard's still calling you a grass.'

McClymont spun his chair back round to face Stringer. He picked up a ballpoint pen and drummed it on the desktop, as if keeping to a beat only he could hear. It was something he did when he was giving a matter his deepest consideration.

Tap – tap – tap.

Big Rab asked, 'You got O'Neill's movements down pat?'

Stringer nodded, waiting.

Tap – tap – tap.

Big Rab asked, 'You think you can pull it off?'

Another nod, still waiting.

Tap – tap – tap again, then a sigh and the pen was dropped onto the desktop. McClymont leaned back in his big chair. 'This wouldnae be necessary if Davie'd done what I asked him to do.'

Stringer kept his silence, waiting for the order.

McClymont reached a decision. 'Do it. Tonight.'

Stringer struggled to keep the smile from his face. He bobbed his head once and stood up.

'Pick someone to drive. Make sure he's dependable,' said McClymont.

Stringer nodded again, this time allowing his smile to break through. He'd already decided on the very boy.

17

THAT NIGHT MCCALL opened up to Donna. Donovan had forced his wife and child away with his silence and years before Davie had let Vari walk out of his life because he wouldn't let her in. Donovan was right – he didn't want to make the same mistake twice. There was something different about Donna, something he'd not felt since Audrey. Yes, she looked like her – slightly, anyway. Same colour of hair, same build, same way of making him laugh, same spirit. But there was more to it than that. She'd got under his skin, somehow, nestled there. He hadn't wanted it, hadn't sought it, but he liked it. So that night they went out for a meal and they made small talk, but all the while he was thinking how best to broach the subject. When they got back to his flat, he began to talk, nervously at first but gradually warming up until the words gushed out. He told her about his father, how he changed over the years, through drink, through rage, through demons eating away him until one night he beat his wife to death.

He told her about Joseph Klein, Joe the Tailor, who took him under his wing and introduced him to The Life. Joe was a crook, but to Davie he was a decent man and his death in 1980 left him rudderless. He told her about Danny McCall resurfacing years later and the havoc he caused, including murdering the woman Davie once believed was his future. He told her about his work, about the people he'd hurt over the years, the things he'd done. He told her it all, holding nothing back.

And he told her about The Dark.

'There was this old guy in the jail once,' he said. 'An old lag, you know? This was when I was doing time for a warehouse job. This guy, old Sammy, he'd done it all over the years. He knew my father, but then, no crook in this city hadn't heard of him. And Sammy, he told me about the Dark Thing. That's what he called it. The Dark Thing. It's something that comes over guys like my dad – and me, although I didn't know that at the time. The Dark blots everything else out, it takes over, like a defence mechanism, I suppose. Without it we'd never be able to do what we do, never be able to function in extreme situations, if you know what I mean.

'But there's a price.

'Every time The Dark comes, a wee bit of you dies. Every time it takes you over and you're the one who walks away, The Dark claims a piece of you until eventually, if you're not careful, there's nothing of you left.'

He paused then and smiled nervously. 'Sounds crazy, doesn't it? But this old guy said he'd seen it happen. He said that's what happened to my dad – The Dark took him over completely. Nothing could make it go away, not my ma, not the drink, nothing. He'd done too much, you see, and it took him over.'

He stopped and swallowed. This was the most he'd ever talked in his entire life, but he couldn't stop now. 'After Spencer, I realised I was almost gone. I don't want it to happen to me. I don't want to wake up one morning and find that there's nothing left, apart from the violence, apart from the Dark. I don't.'

Donna sat on the settee and listened to him without interruption. When he stopped speaking she stared at him for a minute, wondering how to react. Then she stopped herself. This was no time to be playing a part, no time to consider how she should respond to a given situation. It was time to react the way she wanted to. So she stood up, walked over to McCall as he stood in front of the cold gas fire, waiting for her to say something. But she remained silent, letting her fingers and her lips do all her talking. She reached up with both hands to his face, leaned forward and kissed him. It was a long kiss, a soft kiss, a kiss designed to say everything she felt. But even as she kissed him, even as his arms moved around her body, she wasn't sure what she was doing. All she knew was that it felt so right.

The Griffin wasn't a trendy bar or a theme pub or a fancy bistro, despite its location in the city centre. It wasn't a spit in the corner dive, either. It was an old-fashioned Glasgow pub with a U-shaped bar of polished wood and frosted windows looking out onto Bath Street and Elmbank Street near Charing Cross. The walls were wood-paneled, but the old-fashioned charm was offset by a widescreen telly tuned to Sky Sports. It was a favourite for students who liked to keep it real and regulars who enjoyed their drink without expensive frills or the need for earplugs to block out the constant thud of chart hits.

Knight knew Simms tended to repair to the pub on a Friday night to sup a pint or two of real ale and chat up the blonde barmaid he had his eye on. The bar wasn't busy but that wouldn't last. Soon it'd be jumping like a punk on a pogo stick.

Simms sat in a booth alone, reading a copy of the *Evening Times*, a pint glass half full of a rich brown liquid at his elbow. Knight slid into the leather seat opposite him and smiled as Simms looked up.

'Don't look so surprised, son,' said Knight. 'You're no exactly a man of mystery. You were easy to track down.'

Simms tried for nonchalant but didn't quite make it. His voice sounded tense. 'What do you want, Jimmy?'

Knight dove straight in. 'Does your faither know what you're doing with that Fettes cow?'

'What's my dad got to do with it?'

'He was a thief-taker, son, like me. A bloody good one. He wouldn't like you playing politics at the expense of a brother officer.'

'He wouldn't like some of your methods either.'

Knight smiled. 'Don't you kid yourself on that score. There's some things your faither did that don't bear too much scrutiny, if you get my drift. You're what? Twenty-six now? Twenty-seven?'

'Twenty-nine.'

'Old as that? You're wearing well. But once you've been in the Job long enough to do more than wipe your nose you'll understand that to be a good thief-taker takes commitment to getting the job done, no matter what.'

'If by that you mean breaking every bloody rule in the book, then maybe I don't want to understand.'

'Well said, son. Brave words. Spoken like a true lickspittle.' Knight leaned forward, clasping his hands in front of him and lowered his voice. 'Let me tell you a wee secret about real police work, son. Fuck the rule book. It doesn't exist, not for the likes of your dad and me. Aye, we follow it to a certain extent, but when it comes down to it, the rules – the law – just get in the way of hoovering up scroats. Let me ask you a wee history question, you can phone a friend if you want. Apart from keeping the peace, what else were police officers in this fine city expected to do around two hundred years ago?'

Simms shrugged and Knight smiled.

'Not big on the history of the Job, eh? Well, I'll tell you. Part of their duties was to clear up the manure off the roadways, from the horses, you know? And guess what – that's still our job, to keep the shit off the streets. And do you think we do that by following fucking rules laid down by some bloody politicians in Westminster or Holyrood? Just because some bleeding heart liberals say that we have to respect every scumbag's rights, do you think that people like me and your faither stop doing our job? You know we don't.'

Knight looked down at the newspaper on top of the table and saw that Simms had been reading his horoscope. 'You believe in that stuff, do you?'

Simms followed Knight's gaze to the printed page and shrugged. 'I read them like everybody else.'

'Well, I'm here to tell you that it's a load of shit. And I'll tell you why. Because for it to be worth anything there would need to be order in the universe, in life. There would need to be some all-encompassing plan. But there isn't any order, no grand design. Life is chaos. Shit happens and we react to it, that's the way it is and no speywife with a crystal ball and set of tarot cards can predict it.'

Simms sighed. 'Jimmy, what is all this?'

Knight reached out and gripped Simms by the wrist. He leaned closer, his mouth set in a tight line. 'I'm talking here, son, and you'd better listen. This is important stuff. Do you want to know the secret of life?'

Simms shifted slightly in his seat, a bit overawed by the intensity of Knight's gaze and the strong grip on his wrist. He nodded.

'The secret of life is that there is no secret. There's just life. All those books about this prophecy and that prophecy and codes and keys is all just so much bullshit designed to squeeze a few quid out of the gullible. There's just life. No grand design. No secret knowledge. Just people making their way, shagging, fighting. Living. They're all just trying to keep away from the beasts who live in the dark. And the beasts are out there, son, and it's only the flame that keeps them at bay and people like me, and your dad, are the keepers of that flame. And people like you and that ball-buster Vincent and all her fucking rules will be the ones who'll let it die.'

Knight released his grip of Simm's wrist and sat back.

'Where's all this leading, Jimmy?' Simms asked, resisting the urge to rub his flesh where Knight had squeezed.

Knight drew a deep breath through his nose. 'What's this task force got on me?'

'I can't tell you that.'

'Did you listen to a word I just said, son? The more time you spend on investigating coppers means the more chance there is of us weakening. And we cannot afford to weaken, do you understand that? The beasts are waiting out there, snarling in the night, and I haven't the time to worry about my own kind jumping me from behind. I need to know what you have.'

'Don't ask…'

'Your faither.'

'Leave him out of this.'

'I can't leave him out of this. I mean, how ironic is that? Part of the holier-than-thou investigating team out to crucify me is the son of the copper who introduced me to McClymont in the first place. It's classic, so it is.'

Simms stared at the man on the other side of the table, trying to see past the mocking smile to find the truth. 'That's not true.'

It wasn't true, but Knight knew this wishy-washy little bastard couldn't be sure. 'You wish it wasn't. But it is.'

'My dad was a good cop. He retired without a blemish on his record.'

'He knew the score, and that's what made him a good cop. He knew how to win our war – and we're at war, don't you kid yourself that we're not – he knew that to win we had to have allies. McClymont was and is an ally. He also plays for the other side, but that's what makes him so valuable. So he does us a few favours…'

'Bribes, you mean?'

'*Don't take that tone with me.* Your father showed me the way, remember?'

'You're a liar.'

Knight smiled. 'Let me lay my cards on the table, then.'

'Christ, I wish you would.'

'It's simple – if I go down, I take a lot of people with me. Know what I'm saying? Your faither will end up with more than a blemish on his record, he'll have a fucking rash. And think of the effect that will have on his pension. Believe me, I can do it.'

'You're a bastard, Knight, you know that?'

'Aye, it's been said before. Just give me the keys to your office, son. I'll be in and out before you finish another pint. No-one need ever know.'

Simms swallowed hard. Knight waited, guessing what was going on in the younger man's head. This task force was his big chance to shine, his route to promotion. He couldn't just hand over his keys. But he had his father to consider. He was not a well man. His heart. He knew his father had worked with Knight for a time and revelations of misconduct could not only ruin his reputation, they could also kill him.

Knight saw all this working in Simms' eyes and was not surprised when he glanced furtively around to ensure that no-one was watching. He pulled a ring of keys from his jacket pocket and laid them on the table.

'Good lad,' said Knight as he stood up, smoothly plucked the keys from the table and dropped them in his coat pocket. As he passed the bar, he told the barmaid the gentleman in the corner wanted another pint.

He walked up Bath Street, then crossed over and turned right into Holland Street, heading for the rear entrance to Strathclyde Police HQ. The building fronted onto Pitt Street but Knight always entered through here. Dark clouds had gathered and Knight wouldn't be surprised if there was rain before morning. He would not be sorry for a break in the heat. He liked the rain. It cleansed everything.

The security man at the door was gazing at pictures of a nude model in a tabloid and barely glanced at Knight's warrant card as he passed. Knight punched the button for the lift and waited. Unlike a working police station, the headquarters building would be almost totally empty at this time on a Friday night. There would be cops in some of the specialist squads on duty – the drug squad, serious crime – but generally the men and women based here were nine-to-fivers, many of them civilian workers, the rest officers reduced to penpushers in uniform. That was Knight's worst nightmare, being told he would have to police a desk until retirement. He was a frontline copper, a thief-taker and that's the way he intended to stay.

The third floor corridor was empty though brightly lit. As Knight walked towards the task force office he was pleased to see that not one of the other rooms on the floor had lights blazing. He found the correct key on Simm's ring and slipped into the room, pulling a small torch from his coat pocket. No need to advertise his presence to any stray person roaming the corridors. He swung the thin beam around the room, lighting first on the filing cabinets.

There was nothing of interest in the files. In fact, the cabinets were half-empty, which meant Vincent kept everything in her computer. She looked the type, everything stored away neatly on her hard drive. Knight would have placed a bet on her getting all hot and bothered over pictures of stripped-down Apple Macs. He sat down at Vincent's desk and switched on the machine, watching icons flashing on the screen as it fired up. Then it asked for a password and Knight's heart sank. He should've thought to ask Simms if there was a password. He typed in Vincent's name but the computer rejected it. He tried 'password'. Nothing. The cursor flashed mockingly at him as he tried to figure out what sort of password a woman like Vincent would use. It could be anything – a series of numbers, a birthday maybe, or an anniversary; or a word, any kind of word. If it was something personal he was screwed, until he could find out more about her. Just for something to do, he punched in 123456. It didn't work, either. He wasn't surprised. He sat back in the chair and looked around the walls, just in case she had stuck it up there – it's amazing what people will do – but there were no notes. He pulled open the desk drawers but still nothing. He was just about to phone the pub and ask for Simms when his gaze fell on the line of books beside him. James Morton's *Bent Coppers* was there, Martin Short's book on *Lundy*, a couple on Scottish miscarriages of justice, at which Knight snorted because to his mind the only miscarriage of justice was that some fucking publishers had put them out in the first place. The last book, by Peter Maas, made him smile. Surely not, he thought, but he typed in the title all the same.

SERPICO.

The screen flashed a welcome and opened up DCI Vincent's world. *Serpico*, he thought. *Some people think they're so bloody clever.*

He hunched forward and studied the list of files that appeared on screen. One bore his name so, naturally, that was the one he opened first but it didn't tell him much more than he already knew. The O'Neill case's return to the public eye had prompted the investigation. It outlined Knight's career, many of his arrests, raising questions about a number of them. These didn't worry Knight, for he knew there was no way their suspicions would stick. There was a cross-reference to Rab McClymont, but that didn't enlighten him much. There was no mention of MacLeish, though, which puzzled him. He was certain the wee shite was involved in this somehow.

He closed the file marked KNIGHT and looked for one marked MACDOUGALL. And sure enough, after a detailed history of the case – which Knight skipped, because he'd been there after all – he found mention of MacLeish for the first time. What he saw made his blood run cold. He'd known MacLeish had been banged up in Durham, but he hadn't known he'd shared a cell with one Brian Lang. The name sent those now-familiar alarm bells clamouring in Knight's brain. Knight knew Lang, knew he had a liking for young men. He would've been easy meat for a manipulative bag of pus like MacLeish. And Lang would have been saying all sorts of things to the cheeky wee sod, to impress him. Things he shouldn't be saying. And sure enough, Lang had confessed to being on the MacDougall Raid, spilling all sorts of details over six months to MacLeish, who had stored it all away like a sneaky wee squirrel. Knight shook his head and scrolled down, looking for a clue as to where the wee bastard was now, but all he found was that they had sprung MacLeish on the jeweller's charge and spirited him away to an unspecified safe house. He went through that file line by line but there was no hint as to where the safe house was.

He sat back, idly running the mouse over the pad and watching the cursor roam across the screen. So, they had MacLeish with his tale of a fellow con spilling the beans about the MacDougall Raid. It was bad – but not bad enough. MacLeish was a lying wee shite-hawk at the best of times, why should anyone believe him? And Lang might trade on the notoriety to get his wick dipped, but he was not the type to take it to court. They had to have more. There must be something else.

He closed that file and scrolled down the list, finding what he was looking for near the bottom. It was a name he hadn't been expecting but there it was. He clicked on the file and as the first drops of rain struck the window, he began to read.

Jerry O'Neill stood in the closemouth watching the rain bouncing off the pavement. It wasn't forgetting to come down, as his mother used to say. The gutters were already awash, weeks of dust baked by the sun having blocked the drains. He heard his wife and child coming down the stairs behind him, knew they were both tired, and wished his stiff neck hadn't forced him to refuse the offer of a lift from his father-in-law. But the old bastard had really got up his

nose, as usual. O'Neill knew the man had never liked him, even
before he was convicted. Now, of course, he was able to make sly
comments about O'Neill not being able to support his daughter
and grandchild. He'd stuck it as long as he could but when he felt
his temper begin to snap he knew it was time to go. His wife had
given him a sharp look but kept silent. He knew he was in for a
rebuke when they got home and sighed. He glanced at his watch,
saw it was just before 11pm. Later than he'd thought. He
wondered if it really would've hurt to take the lift? Too late now,
though. There was nothing for it but to head for the bus stop on
Crow Road.

His daughter took his hand and looked up at him. He could see
she was dead beat but she was still smiling. 'We're going to get
wet, dad,' she said.

'Naw, hen – we're going to get drookit,' he replied.

'That's the same thing.'

'Naw, it's no. Wet's wet, but drookit's soaking.'

His wife had a bright red umbrella in her hand and she stepped
past them to open it. 'I don't see why dad couldn't have driven us
home,' she said.

Oh God, O'Neill thought, it's starting already. 'We've got to
stand on our own, Sylvy, you know that.'

'A run home doesn't make us beholden to anyone. Certainly
not at this time of night.'

'Tell that to your old man,' said O'Neill, pulling his collar up
around his neck and stepping out into the deluge. His wife sighed,
took their daughter's hand and followed him.

It happened before they reached Crow Road.

The car had pulled in ahead of them and O'Neill had been
aware of a figure climbing out and walking in their direction, but
huddled as they were under the brolly, tipped against the slanting
rain, he hadn't paid any further notice. When the man stopped in
front of them O'Neill barely took in the fact that he was burly and
wore a ski mask. He didn't even notice the gun in his hand until it
was raised, until it was aiming at him, until it was too late.

The two shots ripped through the rain and into his chest. He felt as if he had been punched hard and fell against the wet sandstone of the tenement wall. He hung there for a second, his arm propped against the wall, looking down at the blood dripping onto the pavement. He wondered where the hell it was coming from, then realised it was his blood. His legs gave way and he slid to his knees and he heard something – a scream building and rising. He looked up, rain flooding his eyes, and saw the man still pointing the gun at him. O'Neill tried to say something, anything, but the muzzle flashed and he felt a sting at his temple and then he felt nothing else.

Sylvia O'Neill watched her husband's head snap back and a spray of crimson drench the wall behind him. Her scream had started with the first shots and now it reached a crescendo. She didn't know she was moving until she felt the ski mask between her fingers and the man was twisting in her direction. The gun exploded again and her stomach caught fire and she was falling away, her fingers pulling the balaclava free and she saw the man's face, his bald head and the smile, but then she was on her back, the mask still in her hand, her other hand twitching spasmodically in the air over the wound, though she didn't feel any pain now and something big and red was dancing away from them and she realised it was the brolly rolling down the street, pushed on by the wind and the rain. It was very graceful, like a ballet dancer. she thought, as the darkness closed in on her forever.

Stringer looked down at her and then at the little girl who stood in the middle of the pavement, her eyes wide, her mouth open, staring at the bodies of her father and mother, at their blood flowing in little streams across the concrete and into the gutter. But when she looked up at him, at his face, he saw no fear there.

Perhaps she's in shock, Stringer thought, before deciding it didn't matter. All that mattered was that the wee brat could identify him. He raised the gun again.

'Christ, don't do it, man,' a voice yelled. He looked over his shoulder and saw Jimsie standing on the pavement beside the car, the driver's door open. 'Leave her!'

Stringer smiled and lowered the gun. The girl's gaze followed it down and then moved back to his face. He nodded to her before turning towards the car and yanking open the rear door. Jimsie climbed back in, slammed the door, eager to be away. Stringer was halfway in when he looked back over his shoulder to see the little girl hadn't moved, hadn't said a word, but she was still looking at him.

'Hang on,' he said, then turned and raised the gun. He fired once, saw the blood burst from her raincoat and then her body crumpled.

'Jesus Christ, ya fuckin maniac!' Jimsie screamed and gunned the motor, pulling away from the kerb. Stringer launched himself into the back seat, laughing now, the rear door still swinging as the car gathered speed, leaving the three bodies behind on the rain-slick pavement and the three streams of blood merging into one before flooding into the gutter and on into the darkness.

And half a mile away, on a brick wall near to a school, the rain began to wash away the recently painted words JERRY O'NEILL IS A GRASS.

18

JOE THE TAILOR looked across the chessboard at Davie. They were in the study of his old house near Barlinnie Prison, the old man's books around them, the French windows looking out onto the spacious garden. It was dark out there, but Davie could hear the crows in the mature trees, calling in the night. He felt safe here. He felt wanted. Joe had taught him the game but Davie only beat him once, shortly before the old man died. In this room. In this very room.

The pieces were spaced across the board but Joe wasn't looking at them. He was looking at Davie with a worried expression. Joe seldom looked worried because he always had everything under control. The fact that he was worried now worried Davie.

'You're in the end game now, David,' said Joe.

Davie looked down at the board, thinking they'd only just begun to play. He couldn't have blown it already surely? Joe was good, but he wasn't good enough to take the game after only a few moves.

'Not this game, David,' said Joe and Davie looked back again. He looked older now, older than he had a moment ago. And he was fading. 'You are weak, David, too open. You must be very careful from now on. People you think are friends are not. People you think you can trust you cannot.'

The voice began to grow faint, little more than a whisper as Joe's outline evaporated.

'The end game, David. You are weak, David… too weak…'

And then Davie was alone at the board and all he could hear was the sound of rain rattling at the windows and the faint voices of carrion birds cackling from tree tops he couldn't see.

He awoke to the rain at his own windows, the echo of the crows still reverberating in his ears. He hadn't dreamed of Joe for years, had no idea why he'd done so this night, but the old man's words troubled him.

People you think are friends are not...
People you think you can trust, you cannot...

He knew Joe hadn't really visited him from beyond. He believed the ghosts of those he had lost were with him, but not in a literal sense. They were only memories, a face, a voice, a smile from the past that his mind conjured up. They were part of him. They were born of loss, of need, of guilt. He knew it was his own subconscious speaking in the dream, telling him something, warning him of something. But what? Davie didn't want to mistrust everyone, not anymore. Lying in the dark, listening to the rain pounding on the street outside, he forced himself to consider Donna. Something had changed between them earlier and he wasn't sure what. He'd told her about himself, many of his secrets, things he'd spoken to no-one about, ever. Not Audrey, not Vari. Not even Bobby. But he'd told her. He felt as if he'd spoken for hours, hell, maybe he had. In the end they kissed again, making him feel like a schoolboy once more with his first crush. Then she had returned to her own flat. He'd thought it might've gone further but she didn't seem to want that, although he could sense her hesitancy at the door, as if she was conflicted. Conflicted, yes, he knew all about that. What did he really feel? He liked being with her, wanted to be with her, felt relaxed in her company. When he was away from her, he thought about her. When he saw her, something caught fire in his chest.

But...

You cannot expect this woman to be sucked into your life, he told himself. She's a straight arrow and The Life would kill her – or drive you apart. She's had one loser of a husband and she doesn't need another.

Unless he got out, walked away. He'd told Bobby that was what he wanted. He really was sick of it all. Maybe she was the impetus he needed. Maybe this – finally – was the end game.

And then he heard the hammering at his door. Arrow was instantly on his feet, staring at the bedroom door. McCall looked at the bedside clock and frowned. At half one in the morning there was no way this was good news.

He padded barefoot up the hallway to the front door, Arrow darting ahead of him. A low growl began to build in the dog's throat and he told him to take it easy.

Jimsie stood on his step, his clothing drenched, his eyes red and swollen. He held a Safeway plastic bag with something heavy inside in his hand.

'Davie,' he said, 'I'm fucked! I'm really fucked!'

McCall pulled him into the flat, steered him to the living room and towards an armchair, taking the plastic bag away from him. Arrow had stopped growling but he was still alert, sensing something in the air. The dog knew Jimsie, but he must've been giving off a different kind of scent tonight for he remained on his feet, watching the young man intently. Something cold settled in the pit of McCall's stomach when he glanced inside the bag and saw an automatic pistol nestling at the bottom.

'Jimsie, son,' he said, 'what have you done?'

'I never meant to, Davie, you've got to believe me. I never knew what was going on. I thought he was only gonnae give the guy a slap, you know? I never knew he had a shooter with him. I never knew!'

McCall said, 'Keep your voice down.' It was unlikely anyone would hear but he could tell the young man was on the verge of hysteria.

Jimsie's eyes took on a panicked look but he dropped his voice to a whisper. 'Aw, man, Davie, I'm sorry. I'm sorry. Look, I'll fuck off, okay?' He began to rise but McCall laid a hand on his shoulder and pushed him back down.

'It's okay, Jimsie. Relax. But just keep it down, okay?'

Jimsie dropped back again.

'Now,' said McCall. 'Who was going to get a slap?'

'That guy O'Neill, the one you've been talking to...'

McCall suddenly felt the world around him lurch. 'What happened?'

'Stringer told me to drive him up Crow Road way where the guy was visiting someone. His wife's dad, I think. Stringer said that Big Rab wanted us to deliver a message and I thought we were just gonnae push him around a bit, you know? Tell him to shut his mouth. I was to wait in the motor and Stringer would do the business. Stringer got out and just started blasting. He shot the guy, just like that, and then he shot the woman and then... and then...'

Jimsie began to cry, big fat tears rolling down his face as he remembered the sight of the bodies in the rain-washed street.

McCall knew what was coming but he asked anyway, 'What, Jimsie? What then?'

'The wee lassie, Davie. Oh God, the wee lassie.' He hid his face in his hands, rocking back and forward as he concealed the tears from his friend. McCall's mouth went dry and he felt the chill spread from his belly.

Jimsie's voice was muffled behind his hands. 'I didnae know what to do. I screamed at him not to do it, but the crazy bastard shot her. I drove off and he was laughing in the back of the motor – laughing, Davie! As if he'd enjoyed every minute of it. Davie, what am I gonnae do?'

McCall stared at the young man then held up the bag with the gun. 'He give you this?'

Jimsie dropped his hands and nodded. 'Told me to get rid of it somewhere, but I didnae know how or where. I didnae know where to go. I couldnae go home. I just walked the streets, man, thinking about that wee lassie and the way she looked when her ma and da were shot and then when Stringer shot her.'

McCall nodded, his mouth working against the glue-like consistency of his saliva. 'Did anyone see you there?'

The boy shook his head. 'Don't think so. I was in the motor mostly and it was pishin down so there was nobody walking about.'

'Okay, here's what you do. You get home and lie low for a couple of days. Tell your granddad what's happened but nobody else, understand? I'll get rid of the gun.'

Jimsie stood up, wiped the tears away from his face with the back of his hand and shuddered, as if the cold from McCall's body had reached out and touched him. 'What you gonnae do, man?'

McCall stared at him, hearing Joe's voice again, telling him he was in the end game. 'Hand in my notice.'

Donovan also lay awake that night but he was not pondering the frailties of the human heart. He had instinct on his mind, in particular his own. He had been a bloody good cop before being grassed up by Jimmy Knight, he knew that. He had been good because his instincts had been good. He had a sense for truth, something he'd shared with Knight. He knew when someone was lying and when someone was being straight. He thought that ability was long since dead, but no, here it was back again, nagging away at him.

Jimmy Knight was in it up to his neck, that much was certain. He'd dug up Ricky Ramage, he'd spoken to Howie Lindsay's father before the robbery even took place. That meant he knew something was going to happen and was putting the frame-up in place. The question that remained was why? Why had he set out to deliberately set up Jerry O'Neill? And who was he doing it for? McClymont? Or someone else?

Donovan had interviewed all three members of the MacDougall family now and they had each told the same story, more or less. One of them, or all them, was hiding something. But who? As the Bard said, that is the question, Horatio, my old chum. He thought about Dorrell MacDougall: arrogant, cool, a proper bastard if ever there was one – especially if he had been interfering with his own daughter, as his ex-wife claimed. And then there was Aline herself: beautiful, self-assured, but surely wounded by the sexual assault. Both had been keen to keep Morrigan out of the picture, saying she had been disturbed enough. But Morrigan, so like her mother, seemed clear enough, if a bit confused about events that night. Sure, the sight of her mother being led out of the room had affected her – who wouldn't be affected? – and if it was true her father had been a bit more than a loving parent then it was only natural for her to be psychologically scarred. Being saddled with the name Morrigan wouldn't have helped. But Donovan felt there was something else going on behind those beautiful eyes. She had openly flirted with both him and McCall. What the hell was that about? Donovan felt sure that if either of them had given her the slightest encouragement she would have taken it further. Or was it merely a middle-aged man's fantasy? He closed his eyes, shook his head. No, she was coming on to them, he was certain. The girl liked older guys, she'd said so.

Donovan felt the girl was the key to the whole thing. If you asked him why he thought that he would be unable to answer. But he was certain.

Well, certainish.

Donna awoke with a gasp and sat up in bed. She didn't know what had snatched her from sleep, just that something in her dreams had been disturbing enough to force her awake. Whatever she had been dreaming about had made her heart hammer in her chest and had her casting her eyes around the dark bedroom to ensure there was nothing there. When she was a child, her dad would ease her back to sleep after clicking on all the lamps to show here there was nothing in the dark that wasn't present in the light. Even now, she resisted the urge to switch on her bedside lamp to make sure.

She lay back down, listening to the silence, but could not shake off the feeling that something was wrong, very wrong.

And then the silence was shattered by the high-pitched beep of her telephone. She picked up immediately. 'Hello?'

'We need to talk,' said DCI Allison Vincent.

19

THE CARRIER BAG dangled from McCall's hand, the heavy pistol inside thumping against his leg as he strode through the rain, hands thrust in the pockets of his coat. He didn't notice the weather, he didn't notice the weight of the gun hitting him. The Dark had claimed him as he walked and he welcomed it.

Stringer lived on the first floor of a blonde sandstone tenement that had recently been taken over by the local housing association and sandblasted to its former glory. Although the windows had been replaced with new double glazing and the close had been decorated, they had not yet fitted a door entry system. McCall saw a light in the living room window and smiled thinly. Probably up playing with himself, he thought, thinking about the lives the man had shattered tonight. McCall took the steps two at a time and paused for a second outside Stringer's door. He took the gun out of the bag, crumpled the carrier bag up and thrust it into his coat pocket, then rattled the letterbox.

Stringer took a while to answer the door, so maybe he had been asleep. McCall heard his footsteps in the hallway and then there was a moment of silence while the man no doubt peered through the peephole. McCall held the gun behind his back and stared straight at the eyehole set midway in the door.

Stringer's voice rumbled through to him, muffled by the wood. 'What do you want at this time of night?'

McCall stepped closer, keeping his voice low. 'The big man sent me to get you.'

'What's up?'

McCall made a show of looking round him. 'Aye, that's right, Stringer. I'll shout it out right here in the middle of the landing. Open up, will you?'

McCall knew getting in was going to be the hard part. There was no love lost between them so his turning up in the middle of the night was going to be suspicious. But Stringer thought he could take McCall any day of the week and he was banking on that arrogance winning out over caution. The silence from behind the door stretched so long that McCall thought he had miscalculated but then he heard the satisfying click of the lock being turned and the door swung open.

The roar filled McCall's ears, his flesh turned to ice, the Dark draped itself around him like a comfortable cloak and he was ready.

He hit Stringer's face with the barrel of the gun as soon as the door pulled back. The hard metal opened a deep welt in Stringer's forehead and he rocked back with a small moan, allowing McCall to step inside and kick the door shut with his heel. Stringer stumbled backwards, hand darting to the wound and then staring in an amazed fashion at the blood on his fingers. He was wearing a dressing gown and his legs were bare and Davie guessed the man was naked underneath.

Stringer started to say something but McCall moved again, swinging the pistol, catching him on the jaw with a hard thud and sending him reeling back into the living room, the edge of the weapon slicing a bloody gash. Stringer was tough and recovered swiftly, lunging forward with a roar but McCall was ready for him, sidestepping and slamming the butt of the gun hard into the back of his head. The man went down, blood erupting from the wound on his bald skull. He landed on his hands and knees, where he remained still for a second, then shook his head and leaped up again, fist swinging, but McCall had already stepped out of reach. Stringer bulldozed towards him, both arms raised in an attempt to grab him, but McCall stepped in closer and swung the gun again, clunking the man across the temple once more, opening a new gash. Stringer's eyes rolled and he toppled onto his back. He was breathing heavily now but was still conscious. McCall watched him for a moment then sat down on a chair nearby.

'Stringer,' he said and waited for a response, but the other man lay motionless, apart from the rise and fall of his chest and the blood trickling down his face.

'I know you can hear me,' said McCall and waited again but

Stringer said nothing. 'A wee lassie, Stringer. You murdered a wee lassie. It wasn't necessary.'

Stringer's eyes fluttered slightly but he still kept quiet.

'Why'd you use the boy, Stringer?' McCall said, not really caring if he got a reply.

And then a smile appeared on Stringer's face and a throaty chuckle wheezed from his lips. 'Because I knew it would piss you off, McCall.'

'And you were right. Happy now?'

Stringer looked at McCall. His face was smeared with blood from the craters McCall had opened and his jaw was already swelling but he was still smiling. McCall felt his icy rage wrap itself closer around him. He switched his grip from the butt of the gun to the barrel. 'What are you, Stringer? Right or left-handed?'

'What?'

'Which hand did you use to pull the trigger, Stringer?'

'What?'

'Never mind,' said McCall as he stood up and walked over to the where the man lay prone. Stringer tried to get up but McCall hit him in the mouth and he fell back down, blood spurting from his lip. Without hesitation, McCall knelt down, grabbed Stringer's right wrist and hammered the gun against the knuckles.

Stringer screamed and made a lunge, but McCall jerked his elbow up and shattered his nose. Stringer's head fell back as he drifted into unconsciousness until another jarring jolt of pain from his right hand jerked him fully awake. He screamed again but McCall continued to hammer the gun butt down, shattering the bones of the hand and fingers. He clamped his free hand over Stringer's mouth to stifle the sound but he could still hear screams, another man's screams, Spencer's screams. He ignored them. This had to be done. He pounded at the hand until only a pulpy mess of blood and bruised flesh remained. Stringer no longer screamed – he had long since passed out. Spencer's cries died, too, for he was long ago and far away.

McCall stood up and looked down at the beaten and bleeding body of a man he had hated for so long. Time to finish the job, he thought, time to do the world a favour. He raised the pistol and pointed it at Stringer's head.

And his finger tightened on the trigger.

The rain stopped as McCall reached the loch in the middle of the golf course. It was a municipal green, used by city folk who couldn't afford the membership fees for the swanky clubs on the outskirts. The green was one of the few things the city council had done right. It was well-kept, well-designed and well-used, particularly by councillors who also didn't want to pay costly membership fees. Maybe that explained why the course was so well looked-after.

McCall had found a small screwdriver and some pliers in a cupboard in Stringer's hall and, even though he was no expert, took the pistol apart as best he could. He dumped some of the parts in various drains while he walked to the golf course and now he was left only with the handgrip. As the sun began to rise behind him, he stood on the edge of the man-made loch and threw it as far out as he could, listening for the soft splash somewhere out in the gloom.

He stood for a moment, savouring the cool breeze that whispered round his ears, listening to the birds beginning to stir in the trees while above him the black sky turned a pale yellow and fingers of light began to reach out across the green.

A new day, he thought. And he was going to make a new start.

He hadn't killed Stringer. As he stood there, his finger on the trigger, his hand steady, he felt the dark thing slip away from him. The warmth returned to his body, the raging sea in his ears subsided and the rest of the room came into focus. He looked around him and saw a neat, one-roomed flat with a recess bed, the blankets thrown back, which meant Stringer had been in bed when he arrived. On a small table beside the bed a book lay open but face down; McCall was surprised to see it was the third Harry Potter. Beside it was a framed picture of Stringer with an old couple who McCall took to be his parents. They were all smiling and the man and woman looked so normal. It had never occurred to McCall that Stringer had a family, that he had a life outside his work for Big Rab.

And then he thought of Donna. Would he deserve her if he took that final, fatal step, if he became a killer? He had always believed that if he purposely took a life, then he would somehow lose himself and the demons that had claimed his father would also claim him. Was Stringer worth that?

He had looked back down and saw he was still aiming the gun at the man's bald head. There was blood on the barrel and blood on his own hands and blood dripping from the wounds on Stringer's face to pool on the rug. This was the man who had ruthlessly gunned down an innocent family a few hours before and who had sucked a young man into his game. But despite that, McCall knew he could not kill him. The Dark had brought him here and stayed with him while he administered the beating, but now it was gone.

McCall lowered his arm, slumped into the nearest chair and rubbed his eyes with the fingers of his free hand. He was trembling, but not through fear or cold. He felt a curious kind of excitement because for the first time he believed, really believed, he could beat his genes, beat his father's legacy, beat The Dark.

But not without Donna.

Maybe this really was the end game.

Big Rab watched from the wide picture window of his Bothwell home as McCall's car swung into the driveway. He'd told the lads stationed outside to expect him so they let him through. He watched his old pal climb out and approach the front door. *Davie, Davie*, he thought, *what am I going to do with you?* Knight had phoned during the night, Knight always phoned during the night, with some news. Disturbing news. And Rab couldn't quite bring himself to believe it.

He didn't answer the door, that wouldn't be the done thing, so he let his son do it. He waited in the sitting room, sipping coffee from his favourite mug. He heard the voices in the hallway then young Joseph opened the door, showing McCall in. Rab didn't turn when he said, 'That's fine, son.' He listened for the door to close – he hadn't expected the boy to say anything, he said very little at the best of times. Christ, he was surrounded by guys who said fuck all. Then he turned to face McCall.

'Why'd you do it, Rab?' McCall said.

McClymont gave him an innocent look. 'Why'd I do what, Davie?'

'Don't play that game with me, Rab. I know you too well.'

'Davie, Davie, I don't know what you're on about.'

McCall sighed, then said, 'O'Neill. You had Stringer take him out.'

Rab shook his head. Never admit anything, that was the golden rule. Not even to old friends. But then, if Knight was right, Davie was no longer a friend. 'No way, Davie, no me.'

'Rab, Stringer doesn't fart without your say-so. But he went too far – he took the wife and kid as well.'

Rab already knew this, it was something else Knight had told him. He tried to look genuinely appalled, but something told him Davie wouldn't buy it.

McCall said, 'Shot all three of them in the street. A woman and a wee lassie, Rab. Civilians. And you did it, just as surely as you were there and pulled the trigger.'

'I know nothing about it, Davie, and that's the God's honest,' said McClymont, holding both hands up. 'And you say Stringer did it?'

'Aye. You'd better send an ambulance round to his place before he bleeds to death.'

This was news to Rab. 'What'd you do, Davie?'

McCall gave him a grim little smile as he mimicked Rab's words. 'I know nothing about it, Rab – and that's the God's honest.'

The two men stared at each other across the room, each knowing the other was lying. Finally, McCall broke the silence. 'I've had it, Rab.'

'What do you mean?'

'I want out. Of The Life. I want no more of this.'

McClymont sighed and sat down in an armchair. McCall could tell this wasn't a shock. 'What will you do?'

'I'll find something.'

'Has this got anything to do with that lassie?'

McCall looked surprised.

'Come on, Davie,' said McClymont, 'people talk. You've been spotted – and since you met her you've no been the same. What do you know about her?'

'Leave her out of this.'

'I'm concerned, Davie. I've known you, what? Twenty-five years? You've always been the one I could rely on, but when it comes to women you can be downright undependable. I went through the whole Audrey thing with you...'

'Rab.' there was a warning in Davie's voice, but Rab ignored it.

'And when Vari left there was a wee wobble – you didn't think I noticed, but I did. Now some bitch bats her baby blues at you and you're away like a lovesick schoolboy. Bernadette always said that women were your Achilles Heel, your weak spot.'

'That's enough,' said McCall softly, but it was enough to make Rab stop. He knew he'd touched a nerve.

'I've had it,' Davie went on. 'That's all that needs to be said.'

He turned, yanked open the door and was about to step into the hall when Rab said, 'Davie, let me give you some advice as a pal, okay?' He waited until McCall faced him. He stared into his old mate's face, trying to see any sign of deceit, but saw nothing. Knight must be wrong, he decided, Davie would not do what he'd suggested. He softened his voice. 'There's things going on here that I don't think you know about. Don't let your dick drag you into something you can't control.'

McCall turned away, heading for the front door. Rab followed.

'She's no what you think, Davie.' Rab was shouting now, struggling to make McCall understand. 'Davie, for Christ's sake, listen...'

But McCall had already left the house and was walking down the driveway, his shoulders straight, his head up. Rab watched him go, feeling he should call out after him again, or follow him, but knew it wouldn't do any good. Maybe, long ago, he'd've been able to talk to him but too much blood had flowed under the bridge.

Again he told himself that McCall would not betray him in the way that Knight suggested. But it was half-hearted. Maybe Knight was right. Maybe his old pal had outlived his usefulness.

Rab closed the door gently but remained in the hallway, his big face creased in thought. He wished Bernadette was here, she'd know what to do. But she wasn't. Never would be again. It was all down to him now. Normally he wouldn't think twice – if there were even a suggestion that someone was pulling strokes, they'd be dealt with good and proper, no beating about the bush. But this was Davie McCall. He had to be certain.

20

DONNA WONDERED where the painting had gone. The attractive landscape had been replaced by a large Salvador Dali grotesque and something about that unsettled her. Not because the Dali picture was disturbing – which it was – but its appearance on the wall reminded her how nothing stayed the same forever, things change. Shit happens.

The phone call had been a message to meet in the gallery at ten in the morning. There was no explanation, This was not a scheduled briefing and in this line of work anything out of the usual was dangerous. Donna still sensed something was wrong, badly wrong, and she dreaded the woman's arrival. She had woken with a feeling of dread, the phone call had only served to strengthen it.

And when DCI Vincent made an appearance, Donna knew that somehow the world had changed overnight. She was always impeccably groomed, make-up perfect, hair in place, poised, confident, in control. But today Donna could see her hair was in slight disarray, dark circles shadowed her eyes and she looked as if she'd been wearing the same clothes since the day before. Any one of these would be cause for concern, all of them together meant something cataclysmic had occurred.

'What's up?' She asked.

Vincent looked surprised. 'You've not heard the news this morning?'

She shook her head. After the phone call she'd fallen into a fitful sleep but had managed to lie too long. She hadn't caught the Scottish news as she showered and dressed before making her way across the city to the art galleries at Kelvingrove.

'Jerry O'Neill's dead,' said the DCI, her voice low. 'His family too.'

Donna blinked as this sunk in. Then an uncomfortable thought struck her. 'When?'

'Late last night.'

'When last night? What time?'

'About eleven, why?'

She felt some of the tension drop from her body. Davie hadn't been involved. She'd still been with him at that time. 'No reason.'

Vincent let it pass. 'This changes everything. Killing O'Neill was bad enough, but his wife and child will bring all kinds of attention to the case. I knew we were dealing with monsters, but I didn't realise just how bad they were.'

Donna let the insinuation that Davie was a monster pass by. This was not the time for that argument. 'Any witnesses?'

Vincent shook her head. 'The streets were deserted because of the weather. A few people heard the gunshots but no-one can give a description of the shooter. A car similar to the one spotted at the locus was found burnt out in Partick.'

Donna said, 'So what now?'

The DCI turned her eyes on her. 'Now we bring pressure on your boyfriend. I wanted McClymont and Knight badly enough before, now I can just about taste it.'

'He won't do it.'

'He has to.'

'But he won't. I know him now.'

'Then he'll go down with them. A triple murder means the gloves come off.'

'He had nothing to do with that!'

'How can you be certain?'

'Because I am.'

'Then he knows who was. And he'll tell us, one way or the other.'

She did not respond and Vincent's eyes narrowed suspiciously as she said, 'What?'

'I've said it all before,' Donna said.

The DCI sat down on the bench beside her and tilted her head back, thinking for a moment. Then, still looking at the ceiling, she said, 'Have you slept with him?'

The question should have been surprising but it wasn't. Donna said, 'That's none of your business.'

Allison Vincent straightened and twisted in the seat to face her. 'Oh, really? Let me see, then. I take an officer from Central for some undercover work, something with which she is not unfamiliar. I've been assured that she knows her job, is a consummate professional. I place her with a known criminal in this city, with the specific brief to get close to said known criminal and help turn him so that I can bring one particularly nasty crook and an even nastier bent fucking cop to court. Said officer takes the word undercover too far and screws said known criminal, placing just about everything we have done to date in fucking jeopardy and I'm told that it's none of my business! So I'll ask you again, have you slept with David McCall?'

Vincent was staring at her with a blistering intensity but Donna held her gaze easily. 'No,' she said and Vincent visibly relaxed. Donna waited a moment and followed up with, 'But I wanted to.'

Vincent gave herself a grim little nod of satisfaction. 'I was right, then. You've fallen for him.'

Donna kept her silence. She didn't know how she felt.

Vincent sighed and stood up, paced around the room, considering the situation. 'Well, isn't this a fucking mess?' She stopped, turned back to Donna. 'Where is he now?'

'I don't know.'

'You don't know?'

'I don't know. He must've left in the middle of the night.'

'You were with him last night?'

Donna nodded.

Vincent narrowed her eyes, obviously wondering if Donna had actually been to bed with McCall. 'But not all night?'

'No, but I was with him when the O'Neill family was killed, if that's what you're thinking.'

'Alone?'

'Yes, we were alone.'

'Uh-huh. What were you doing?'

'Talking.'

'Just talking?'

Donna thought about how she had kissed him, how she had

wanted it to go further, how he had wanted to go further, but her professionalism had stepped in where her common sense wouldn't and she had held back. It'd been close, though. She'd told Vincent the truth – they hadn't slept together, but she wanted to. She really wanted to. 'Yes, just talking.'

'About what?'

This was it. In the end, this was what it was all about. Davie had opened up to her, told her about his life, told her some of the things he'd done for Rab McClymont. That was Donna's mission, get him to incriminate himself and hopefully others so that his own words could be used to turn him, make him inform, tell them more about McClymont's organisation and his connection to Jimmy Knight. Donna had performed similar functions before and she had done her job well. This time, though, it was different. She thought about telling Vincent a pack of lies but the DCI was ahead of her.

'Detective Sergeant Bronson, choose your next words very carefully. You have a career to consider here and if you keep anything from me, you're not only placing that career in jeopardy, but you could leave yourself open to criminal charges. Now, what did you talk about with David McCall last night?'

Donna took a deep breath. Vincent had purposely used her rank and real surname. She'd kept her first name because it was more natural to her but the rank and second name were never used by her handler in order to keep her in character. Using them now was Vincent's way of telling her the job was over. Now it was time to put up or shut up. She had no doubt Vincent would follow through on her threat but she didn't care. She knew she was being rash, she'd worked hard to find her place on the Job, but she still shook her head. 'Nothing.'

Vincent breathed out with a sibilant hiss. Her look told Donna that she didn't believe her. 'Then I'll speak to him. If you won't do your job, I'll do it for you.'

'I've done my job,' said Donna, her voice sounding firmer than she felt. She was wading through deep waters here and she could feel it going over her head. But she still didn't care. 'Why is Davie so important?'

'Oh, Davie, is it now?'

Donna ignored the heavy sarcasm. 'He's never going to tell you anything. He still thinks McClymont's his friend.'

'So you have discussed McClymont?'

'In passing. But he's never mentioned Knight, not once. I don't think he can tell you anything about him.' Another thought struck her. 'Anyway, I thought MacLeish was the key?'

It was Vincent's turn to look ashamed. 'Well, there's a small problem with MacLeish,' she said. 'We've lost him.'

Shoog Macleish had given his watchers the slip the night before, just about the time Jimmy Knight was hacking into Vincent's computer records. They'd stashed him in a rented flat in the city centre, not allowing him out in the open for a minute. The flat was spartan, a couple of beds in the single bedroom, an electric cooker in the kitchen that didn't work so they had to rely on take-away and some lumpy chairs in the living room with a telly with a video for entertainment. There was a selection of movies and more adult material for his entertainment but the one thing they didn't provide was mood-enhancing substances. And Shoog was the kind of boy who couldn't do without a bit of chemical uplift for long.

Vincent knew he'd made straight for the East End and his old haunts, because that's what boys like Shoog MacLeish do, predictability being their middle name. They were like salmon returning to spawn. Vincent had eyes and ears open and was confident that she'd hoover him back up again within a couple of days.

But there were other eyes, other ears, and they weren't working for Vincent. They knew of his habits, they knew his haunts and they knew his appetites.

Knight was in Queen's Park talking to McClymont when he got the word. They were standing on the raised area around the flagpole, just two blokes taking in the view towards the West End and the spire of the University of Glasgow. It was one of Knight's favourite vantage points to see the city.

His mobile rang and he heard Ricky Ramage's voice.

'The item you're looking for has been spotted in Flanagan's. It'll be back there tonight.' Then he cut the connection, leaving Knight listening to a dead phone and thinking 'the item'? The nervy wee bastard had seen too many movies. He folded the phone together, dropped it into his pocket and looked back to Big Rab, who was looking decidedly unhappy. He'd told Knight about his conversation with McCall and how he couldn't accept that he'd turned grass.

'I still cannae believe it, man,' he said, shaking his head. 'Davie and me, we go way back. He wouldnae roll over on me, no way.'

'Look,' said Knight, wondering if this show of loyalty to an old friend was feigned, 'I'm telling you what I saw on that computer. They've put this bird in with Davie and she's to lure him over to their side, get him to talk about you and me somehow. These people are good at what they do. She'll shag his brains out and get him talking and then they'll blackmail him into giving evidence.'

'But the report didnae say that Davie'd talked, did it?'

'No, but...'

'There you go, then.'

'But there's couple of other things I've no told you yet. Did you know he gave some lads a doing up a few days ago?

'I heard. Somebody with a personal score to settle.'

'Aye, but did you know that one of the boys fired Davie McCall in for it – but that DCI Vincent pulled strings to stop him from being lifted?'

Rab seemed to visibly pale and Knight now actually believed the man was as crestfallen as he seemed.

'And he's been poking his nose into the O'Neill thing with Frank Donovan. You remember Frank Donovan?'

'Thought he was dead.'

'Dead drunk, maybe. But he's sober for now and he's asking around about the case – and your boy McCall is right there at his side. He's up to something and it's not to your benefit, you can bet on that.'

Knight let this sink in before he continued.

'Face facts, Rab,' the cop went on. 'He gave Stringer a right going over. He's told you he's walking away.'

'Aye, I know,' said Rab quietly.

Knight didn't understand McClymont's hesitation. He knew McCall had been a mate, but this was business. 'Jesus, you had O'Neill and his family killed without turning a hair.'

'I never had nothing to do with that, I told you.'

'Aye, sure, and The White House is at Defcon Three because pigs are invading by air. Look, I don't give a toss what happened to O'Neill and his family, okay? Far as I'm concerned that's something less I need to worry about, know what I'm saying? So maybe it was a bit over-the-top, taking out his wife and wean, but there's no point crying over spilt milk. But this Davie McCall thing, that's a worry. And if you don't do something about it, I'll need to.'

'I'll deal with it, I'll deal with it,' said McClymont. 'I just wish I didn't have to deal with it, that's all. Twenty-five years he's been my mate, man, that's a long time.'

'See how long it feels when you're looking out through prison bars.'

Shoog had been going out of his head in that flat with the two wankers who'd been assigned to watch him. He'd got halfway into *Dances With Wolves* before his patience snapped. He thought it was a cowboy picture but it had subtitles, like some foreign piece of shite they'd show at the GFT, which, as far as he was concerned, stood for Guff For Tossers. Bugger that for a game of soldiers. He was a free spirit that needed the open streets to thrive. So when he saw his chance to leg it, he took it.

Now he was back where he belonged – on the streets where he lived. It never occurred to him that he was in any danger. As far as he was concerned no-one, not even Knight, knew he was talking to the polis. If that big bastard had known he'd never've walked out of his own flat alive when they lifted him for the jewellers' job. No, the Black Knight didn't know anything about what Lang had told him on those long, dark nights in the jail. He told him all about Knight hiring them for the MacDougall job and letting them part company with half of the two hundred grand. Doing the wife was a wee extra Knight had specified for some reason. Of course, Lang held the young lassie throughout all that because his tastes ran in a different direction. He'd recruited a bloke from Liverpool who was into that sort of thing. That guy found himself face down in the Mersey shortly after he returned to his home town. Funny how things work out.

He knew the gen he'd gleaned from Lang was his get out of jail free card and he'd played it. That introduced him to DCI bloody Vincent – and that was who he got his lawyer to call when Knight had him lifted for that jeweller's job. Next thing he knew he was walking out the Sheriff Court a free man. Mind you, he walked straight into the arms of the two wankers who whisked him off to that soul-destroying dump in the city centre, but there you are. Vincent was unhappy with Knight being involved in the arrest and wanted Shoog out of harm's way.

Once free again, he went to see his old mum first off, not because he felt anything for the old bird, but because he always kept a change of clothes at her place. She was as pleased to see him as usual, which meant she never lifted her face from *Who Wants To Be A Millionaire?* on the telly. Then he paid a visit to a pal of his who was holding a wee bundle of powder for him. He'd shared some with his mate, heating it on some tin foil and smoking it through the plastic casing of a ballpoint pen. He'd never liked the idea of jagging the stuff in his arm. Ever since he was a boy, he'd had an unnatural fear of needles. After a hit, he was ready to face the world. Or at least the Flanagan's Bar part of it.

The first night he'd sat there for a couple of hours, sipping a coke because he'd never developed a taste for anything stronger, and watching the sports channel on the telly. There wasn't much doing in the bar because the rain had kept most people in. The one thing Shoog really wanted after a hit was some female company. The stuff really got his juices flowing, but there was no talent to speak of that night. So he'd gone back to his pal's flat and crashed until lunchtime the next day. When he woke up it wasn't raining and things looked good for a night on the batter. Tonight, he thought, I'm going to get lucky.

21

MCCALL GOT BACK to his flat at about ten that morning determined to tell Donna that he'd cast off The Life. He felt as if a weight had lifted and he couldn't wait to tell her and he hoped she'd be pleased. He raced up the stairs, two at a time, rang her doorbell, but there was no answer. Disappointment carved away at his bright mood but he told himself she must be at work. He opened his own door and let Arrow bound out, bright and eager and relieved he was no longer alone. McCall walked the dog to the supermarket where Donna worked but one of the girls on the check-out said she'd not come in that morning. His mood darkened as he made his way to Sammy's flat knowing that he'd find Jimsie there. The boy wouldn't have gone home to his mum's in Castlemilk, he'd've gone straight to his grandad. All the while, Big Rab's words echoed in McCall's head.

She's not what she seems, he'd said.

Not what she seems.

Old Sammy led McCall into the kitchen. A half-constructed model bomber sat on the table but the old man was paying no attention to the scale replica. He sat beside the unlit gas fire, his face grave as he absently stroked Arrow's head.

'I'll kill that bastard Stringer, so I will,' he said.

'Just leave it, okay?' McCall urged. 'Stringer's been sorted.'

The old man understood what that meant. 'Permanent?'

McCall shook his head. 'But he'll no play the violin again.'

'Too good for him, so it is.'

'Aye, maybe. But don't you go making things worse for Jimsie, okay?'

The old man sighed, knowing McCall was talking sense. 'He's no taking it very well,' he said.

'Where is he?'

'In the room.' Glasgow-speak for any room other than the one they were in. 'He's no come out all morning.'

'Keep him close and things'll be fine,' said McCall. 'What'd you tell his mum?'

'That he'd been out on the batter. She wasn't pleased, but...' Sammy shrugged, saying that her believing her son had merely had a drunken night was better than the truth.

The old man made a pot of tea and the two men sat talking for a time. They talked about Big Rab, about Knight, about O'Neill. They talked about McCall's father. McCall told him about Donna and said he was finished with The Life and the old man nodded.

'Get out now, Davie, son,' he said. 'Take that lassie and get away from this city, far away.'

Back in Sword Street, McCall unlocked his flat and let Arrow in, then climbed the stairs to Donna's. This time she answered the door and he felt relief wash over him.

'Listen,' he started, 'I'm sorry about last night but...'

She shook her head, not looking him in the eye. 'You'd better come in, Davie. There's someone who wants to speak to you.'

Frowning, McCall followed her along the hall and into the living room. Standing by the fireplace, the word BITCH still etched on the wall, was a tall woman with jet-black hair and the look of someone who meant business. Immediately McCall felt himself on his guard.

'Davie, this is Detective Chief Inspector Vincent,' said Donna.

McCall glanced at her in surprise, but her eyes were lowered.

'I'm with Lothian and Borders,' said the woman. 'And Donna here is a DS with the Central force.'

McCall continued to look at Donna, who had moved round the back of the settee as if she needed something between them, her face still averted. He suddenly felt sick.

She's not what she seems.

'We're part of a special task force investigating police corruption and organised crime in this city,' the woman continued. 'We're targeting a DI James Knight. We think you can help us.'

Donna still hadn't looked at him. Something stung at the back of his eyes, something he'd felt only a few times before, when his mother was killed, when Audrey was killed, when he had to part with his dog, Abe. He didn't speak. He didn't trust himself to speak.

'We're not particularly interested in you,' the woman was saying, 'but we can be if you don't co-operate. You've spoken to my officer here of a number of things, including your association with Robert McClymont. None of it admissible as evidence, of course – unless it was repeated in front of another officer. A ranking officer.'

McCall took his eyes away from Donna and looked at DCI Vincent, who watched him with cool and steady eyes. McCall knew what she was implying. She would lie in court. She'd swear under oath that McCall made the statements in front of them both. And Donna would repeat the lie. Donna was her officer. Donna was a cop and all cops stick together.

Vincent continued, 'And, of course, if we look back at some of the incidents you've described, I'm sure we'll find something that can be used as corroboration. It won't take much. There was an incident in a lane outside a pub not long ago. Two men were injured and I feel certain I could turn local eyes in your direction. All it would take is one phone call.'

'And if you don't find enough evidence, you'll make it up,' said McCall, his words thick, his tongue numb.

'If necessary, for the greater good. But as I said, I'm not particularly interested in you. It's Knight I want – and McClymont, if we can get him. But Knight is more important.'

'Can't help you.'

Vincent sighed and looked at Donna. 'Donna here tells me you were trying to help O'Neill somehow. Why?'

'None of your business.'

'You know he's dead. You know they killed his wife and child. Are these the kind of people you want to protect? Child killers?'

'I told you, I can't help you.'

'Can't or won't?'

'Take your pick.'

Vincent shook her head and sat down on the settee. She moved gracefully, like a dancer, and looked as if she owned not just this place but the whole world. Donna didn't move.

'I was led to believe you were different from the rest, McCall. I know you had nothing to do with the murders as you were otherwise engaged, with my officer.'

McCall's eyes darted back to Donna again. So she had told her that too. Jesus, how wrong can you be about someone?

'But by shielding the people who are responsible, you are only making yourself one of them. Do you understand?'

'I told you,' said McCall, 'I can't help you.'

'Take some time. Think about it. Big Rab ordered the killings and someone on his crew pulled the trigger. Jimmy Knight almost certainly knew it was going to happen. Are they worth going down for? Are they worth your liberty? Think about it, Davie. You want out, I know that, and I can help you. Think about it.'

McCall heard her talk but he wasn't paying attention. He stared at Donna, feeling a mixture of anger and pain. He'd made a complete fool of himself over her but it would never happen again. He wondered if, on some level, he'd always suspected her but had ignored it. What was it Rab had said?

Bernadette always said that women were your Achilles Heel.

Rab's wife certainly knew that. She'd played on his weakness, too.

He became aware that Vincent had stopped talking and he dragged his gaze back to her. McCall asked, 'Anything else?'

The woman shook her head and McCall forced his voice to be calm, measured. He didn't want Donna to know how much she had wounded him. He said to Vincent, 'Your man did a good job on the drunk act the other night.'

'Thank you, I'll pass on your praise.'

'I really thought he was drunk.'

'He'll be pleased you thought that.'

'If there was an award for it, I'd vote for him.'

Vincent's mouth tightened. 'Don't make a mistake here, McCall. We can help you. If you turn your back now there's nothing we can do.'

McCall ignored her. 'But it wasn't the only award-winning performance, was it?' This time Donna looked up and into his eyes. He nodded to the word on the wall. 'Not everything was a lie, was it?'

He saw the pain burn deep in her eyes before she said, 'I had to do it, Davie. It's my job.'

'Some job,' he said.

She looked away again, just briefly, then her eyes snapped back and he saw the first kindle of defiance. 'You're the bad guy, Davie. Don't forget that.'

The words rammed home like a knife strike. He felt them slice deep inside his chest. He couldn't say anything, all he could do was turn and walk out.

Frank Donovan slumped low in his car, thinking it was a hell of a way to spend a Saturday afternoon. He kept his eye on the front door to Morrigan MacDougall's building while he munched slowly on a pre-packed sandwich he'd bought in a shop on Byres Road. It was billed as a BLT but the 'B' must've stood for bullshit because so far he'd detected only the faintest trace of bacon. The programme selection on the radio wasn't helping much. Currently, a comic with a permanent sneer in her voice was trying too hard to be funny and not quite making it. He'd tested other channels, but all he had to choose from was some tuneless wailing on Radio 1, some tuneless modern classical on Radio 3, some posh bloke talking to an upper-class prat on Classic FM, more upper-class prats talking about poetry on Radio 4 and don't even get him started on the commercial stations and their increasingly annoying and frequent adverts. Or maybe he was just bad-tempered because he was bored and he hadn't had a drink in a week.

He'd made that stunning realisation earlier that morning. Seven days without a sip of anything distilled, brewed or mixed in a bathtub somewhere. That was really quite something for him. He should have gone out and got rat-arsed to celebrate, but instead here he was numbing his backside in the car, the Metro City not renowned for its spaciousness, waiting for who-knew-what to happen.

He couldn't shake off the feeling that the girl knew more than she was saying. He'd gone back to visit both the father and the mother that morning but he'd refused to say anything more, threatening to resort to a lawyer if he was harassed any further. Aline knew he'd visited her daughter, of course, and demanded to know how he had found her address. Donovan, naturally, was not about to confess to rifling through her address book, so gave her the standard reply that it was his job to find people. Her demeanor was considerably frostier than their first meeting. He gleaned nothing further, apart from the nagging feeling that there was something further to glean.

So he headed to Huntly Gardens, but there was no answer to his insistent pressing on the security buzzer. That was when he bought the phantom bacon, lettuce and tomato sandwich and settled himself in for a wait.

Mid-morning gave way to lunchtime, when he attacked the sandwich, and then into early afternoon. By about three he was beginning to think he was wasting his time when he saw a flash motor stop across the road from him and Morrigan climbed out. She was wearing a grey trouser suit and white blouse and again Donovan was struck by the resemblance to her mother. She carried a number of bags bearing the names of high-class city centre stores – the kind that demand a credit reference just to look in the window – so obviously she'd been on a shopping trip. He debated with himself whether to buzz her up right away, or let her get in and get settled. There was a lot to be said for both approaches and he couldn't really decide which way to go.

He was still weighing up the options when another car drove into the quiet street. Donovan recognised the man behind the wheel immediately and felt his chest tighten and the nerves in his fingers and hands tingled. *What the hell is he doing here?* He watched the man lock his car door then walk nonchalantly towards Morrigan's building. He didn't use the buzzer, but pulled a key from his coat pocket and let himself in.

Jesus, thought Donovan. *Oh, sweet Jesus.*

Bobby Newman hadn't spoken to Big Rab for over a year, so it was something of a shock when he sauntered into the shop on Duke Street just before closing time, two of his lads at his tail. One of them locked the door behind him, twisting the OPEN sign to CLOSED. Bobby would've protested, but Rab's face told him he wasn't here to shoot the breeze.

'Long time no see, Rab,' he said.

Rab bobbed his head in acknowledgement and leaned on the counter, his fingers absently poking through a box of cut-price paintbrushes. 'No a social call, Bobby,' he said.

Bobby looked over Rab's shoulder to the two men. They were keeping a respectful distance but their tough-guy glower spoke volumes. Bobby said, 'Where's Stringer?'

'Indisposed.' Rab didn't look Bobby in the eye. He kept playing with the brushes.

Bobby didn't press the Stringer matter. Something told him he didn't want to know. He felt the air around him thicken and a host of anxious butterflies fluttered in his belly. He hadn't been in anything like harm's way for five years, not since an encounter in a ruined church, and he was out of practice. He knew this was the side of Big Rab that others saw, just before something bad was about to happen. 'What's up, Rab?'

Now the big fella looked up, his dark eyes blank. 'It's Davie.'

Concern for his pal made the butterflies flap hard enough to cause a hurricane in New Zealand. 'Is he okay?'

Rab didn't answer. He half-turned to his boys, checking where they were, then turned back to Bobby. 'I need to know what's going on. You're the only one who'll know.'

'Going on how?'

'That's what I want to know.'

Bobby couldn't help but smile. 'Shit, Rab – you been taking those enigma pills again? You want to be a wee bit clearer, mate?'

Rab gave Bobby a long stare. 'This bit of skirt he's got – what do you know about her?'

'Donna? She seems alright. Davie likes her.'

'She's a cop, Bobby.'

That floored him. He struggled to take that in. Rab leaned on the counter. 'What I need to know is, does Davie know? And what's he telling her?'

Bobby said, 'I don't think he does know. Come on, Rab – you think he'd tell her anything? This is Davie!'

'Aye, that's what I keep telling myself, but you know what? There's a wee voice in my head that tells me I'm getting screwed, and not in a good way. There's been things happening, Bobby, strange things, and I think Davie's turning on me.'

'No – not Davie. And even if he was, what makes you think I'd know?'

'If there's anyone who would know, it's you. He tells you everything.'

Bobby said, 'He's told me nothing.'

'I don't believe you.'

The air between them had deadened considerably. Rab had a reputation for not accepting betrayal, even though he'd betrayed many a friend in the past. Including Bobby. Rab had involved him in a murder twenty years before, an old pal who Rab said had turned grass. It had been one of the reasons Bobby had got out of The Life. Now Rab thought Davie was ratting on him and Bobby was in the middle. It was not a good place to be.

'Rab,' he said, keeping his voice low and even, 'I'm telling you I know nothing. Why don't you go ask him?'

'He's not in his flat. No-one knows where he is. Do you know where he is, Bobby? I'll bet you do.'

Rab stared straight into Bobby's face, his expression blank, his eyes dark and deep. This was a part of him Bobby had only witnessed from the other side, Rab's side. Now, viewing it from this perspective, he saw why Rab was so feared. He didn't just send out guys to do his dirty work, he was more than capable of doing it himself.

The two guys each edged forward. Bobby swallowed. He'd often wondered how he'd fare in a set-to with Rab. and he suspected he'd come off worse. Bobby was capable of looking after himself, but he didn't have Rab's killer instinct. And with two boys backing him up? Well, he knew the odds were not in his favour. He knew Rab's game – hurt Bobby, maybe even kill him, and draw Davie out. Friends being hurt was something that would bring Davie running without a care for the consequences.

'Rab, I'm telling you I've no clue where Davie is, or anything else for that matter.' Bobby was proud of the hard edge to his words, even though he was ready to soil himself. 'But here's one thing I'm certain of – Davie's no grass. And what's more, you know it.' His hands slid under the counter to rest on the baseball bat he kept on a shelf. If the shit hit the fan, he'd go down swinging, that's for damn sure. 'Think about it, Rab – it's Davie McCall. He's a pal, Rab. Yours. Mine. We all go back a long way. You honestly think he'd turn tout? Cos I don't, never in a million years.'

Bobby saw light seep back into Rab's eyes but there was still doubt. The threat wasn't over and he decided to be more direct. 'Tell your lads to back off, Rab.'

Rab craned over his shoulder at the two men beginning to crowd in. He turned back but said nothing. Bobby's grip tightened on the Louisville Slugger. 'I mean it, Rab. I know your game, I know what's in your mind, and you'll do me a damage, no doubt about it, but at least two of you will leave here with lumps of your own. The question is – which two?'

Rab's gaze dropped to the counter top, as if he was trying to penetrate the wood to see what Bobby had hidden under there. Then the eyes slowly raised and he stared at Bobby once more. The two old friends faced each other, the counter, the years and a myriad of memories between them. It must've only been a few seconds but for Bobby it was as if time had frozen, each moment suspended in the dense air surrounding them. He raised the bat gently from the shelf but kept it hidden from view, spaced his feet to bolster his swing and braced himself.

Then Rab smiled. It wasn't much of a smile but it eased the tension considerably.

'Relax, Bobby, no need for that. We're all pals here.' He waved the two men back again. 'Do me a favour – you see Davie, tell him we need to talk. Can you do that?'

'I can do that,' said Bobby, still on edge.

Rab smiled again, nodded and turned to walk away. Then he turned again. 'And, Bobby, mate – you know if I wanted you hurt, you'd be lying on the deck now, don't you? Unless that's a bazooka you've got under there.'

He didn't wait for a response. He left Bobby standing behind his counter, his hands still on the bat, his heart hammering in his chest, the final remnants of a friendship breathing their last on the shop floor.

22

SHOOG MACLEISH couldn't believe his luck when the lassie gave him the eye. She'd been in the pub when he arrived, sitting on her own at a corner table, sipping a something and tonic. He'd gone to the bar as usual, ordered a coke as usual and when he scanned the room to check out the talent – as usual – he found her looking at him. She'd turned away immediately, of course, but he'd still caught that interested gleam in her dark eyes. She was a looker, all right. Twenty, maybe, twenty-one. Well-dressed – too well dressed for this place, he'd thought, but he wasn't going to quibble. He sipped his coke and glanced back at her, and there she was, giving him the eye again. *Shoog, ya lucky bastard, you've scored. But play it cool. Chill, man.*

For the next twenty minutes he pretended to be watching *Surprise, Surprise* on the box while surreptitiously checking her out. He saw her give two guys the fish eye when they tried to chat her up but when they walked away he caught her giving him a wee fly glance. Finally, he picked up his glass and sauntered over to her table, fixing his most charming grin on his kisser.

'You here alone, doll?' He asked.

'I'm waiting for someone,' she said. Nice voice, Glasgow posh. Definitely a cut above the usual wee hairy this place attracted.

'Well,' he said, sitting down in the chair opposite, 'I've arrived.'

She smiled and glanced at the door. 'You're very sure of yourself, aren't you?'

'Look, doll, we can do the wee chat-up shuffle but I saw you checking out my merchandise as soon as I came in, okay? And you've given two blokes the verbal two-fingers while still giving me the come hither, know what I mean?'

She looked down at the table, a smile flirting with her lips. 'I don't know what you're talking about. But as you're here, you can buy me a drink.'

'Nae problem. What'll you have?'

'Gin and tonic.'

'Back in a jiff.'

He motioned the barman as he moved, got the order and was back at the girl's table before you could say Safe Sex.

'There you go, darlin. Get yourself around that.'

She lifted the glass to her lips. 'I can't wait long. I'm going to a party tonight and I've got rather a long way to travel.'

'Where's the party then, doll?'

'A house in the Campsies. It's a friend's twenty-first and her daddy's allowing her to use it.'

A house in the Campsies, thought Shoog, and a rich daddy. Darling, what the fuck are you doing in this postcode, let alone this shithole? As if she'd read his mind, the girl went on, 'I really was supposed to meet someone here, but it looks like I've been stood up. And my car is just around the corner and I've already had three of these.' She raised her glass to her lips and sipped the drink.

'This isnae the kind of place a guy should be meetin a girl like you.'

She lowered her voice and widened her eyes. 'Don't I know it. But my friend is a fireman at the station up the road. I don't know, maybe he's been called out, you know? Anyway, I nearly died when I walked in. I mean, no offence but it's not the Hilton, is it?'

Shoog looked around, as if seeing the bar for the first time. It wasn't too bad for this area, but she was right, they didn't sell many pina colladas.

'My name's Jenny, by the way,' she said.

'Harry,' Shoog said, holding out his hand. 'Harry Weaver.'

'And do you come here often, Harry?'

'Is it not me that's supposed to use that line?'

She laughed. 'You've already done the what's-a-nice-girl-like-you-doing-in-a-place-like-this. More or less, anyway.'

He smiled. 'True. No, I don't come in here that often. I don't drink, see. Pubs don't have much appeal for me.' Unless of course he was doing a bit of business or randy. Or both. But he didn't say that, of course.

'What about parties?'

'How do you mean?'

'Well, I was thinking… I've been drinking, so I can't drive. My friend has stood me up. You've not been drinking. You do drive, don't you?'

'Aye.'

'Well, why don't you come to the party with me? You'll have a great time, I promise.'

He liked the way she said he'd have a great time. He liked the cheeky wee smile when she said it. He liked the idea and he told her that.

'Great!' She said. 'Let's go then.'

She stood up so fast Shoog got the impression she didn't want to hear any more of his outstanding banter. She drained the drink as she stood – God, she was his kinda gal – and then began to walk to the door. He seized the opportunity to stare at her legs. They were long and shapely and encased in black stockings, not tights. Shoog spotted the other guys in the bar giving her the look and he thought, *eat your heart out, lads, she's with me the night.*

She handed him the keys to her car – an Aston Martin fob, he noticed, and once again he was impressed – and told him it was parked just around the corner. She took his arm and he felt the swell of her right breast pressing against his upper arm. He could smell her perfume in the night air. He had no idea what it was, but it even smelled expensive. Christ, he was getting a hard-on here.

Speaking of hard-ons, the car was a Mendip Blue DB7 Coupe V12 Vantage and he ran its specs through his head with a near pornographic delight – leather interior, 5.9 litre 12-cylinder engine, 0–62 mph in just over five seconds and a price tag that gave him a headrush. Shoog, who'd never driven anything more expensive than a nicked Ford Focus, fell in love immediately. He just might marry this girl, he thought. He pressed the button on the key but there was no sound of the alarm deactivating.

The girl shrugged. 'I must've forgotten to lock it.'

'Dangerous thing to do in this part of town,' he said. 'You could get it stole.' Aye, and I might've been the one who stole it, he said to himself.

'So what?' She said. 'It's insured.'

He shook his head at the arrogance and followed her round to the driver's door. She pulled it open, jerked the seat forward and ducked into the back seat. So she wants a chauffeur, he thought. Fair enoughski, just as long as I end up polishing her headlamps. Shoog bent into the car and came face-to-face with Jimmy Knight.

'Shoog, old son,' said the cop. 'Been a while.' The man's hands hooked him by the lapels and dragged him fully into the car. Once in the driver's seat, Shoog glanced at the girl behind him and she smiled, tossing her long hair back at the same time. She waved another keyfob in the air and pressed the button. The click of the locking mechanism was, to Shoog, deafening.

'Now, Shoog,' said Knight. 'I hear you've been talking to some people about me.'

'No, I havnae, Mister Knight.' All his earlier confidence was gone, replaced by the voice of a frightened little boy. He shrank back into the soft ivory seat.

Knight waved a finger at him. 'Ah-ah! Don't be telling me porkies. My ears have been burning, so they have.'

'Honest, Mister Knight, I've never said a word. They wanted me to, but I didnae! I've been stringing them along, know what I'm sayin? Keeping them sweet, so's they'd help me, but I've no said nothin about you.'

Knight's face turned dark. 'Can it, skidmark! Give me your arm.'

'My arm? What for?'

'Never mind the questions and gimme your fuckin arm!' Knight didn't wait, though. He grabbed Shoog's right arm and clamped it across his chest. Then he ripped at the sleeve of the jacket. Shoog tried to pull himself free but he was thin and weedy and Knight had him in an unbreakable grip. Shoog poked around with his free hand in his jacket pocket and pulled out a switchblade. He clicked it open and lunged at Knight but the big cop caught his wrist and twisted until the pain made Shoog drop the weapon.

Knight looked at the blade lying in the well of the car at his feet. 'That's a nasty lookin wee toy, son. I hope you know they're illegal and I'll have to impound it.'

'What you gonnae do?' Shoog's voice trembled as he looked back again at the girl, his eyes willing her to help him. She blew him a kiss and handed Knight a hypodermic syringe. The sight of it horrified Shoog. Knight didn't say a word as he wedged the syringe sideways between his teeth and with his free hand squeezed the top of Shoog's arm.

Shoog felt terror stab at his bladder. 'Mister Knight?'

Knight continued to ignore him as he watched a vein bulge in the cup of Shoog's elbow. He removed the syringe from his mouth and jabbed the needle into the vein. Shoog cried out, struggled again, but still could not break free. He looked down at his arm, at the needle puncturing his flesh, at Knight's hand slowly depressing the plunger. The fluid in the hypo squirted into his bloodstream and Shoog was certain he could feel it flooding through his body. 'Mister Knight, what have you done?'

'You're going to experience the ultimate high, Shoog,' said Knight as he leaned over the seat and dropped the syringe into a plastic bag being held by the girl. 'See, pal, I know you've been talking to that bitch Vincent about me. And I can't have it, you know that, don't you? I don't know what antics you got up to in Durham with Lang and I really don't care, but I know he told you things he really shouldn't've.'

'He never said nothin.'

'Please, Shoog, you've only got a few more minutes. You're about to meet your maker, son, don't blacken your soul any further with silly wee lies.'

The young man looked at the hole in his arm. It looked huge. It looked like a fucking crater. He pressed his fingers down on top of it, as if that could stop the drugs coursing through his body.

'Shouldn't do drugs, Shoog,' said Knight. 'Did no one tell you they're bad for you?'

'Mister Knight...' Shoog began but he couldn't find the words. His eyelids were already growing heavy and he blinked to keep them open.

'Not in the car, Jimmy,' he heard the girl say, but her voice seemed to be so far away, so far away. 'I don't want him vomiting over the seat.'

'Don't worry,' said Knight and Shoog heard the click of the locks opening again. His head fell back against the rest and he felt the press of Knight's body across him as the cop leaned over to push open the car door.

'Shoog.' Someone was talking to him, shaking him. It was Jimmy Knight. He opened his eyes and the cop's face swam through the murk. 'Shoog, time to go now. Out you go.' He felt a hand on his arm shoving him and he tumbled out of the car. Instinctively his hands went out to stop his face from crashing into the hard concrete. He moved one leg then the other and managed, somehow, to raise himself to his feet.

He heard a voice as he swayed in the night air. He knew it was Knight's but it sounded alien, hollow, like it was floating down a long tunnel. 'Maybe you'll make it to a hospital, son, maybe you won't. I'm betting you won't. Your breathing's already becoming shallower, son, and your heart rate'll drop, too. Before you know it, your body'll just call the game a bogey and you'll slip away.'

Shoog tried to speak. At least, he thought he tried to speak. His mouth was dry, his tongue sluggish.

'Christ, he's wasted!' That was the girl's voice and she was laughing. He heard the door slamming shut and then the car was gone. He didn't see it go. First it was there, then it wasn't. Like fucking magic. Like someone spirited it away. Okay, where's the ship? That was the ending to some joke but he couldn't remember the rest. There was a parrot and a magician, he knew that. Okay – where's the ship? He'd laughed like a hyena when he first heard it, years ago, but now all he could remember was the punchline.

Another car drove past him, a smaller one, and he saw a man's face staring at him as he went by. Shoog raised his arm to try and flag him down but he felt so tired so all he managed was a small wave. Then the moment was past and the car was gone and Shoog was walking but he didn't know where. He didn't know where he was. Slip away, that's what the bastard Black Knight had said. He'd just slip away. But he wasn't going to let it happen. He was going to win the day. He was going to hospital. He was going to get to Accident and Emergency and he was going to be all right. But first, he had to lie down.

He was down on all fours before he knew it, his body twisting as his guts spasmed. He slammed into the pavement – or was he in the middle of the road? He really didn't know or care. All he knew was that there was something wrong with his breathing and his mouth was dry and the jolts of agony from his stomach were unbearable. He tried to get up but found he couldn't. He tried to pull his feet up under him but his body wouldn't move. He heard footsteps and looked up to see a young couple, arm in arm, coming towards him. He wanted to tell them he needed help but all that came out was a jumble of incoherent noises. The guy seemed frightened but the girl just looked revolted. They gave him a wide berth and he raised one hand to stop them but all he succeeded in doing was falling over. He didn't see them go. He wasn't even sure they were there in the first place. Maybe if he closed his eyes for a minute he'd be able to move again. Just a wee drowse and he'd be right as rain.

He lay on his back, his breathing quickening, no longer feeling the pain, and soon drifted into the welcoming darkness.

When Donovan saw Knight letting himself through Morrigan's front door, something clicked in his brain.

Jimmy Knight.

Jimmy Knight, with a key to her front door.

Holy shit – Jimmy Knight was the boyfriend she'd mentioned. He hadn't expected that, although now that he thought about it he was surprised he was surprised. Everything in this case circled the Black Knight like dirty water round a plughole.

Donovan sat very still for a moment, trying to piece everything together.

Someone robs the MacDougalls. The crew appear to be professionals, but they rape the mother. That sounded personal. They knew about the security code to the house, but not the combination to the safe, which only Dorrell MacDougall knew. That sounded like inside information. Jerry O'Neill is fingered for the job. He's a friend of the family and is banging Mrs MacDougall. She could have given him the security code by mistake, but how do you suddenly blurt out a series of numbers? She could have given him the security code on purpose, which means she was in on it. But to allow herself to be raped? No way, Jose. And if O'Neill was the mastermind, why does he get the men to do that? That's cold-blooded brutality. It was also unnecessary, because the threat of violence alone should have been enough to make MacDougall part with the combination. But from all reports there was very little preamble. The threat was made, Dorrell refused and Aline was dragged away.

Davie had to hear about this, Donovan decided. There was a call box where the gardens ended and he'd opened the car door and had one leg out when Knight and Morrigan came out of the flat. She was wearing a black leather jacket and black mini skirt that showed off her long legs. They got into her blue sporty model and drove off. Davie could wait. Donovan decided to stay with them and see where they were going. He turned the key but waited until the car had almost reached the junction with Byres Road before he set off.

He kept a decent distance behind them, ensuring he never lost sight of them. They weren't speeding, for which he was thankful as his old car was in no state to keep up with that sporty number. As he drove he kept turning the details of the case over in his head.

The rape was the most troubling part of this entire thing. It was nasty and brutish but it was not a case of the raiders deciding to show off how big and powerful they were. It was part of the plan. So was the whole thing worked out by Dorrell MacDougall as a means of punishing his wife for her affair? And he worked with Knight not only to organise the thing but also to fit O'Neill up? And Knight, who has a close working relationship with Big Rab, saw a way of helping everyone out? But how did MacDougall latch on to Knight in the first place? Did he use his underworld contacts?

They had headed down Byres Road onto the Expressway. The

sun was low but there was still more than enough daylight to keep them in view as they headed towards the city centre. Donovan wondered if they were headed out for a night on the town. He wondered where a guy like Knight took his conquests. Somewhere expensive, no doubt, where discretion was guaranteed. Donovan had heard stories of his old partner's inability to keep it in his pants, had seen some evidence of it himself over the years. He'd be well-versed in keeping his infidelities low profile.

However, the couple weren't going into town. They took the on-ramp to the eastbound M8. Christ, thought Donovan, maybe they're going to Edinburgh. He glanced at his fuel gauge. He had almost a full tank but did he really want to tail them all the way? He decided to stay with them a little while longer.

Morrigan was a puzzle. She'd been abused by her father, was there something in there that made her fixate on an older man? In the course of the investigation Knight must've met her, she was a witness, after all. So did he seduce her back then, as a teenager? He wouldn't put it past Knight. Or was this liaison more recent? Was that what both MacDougall and his ex-wife knew and weren't saying? Or was it simply that they didn't want damaging memories being rekindled?

Donovan sighed. There were still more holes in this case than a string vest.

They signaled they were taking the Blochairn turn-off, then turned right to head to the East End. Where the hell were they going in the East End? Knight was too well known there. They followed the road to Duke Street and eventually parked in a side street. Donovan pulled in on the main road and watched the girl get out of the car and click on her high heels round the corner and into a bar. Knight stayed in the car. Donovan was puzzled, wondering what the hell they were up to. The bar was not the sort of place a girl like Morrigan would normally be seen dead in. Yet, there she was, walking in there alone.

About forty-five minutes later she came back out, but she wasn't alone. Donovan didn't know who the gangly young man was but he knew by looking at his Miami Vice get-up that he really wasn't her type. He was surprised to see her take his arm and snuggle closer to him, leading him to the car. He went around to the driver's side while she stood on the pavement for a moment before climbing into the back. A momentary look of bafflement crossed the young man's face before he gave a wee shrug and opened the door. Just as he was about to climb in, Donovan saw the guy hesitate before he was jerked inside.

Ten minutes later he saw the guy fall out of the car then pull himself to his feet. The car's brake lights flickered and Donovan started his own motor, pulled out and cruised into the side street. He passed close by the guy, who was standing in the middle of the road looking like someone had just told him his mother was dead, his dad was dying and his dog was feeling under the weather. The guy gave him a wave as he passed but there was no way Donovan was going to let the flash vehicle out of his sight.

The Aston Martin wound its way through the streets onto the motorway and headed back across town. It looked like they were going home to Huntly Gardens. Donovan hoped so, because he was desperate to get to a phone and tell McCall the latest development. Sure enough, the car came to a halt outside Morrigan's flat and both she and Knight went inside. Donovan waited for fifteen minutes to see if Knight would come back out, but the blinds and the curtains were drawn over the windows and he had the impression they were settling in for the night. Feeling strangely jealous, Donovan sprinted to the phone box tucked up against the fence around the gardens. He punched in McCall's number and listened to the ringing at the other end, then McCall's answering machine came on.

'Davie, Frank,' said Donovan, feeling somewhat disappointed. 'Listen, you'll never guess who Morrigan's boyfriend is. Jimmy Knight. Can you believe it? I've been following them about all night. They went to Flanagan's, or she did anyway. I don't know what they've been up to, but it all looked kind of strange. I'm heading off home now so if you want...'

He heard the phone box door open and he turned and snapped, 'Hey, I'm on the phone.'

He stopped when he saw Jimmy Knight smiling in at him.

'Hang up the phone, Frankie,' he said and Donovan laid the receiver back on its rest. Knight leaned against the open door, making no attempt to move. 'You know, Frankie, you really should brush up on your tailing skills. I spotted you just after we left here today.'

'What are you up to, Jimmy?'

'Whatever she'll let me,' said Knight with a lecherous grin. 'And she's up for just about anything.'

'I'm not talking about the girl.'

'I know you're not. But it's far too complicated to go into just now. I've not really got the time.'

'You got something better to do, then?'

'Aye,' said Knight, straightening up, his hand in his coat pocket, his eyes darting quickly up and down the deserted street. 'This.'

Donovan heard a click and saw something metallic glitter in Knight's right hand while his left snapped up and smashed the overhead light. Pieces of glass and plastic rained down on both men as Knight forced Donovan back against the phone and then jabbed in and up with the switchblade. Donovan fought back but something ice cold pushed itself into his stomach, just under his ribs. Then a burning pain seared its way through his body and he looked up into Knight's face, saw the grin contorted into a snarl, saw the eyes bright with madness.

'Sorry, Frankie boy, but you shouldn't be sticking your nose into my business,' he said as he jerked his hand upwards and another jolt of agony squeezed at Donovan's guts. A jagged breath hissed in his throat and his hands fluttered against Knight's shoulders as he tried to push him away, tried to block the pain, tried to get the red-hot poker that was lodged under his ribs away from him. But Knight just jammed the blade in tighter and the fire engulfed Donovan's body. He moaned once and his eyelids flickered and he felt his legs give.

Knight pulled Shoog's switchblade out and stepped back to watch Donovan slump against the glass wall of the phone box and slide down to his knees, blood pumping from the wound and streaming down his belly. He tried to say something but no words came. Knight took out a paper tissue and wiped the blade as Donovan's head sank slowly onto his chest.

'Night, night, Frankie,' he said. And with a final look to make sure no-one was watching, he walked quickly back to Morrigan's willing embrace.

23

MCCALL HAD WANDERED the streets for some time after he left Donna and Vincent, Arrow on his lead. Earlier, the dog had sensed something amiss and had laid his head on his lap, unsure of what was happening. McCall had felt a bit better as he stroked Arrow's head. What was it they said? The more I know people, the more I love my dog? God knows that was true. She wasn't worth his tears, he told himself. She wasn't worth the pain. But that didn't help. It didn't help at all. So he hit the streets and after a few hours found himself at Bobby Newman's place.

Bobby told him that Rab wanted to see him, that he knew Donna was a cop. McCall wasn't surprised. *She's not what she seems*, he'd said. That meant Rab knew what she was. He told Bobby and Connie what had happened.

'Jesus, Davie,' said Bobby, catching his pal's tone, his voice low because his daughter was upstairs sleeping. 'I never thought... not after Audrey.' No-one other than Bobby would get away with mentioning Audrey but McCall still felt something inside wince. 'So what you going to do?'

McCall stopped and thought about that. What was he going to do? 'I don't know,' he answered, truthfully.

'You could always forgive and forget,' ventured Connie, but McCall shook his head.

'I'm better off this way,' he said. 'If people get to you, they just hurt you. Eventually.'

'You can't go through life that way,' said Connie, gently.

'I can't go through life any other way.'

And when he looked up she saw – for the very first time – the pain in his eyes.

Lorraine Armstrong thought swearing showed a limited vocabulary so curse words never passed her lips. She did, however, spell them out in her head when she was annoyed. And when Buffy began scratching at the door just after eleven, she became very annoyed indeed. Her husband was snoring in the armchair and it was his turn to take her out. He was, she decided, a bit of an S-O-D. She debated waking him up and making him fulfill his part of the routine, but knew if she did that the poor pup would be outside for two minutes and then brought back in whether she'd done her business or not. He was more than an S-O-D, he was a B-A-S-T-A-R-D.

So she pulled on her dog walking boots and her dog-walking coat and fastened Buffy's tartan collar. Buffy – named not for that silly television programme but the nickname given to the Queen Mother when she was a girl – was a Westie and her pride and joy. She was not an unkind woman, but sometimes she did wonder if she cared for the dog more than she cared for Mr Armstrong.

She stooped at the front door of the building to click the lead onto the dog's collar and stepped out into the street, heading towards the main road because she refused to allow Buffy to soil the gardens. She had a pocketful of plastic bags with which to pick up the droppings, but it was easier to lift from concrete than grass.

The first thing she saw was the door of the phone box lying open, then she realised that a man's legs were wedging it like that. A drunk, she thought, a drunk asleep in the phone box. It had happened before and no doubt it would happen again.

'Buffy!' She said sharply, jerking the dog away from a stream of something dark leading from the phone box to the gutter. The man was not only drunk and asleep in a public place, he'd P-I-S-S-E-D himself. This was disgraceful and should not be tolerated. She was kind, but Mrs Armstrong was not about to tolerate something that should not be tolerated.

She nudged one of his legs with her foot. 'Excuse me,' she said, because she always remembered her manners, even when dealing with someone who clearly had none. But the man did not respond.

Another nudge and a repeat of 'Excuse me' provoked nothing. Mrs Armstrong, her anger rising, stepped over his legs and peered into the phone box, being careful to keep her feet and Buffy away from the liquid draining across the pavement. That was when she realised the light had been smashed and wondered if this man had done it.

'You can't sleep here,' she said. 'It's not a hostel or a public convenience.'

But the man simply lay there, not saying a word, not moving. Mrs Armstrong clicked her tongue, decided he was being a right pain in the A-R-S-E, and leaned in further in order to deliver a proper scolding. But something about his position and the deathly white of his flesh made her realise she was wrong.

'Are you all right?' She asked, her voice losing its earlier edge as she leaned closer.

And then she saw the liquid streaming from him wasn't urine, but blood. And that he wasn't drunk at all.

'Oh, fuck,' she breathed.

The arrival of the ambulance and the police woke a lot of people up. The flashing blue lights bounced from the windows of the buildings on both sides of the gardens and lamps soon flicked on. A few curious residents even came to their front doors in dressing gowns or hastily-donned clothing to see what all the fuss was about.

Mrs Armstrong had recovered her composure and was talking to a policewoman in a calm and dignified manner. She had been near to hysterics when she ran back to her home to dial 999, as there was no way on God's green earth that she was going to step into a phone box with a dead man lying there. Anyway, she could be tampering with evidence – she'd seen *The Bill*. Contrary to Mrs Armstrong's belief, the man was not dead, although he wasn't far from it. The police officers milling around the blocked off road and talking to anyone who might have witnessed anything knew they might yet be investigating a murder.

McCall found Donovan's message on his answering machine and the sound of Knight's voice at the end sent him dashing back out again. He still didn't enjoy driving and avoided it as often as he could, but he drove like a maniac from east to west to be halted at the mouth of the Gardens by a young police officer. He parked his car illegally outside the Grosvenor Hotel and ran back just in time to catch sight of Donovan's white face as the double doors of the ambulance were slammed shut and the vehicle pulled away from the kerb with lights blazing and siren blaring. He knew he wasn't dead – they had him on a drip and the paramedic was working on his chest.

For the first time in his life he didn't know what to do. He watched the ambulance screech past him and career towards the hospital and he still didn't know what to do.

'What happened?' He asked the young cop.

'Guy was stabbed in the phone box,' said the officer.

McCall nodded. If they could trace the last call made from that box they'd know Frank had phoned him.

'His name's Frank Donovan,' he said. 'He was phoning me when he was attacked.'

The cop just stared at him, his face a picture of surprise.

'I think you'd better tell someone senior,' said McCall.

As soon as they found out who he was, the police gave McCall a hard time. Up until then they had been polite and offering tea, which of course McCall refused because in The Life you never accept anything in a police station. Handle a cup, a glass or even a cigarette packet, they said, and you never know where your fingerprints would end up. But once their routine computer search revealed he was *the* David McCall they were no longer so polite, but still offering tea. And cigarettes.

They put him in an interview room and two CID officers sat opposite him, treated him to the stare. One was big, the other small. One had hair, the other had a fine head of skin. One spoke, the other didn't.

'Why did this guy Donovan phone you?' It was Baldy who asked the questions.

'He's a friend,' McCall said. 'How is he?'

'Guys like you don't have friends,' Baldy said, smiling like he'd beaten Billy Connolly to a punchline.

McCall remembered Donovan saying the same thing. 'He used to be one of you guys, you know that?

'We know that. And he was a scumbag, the way we hear it, so maybe you and him were best buds. He went private after we tossed him out on his arse. What was he working on?'

'He didn't confide in me,' McCall lied. 'How is he?'

Baldy ignored the question again. 'We know he phoned you from that call box. What'd he say on the phone?'

'Didn't speak to him. He left a message on my machine. Is he still alive?'

'So what made you rush all the way west if you didn't speak to him?'

McCall didn't need to hesitate. Instinctively he'd replaced the micro-cassette from his answering machine before he left the house. He'd recognized the other voice and didn't know if Knight was aware Donovan was in the process of leaving a message so there was no way he was leaving that evidence in his flat. Knight wasn't above a bit of breaking and entering and he doubted if Arrow would be a sufficient deterrent. The original tape was in his car, which was still parked up the West End.

'He wanted to go for a drink. There are good pubs in Byres Road and that's just around the corner. Will someone tell me how he is?'

'What was he doing in Huntly Gardens?'

'Beats me.'

'Why did he phone you?'

'Already told you...'

'What was he working on?'

And so it went on. And on. And on. They kept McCall cooped up in a small windowless room until daybreak, hammering him with questions, repeating themselves, backtracking, going over the same ground, over and over until everyone concerned was exhausted. Eventually, they let him go because there was nothing to hold him on. But McCall was left in no doubt that knew he was involved somehow. He was David McCall, Danny McCall's son, Big Rab's enforcer. He was the bad guy.

Donovan was still hanging on, but the thread holding him to life was thin and stretching all the time. The knife had punctured a lung and nicked the heart, a friendly nurse had told McCall after first asking if he was family. McCall told her that apart from a wife and child somewhere, Donovan had no family. He was a friend, he explained. Donovan was in the Intensive Care unit, on a respirator and some sort of IV. McCall could only see him through a window and he listened as the nurse explained the injuries and what the doctors had done. He heard words like extreme blood loss and tamponade and transfusion but all that sunk in was that it had been touch and go, They were still not certain of his chances, but they would use all their skills and resources to help him pull through. McCall nodded and looked at the man lying in the bed on the other side of the glass. He appeared to be so small and frail as he lay there. He looked old, though he was only in his forties.

When the nurse left him alone, McCall leaned his head against the glass, feeling it cool against his forehead. He wanted to speak to Frank, to tell him how sorry he was. Their connection had been unlucky from the start and this was not the first time he'd ended up in hospital because of him. He'd got the man into all this and he should've been with him last night. He should've been there. If he had been, Knight would never have got close to Donovan. Donovan couldn't take Knight, but McCall could. Because that's what he did. That's what he was.

'I'm sorry, Frank,' he whispered into the glass, then pushed himself away and walked down the quiet corridor, heading for the sunlight, each step filled with purpose.

He hadn't known what to do the night before as he watched the ambulance speed away. He hadn't been sure what to do when the police were questioning him.

But he knew now.

He needed the Dark one last time.

24

MCCALL WAS MILDLY surprised when she let him in. After all, the last time he'd been there the girl had thrown a strop – and then him and Donovan out. But she buzzed him in without any hesitation and was waiting at her front door when he climbed the curved staircase.

Her first words, though, were far from welcoming. 'What do you want now?'

She leaned against the doorframe, a hand resting lightly on a jutted hip. She was wearing a loose t-shirt with a thick black belt tightened at her waist and black denims. She was casual but looked smarter than some people he knew when they wore their Sunday best. Some people have that knack. Donovan said her mother was like that. McCall wasn't a betting man, but he'd lay odds DCI Vincent was the same. The thought brought Donna back to mind but he forced her away to concentrate on the young woman in front of him.

'A few more questions,' said McCall, keeping his eyes on her face.

'What if I don't want to answer them?'

'Then I'll go away and take what I've got to the law.'

She looked deep into his eyes, trying to gauge if he was bluffing. He kept his face impassive. He was good at that.

'Take what to the law?'

'Why don't I come in and we'll talk about it?'

She hesitated, then turned swiftly and walked into the flat, leaving him to close the door. She took up her position at the fireplace and fired up a cigarette. McCall sat down in the same place on the settee as before.

'So,' she said, blowing smoke towards the ceiling, 'what's your problem?'

'A friend of mine was stabbed outside here last night. I don't like that. A family was gunned down in the street the night before that. I don't like that either. Six years ago, a woman was raped in her home by some scumbag thief. You can guess what I think of that.'

'I didn't find it much of a picnic, either. But what's the rest got to do with me?'

'Your boyfriend is up to his neck in it all.'

A smile came into her eyes. 'My boyfriend?'

'Jimmy Knight. DI Jimmy Knight.' He paused, then said, 'The DI stands for Deeply Involved.' It was something Donovan would've said and McCall was glad he was channeling the man somehow.

She drew on the cigarette and sat down in the nearest armchair. 'I know him. He investigated the robbery. But what makes you think he's my boyfriend?'

McCall smiled. It was a thin smile, but a smile nonetheless. 'I know.'

There was a silence for a few moments as he stared her out. She shifted her gaze first, but that was a foregone conclusion. She said, 'What if I deny it?'

McCall kept his smile in place and fished around in the pocket of the long coat he was wearing. He took out a mini tape recorder and held it up to let her see it. He pressed the PLAY button and Donovan's voice crackled into the room.

'Listen, you'll never guess who Morrigan's boyfriend is. Jimmy Knight. Can you believe it? I've been following them about all night. They went to Flanagan's, or she did anyway. I don't know what they've been up to but it all looked kind of strange...'

McCall clicked the tape off and stared at her again, letting the words sink in. Then he said, 'That's from the answering machine at my home. There's another voice just after it. I think you'll recognise it.'

He pressed PLAY again and the recording continued.

'I'm heading off home now so if you want – hey – I'm on the phone.'

'Hang up the phone, Frankie.'

McCall stopped the tape but kept the player in plain view.

While he waited for her to speak he watched her mind work in her eyes and the way she jiggled the cigarette between her fingers. Finally he decided to give her another push.

'I went to Flanagan's, spoke to a guy there I know. Seems a boy died round the corner last night. OD'd, right there on the street. He'd been in the pub just before and left with a lassie. Good-looking lassie, my mate said. He'd never seen her before but he was able to describe her. You can get good-looking lassies in Flanagan's but this one was seriously out-of-place, he said.'

'I know nothing about a place called Flanagan's.'

'Fair enough. So maybe I should just take this...' He held up the tape machine again. '...to the police. Donovan is at death's door and a thing like this... well, it's as good as a death bed statement. And you've heard of them, haven't you? Cops and prosecutors and juries tend to take a very serious view of them, so they do. Might just tell them what I know about the dead boy in the street, too. Pass on the description I've got. And the flash car seen nearby.'

She glared at him, not knowing whether to believe him or not.

'What do you want?' She asked eventually.

'I want the truth.'

'About what?'

'What happened six years ago.'

She stood up again and stubbed the cigarette out in an ashtray on the mantelpiece. 'If I tell you, what will you do with the information? How do I know you won't go to the police with it all?'

'Look, I'll be honest with you – I don't like the police much and they don't like me. But I'll go to them if I have to. I'd just rather not have to.'

She glanced at him nervously. 'You'll go after him yourself? He's a dangerous man. That's why I've stayed with him all these years. He scares me because I know what he's capable of.'

'I can handle him.'

'He'll know I told you.'

'I can handle him,' McCall repeated, deadpan. That wasn't Donovan speaking, that was all him.

She lit up another cigarette and paced back and forward along the front of the fireplace, sucking on the fag with one hand, the other arm crossed over her midriff, as if she was in pain. Then she reached a decision and came to a halt. She faced McCall and began to speak softly.

'I was fifteen when I met him for the first time…'

For two days Jimmy Knight had the feeling he was being watched. In anyone else it could have been a guilty conscience, but with him that was unlikely. He had taken immense satisfaction from discovering that Shoog had been found dead in the middle of the road about an hour after they'd pumped the brown into his veins. That satisfaction was marred somewhat by the news that Frank Donovan was still hanging on, but he was assured by the cop handling the case that the man was not expected to survive his injuries.

After he'd left Donovan bleeding in the phone box, which served the bastard right for sticking his nose where it didn't belong, Knight had gone back to Morrigan. She proved to be very, very inventive that night and Knight hadn't even brought any Colombian marching powder. Obviously killing a man – two men, effectively, although she'd been tucked up in bed when Knight stabbed Donovan – was aphrodisiac enough for her.

He'd stayed away from Huntly Gardens for two days, knowing that it would be the focus of the investigation. He was well known in the force and he didn't want to run the risk of being spotted. She'd tried phoning his mobile a couple of times but he just switched it off when he saw her number on the LCD. Treat them mean, keep them keen, that was his secret – when he did turn up, she'd be all the more appreciative. He went about his lawful business, investigating a couple of break-ins, an arson attack and the rape of an eighty-four-year-old grandmother. That last one had even him shaking his head, thinking the world was going seriously to hell in a hand basket.

But he couldn't shake off the sensation of unseen eyes upon him. He didn't feel them all the time, just when the hairs on the back of his neck bristled, but when he turned round he saw no-one paying any attention to him. He had grown older and richer relying on his instincts and he knew not to ignore them.

He decided to give Shoog MacLeish's mother a visit, just to pay his respects. Well, he reasoned, it's what you do, isn't it? And she wasn't a bad sort, Mrs MacLeish. It wasn't her fault her son was a waster. So he called in around tea-time on the Tuesday after Shoog died, expressing his regrets to the grey-haired woman as she stared at some kids show on the telly. And of course the lies flowed like sewage from his mouth.

'He wasn't a bad lad, just ill-advised.'

'I always had a lot of time for him.'

'If only I could have helped him more.'

'I had no idea he was doing drugs.'

'I'm sorry for your loss.'

'If there's anything I can do.'

And so on.

And so forth.

He left her still gazing at the TV screen. He couldn't tell whether she cared if Shoog was dead because apart from opening the door and leading him into the living room, she'd given little indication as to whether she knew Knight was there or not. So he said goodbye and left the flat, shaking his head as he walked down the tenement stairs. The lives some people lead, he thought.

The tenement had been built on the crest of a hill so the rear of this building was on a lower level than the front entrance. The voice came from the dark well leading down to the rear door, which in turn led to the concrete back court.

'Jimmy,' said the voice and Knight whirled, his hand already in his pocket, fingers closing on the switchblade.

'Who the fuck is it?' Knight asked, every nerve in his body tingling.

'We need to talk,' said the voice.

'I'm no talkin to a fuckin shadow.'

There was a pause, followed by a movement and a face emerged from the gloom. Knight smiled. 'Well, well, you still walkin about?'

McCall kept his distance from Knight and nodded. 'Looks like it.'

'Still shaggin that bird?' Knight smiled again when he saw the look of surprise flash across McCall's face. 'Oh, aye – I know all about it. Hope she's worth it.'

McCall ignored him, knowing Knight was more than capable of picking at a scab to draw blood. 'We've got things to discuss.'

Knight frowned then, a thought striking him. 'You wired for sound, Davie boy?'

'No.'

'How about you let me pat you down, just to make sure?'

'How about I don't.'

Knight stared at the man, trying to divine something from the way he was standing. The boy seemed relaxed enough, but you could never tell with his kind. That long coat of his could hide all sorts of things. He could even have something in his right hand, which was hidden beneath the folds of the coat. But then, Knight himself had something in his hand – the knife, the one he'd taken from Shoog, the one with which he'd gutted Frankie Boy, which he had eased from his own coat pocket and carefully clicked open. He held it loosely half behind his back.

'What do you want, Davie.'

'Frank Donovan.'

Knight snorted. 'Nothing to do with me, Davie. Frankie just got in the wrong person's face, know what I'm saying? Probably the husband of some client he'd been snooping on.'

McCall shook his head. 'No, Jimmy, it was you. We both know it.'

Knight shrugged. A shrug doesn't show up on tape. Not that he thought McCall really was wired. It wasn't his style.

'I know you helped plan the MacDougall robbery, Jimmy,' said McCall.

'Don't talk shite, man.'

'I've been thinking a lot about this over the past couple of days. While I've been watching you.'

'So it was you I could feel like an itch on my back?'

'Aye.'

Another half step forward, the knife still behind him. McCall had made a better fist of tailing him than Donovan. He'd've congratulated him if he wasn't still being canny about a possible wire.

McCall shrugged and continued with his thoughts. 'Whoever organised the thing had to have the know-how to pull together a crew from outside the city. MacDougall knew some people but not the kind who could do that. So who was involved in this and knew who to speak to?'

He paused then and looked directly at Knight.

'You, Jimmy,' said McCall. 'You pulled together the crew, you organised the whole thing, you pocketed half the two hundred grand.'

Knight laughed. 'You've got this all worked out, haven't you? Okay, mate, we'll play your wee guessing game. So who gave me the code for the alarm system, then?'

'For the answer to that we have to jump to a year before the robbery. A fifteen-year-old girl is caught in possession of some cocaine. She's a good-looking girl and she comes on to the cop who arrested her. Her father has sexually abused her for three years or so and she's mixed up. She needs help, not another man treating her like a twenty quid whore. But the cop agrees to forget about the drugs in return for sex. To be fair to him, he did think she was older. Does any of this sound familiar?'

Knight refused to answer but his hand tightened on the handle of the knife. Just another couple of steps, he was thinking, and I'll cut any fucking microphone out of him.

'You've been using that girl ever since, Knight. You give her drugs and she gives you her body. You're no better than her abusive father, Knight.'

'This is all fantasy,' said Knight, softly.

'Then you hatched the robbery plan. You got her to give you the alarm code. You used her, Knight. A teenage lassie.'

Knight smiled. 'You're very outraged for a man in your line of work, Davie.'

'I've done some things, sure. But if I'm the bad guy, that makes you some sort of demon, Jimmy.'

Knight edged slightly closer, keeping his voice low. 'Are you wired, Davie?'

'I told you I wasn't.'

Knight believed him this time. 'Then why you here?'

'To make amends, Jimmy. For Frank Donovan, for the O'Neills, for all the people you've hurt over the years, including Morrigan.'

Knight's fingers tensed on the knife handle. Closer now. Another few seconds. 'You some sort of avenging angel, that it? Or is this all to make up for the things you've done, the harm you've caused?'

McCall thought about this. 'Whatever you like, Jimmy.'

Knight nodded, accepting this. 'Fair enough, son. But don't be doing it for that lassie. She doesn't deserve it.'

'Jimmy, she told me.'

Knight stopped edging forward. 'What? You spoke to her? She told you it was me?'

McCall nodded. Knight was stunned for a minute, then he threw his head back and laughed. 'The wee cow! She told you the robbery was my idea? Oh, that wee bitch! That wee fucking bitch! Davie, son, I hope you got some from her because she's spun you a yarn!'

McCall took a step back, puzzled. Knight stopped laughing, not caring now if McCall was wired. Wouldn't matter in a moment or two. 'It was *her* idea – the whole bloody lot of it! Sure, I was shagging her before that. And she was worth it, believe me. She's a nimble wee lassie, always was. And you're right, I did think she was older that first time, not that it would've made any difference.'

Knight paused, took another half step closer to McCall. 'But then she came to *me* with the idea for the robbery. You think I was using her? It was the other way around. She'd made a video tape of me and her in a hotel room, doing all sorts of things. She was active that night, let me tell you. She had me tying her up, pretending I was forcing her. She's used that video against me ever since.'

Knight paused, as if he was remembering that night but in reality he was sliding even closer, the knife ready. Softly, softly, catchee monkey, he thought. 'Then she talked about robbing her dad. I knew the old man had been humping her for years – and he'd taught her well. She was very talented, if you know what I mean...'

'Nimble,' said McCall, the distaste evident in his voice.

'Yeah,' said Knight, paying no heed to McCall's tone. 'She wanted payback on him and on her mother. She knew all about the affair with O'Neill and was afraid she'd be left alone with her father. So she came up with this robbery plan, complete with the rape. It was all her idea, the whole thing. My job was to pull the guys together and then, later, plant the evidence against O'Neill. That was his punishment, for threatening to take her mother away. The rape was her mother's punishment for thinking about deserting her. Truth is, I thought it was a bit too much, but shit – hell hath no fury and all that. Stupid wee bitch – she's never understood that it was a casual thing between her mum and O'Neill.'

'And was it just a coincidence that you were investigating the case, too?'

'Let me tell you something, Davie boy – with that lassie there are no coincidences. She planned it so that I would be on duty the night of the robbery. She was leaving nothing to chance, that girl. Nothing. She's smart, I mean genius smart.'

'So you're just a victim, Jimmy, that what you're saying?'

Knight smiled. While he'd been talking he'd come within striking distance – and this prick hadn't even noticed.

'There are no victims,' he said. 'There's just the stupid – and the dead.'

That was when he moved, swinging his arm out from behind his back, knife pointed upwards towards McCall's ribs. Dumb bastard, he thought as he stepped in for the kill, he should have been paying attention.

But McCall had been paying attention. He'd noticed Knight creeping forward, he'd noticed the hand hidden behind his back. And when the cop made his move, McCall made his, stepping back and revealing his own hand, the one hidden beneath the folds of his coat.

Knight's knife sliced harmlessly through the air just inches from McCall's chest. He swung back for another go – and that was when he saw the gun in McCall's hand, pointing straight at his face. He looked from the unwavering black hole of the muzzle to the grim face behind it. 'I thought you didn't like guns,' said Knight.

'I don't,' said McCall and for the second time in his life he squeezed a trigger.

This time, he fired.

25

ACCORDING TO THE sign on the wooden barrier on the pavement, the row of tenements was due for demolition. The windows had been boarded up, the entrances blocked by metal grilles over a year before, but there was still no sign of any wrecking crews. As far as McCall was concerned, the place should have been razed to the ground years ago. He'd found a way in through a back close where kids or junkies, or both, had long since prized the metal bolts holding the grilles away. He'd stepped over puddles of what could have been rainwater but more than likely wasn't and climbed the stairs to the second floor flat, hearing the scurrying of rats somewhere in the dank darkness. He kicked the front door in, for there was no-one in this dead building to hear, and stepped over the threshold. A startled crow flapped through the gaping window and merged with the night.

He hadn't been back since that night. He'd passed by, he'd even stood outside and looked up at the lifeless windows but never actually set foot inside. Now he was here and he fancied he could still see the blood on the wall near where his mother had died but he knew that was merely his imagination; the ancient plaster had long ago flaked away, leaving only weathered strapping visible. Be it ever so humble, he thought as he walked around the room, gingerly feeling his way with his feet as the ageing floorboards, rotted by generations of damp, groaned under his weight.

He remembered the room as bigger. It had certainly been cleaner and tidier. The ceiling had given way in one corner and pieces of blackened timbers and slates lay heaped on the floor.

An old wooden chair lay on its side and he righted it, wiped the seat off and sat down. He slid a piece of paper from his pocket, unfolded it slowly and stared at the sketch of Donna's face. It was unfinished, which he thought ironic. He never did get her mouth right. But then, he'd got nothing right about her, had he? God, she had played him like an old violin and he had been strung right along. He held the drawing in front of him in both hands, elbows on his knees, and felt the rage and the sadness sting at his eyes. He'd wanted to change for her. But she'd betrayed him. Suckered him. Made a fool of him.

For once he wanted the Dark to insulate him against the pain. He called on it, needing it, wanting it.

But it didn't come. The tightness still clutched at his throat and his chest and his eyes. But he refused to let it burst through. He held it in check and forced it back down. He would never let it get through. He would never again let anyone get to him the way she had.

He stood up and looked around the room. You're still here, dad, he thought. I can feel you, feel your rage seeping out of these tired old walls. You tried to get at me through Spencer, even through Stringer, but you didn't get me and you'll never get me. Not now. You'll never be able to touch me again. No one will. Knight was the last. Knight was the end of it.

The drawing slipped from his fingers and floated down to the floor where it lay face up. Her eyes watched him as he stepped away, charcoal grey in the picture but in his mind clear and blue and sparkling. He walked out of the derelict flat, leaving her and his father's demons behind.

Donna dropped the last of the boxes in the back of DCI Vincent's car and glanced once more at the second-floor windows. The blinds were drawn but she felt McCall was behind them, watching her. She wanted to speak to him again, but she would never try while Vincent was around. The two suitcases and the boxes in the boot were her personal possessions from the flat. The furniture and ornaments would be moved out later in the week.

She felt eyes on her and she looked over to see the DCI leaning on the open door of the driver's side, a curiously amused expression on her face.

'Forget it, that ship has sailed,' Vincent said, guessing her thoughts.

She glared at her and turned her attention to a car that had just pulled up. She recognised Jimsie as he climbed out. She exchanged a few words with him, then joined Vincent.

In the car, Donna silently watched the buildings and shops and streets shoot past. Vincent glanced at her as she drove.

'He's not worth it,' she said. Donna looked at her once, then back out of the side window again.

'Remember what he is, Donna,' said Vincent.

'What is he?' She asked, her anger rising. 'The bad guy? That's what I told him. He was the bad guy and I was just doing my job. Using him to get at an even worse guy. Now that guy is dead and everything – everything – was for nothing.'

'Not for nothing. We still have McClymont to get.'

'And what chance is there of that? O'Neill's dead, not that he could tell you anything anyway. MacLeish is dead. Knight's dead. And Davie won't play ball. What was it all for? Tell me – what exactly was it all for?'

'The greater good.'

'Oh, don't hand me any of that shit! Your career, my career, that's what it's all about. That's why we do these things. That's why we lie and cheat and lie some more to get what we want. And what's our lying got us this time? Five people dead and no closer to getting McClymont. We'll never get him. Your only hope was Davie.'

'Not the only one,' Vincent said quietly and Donna froze, waiting for her to expand on her comment. 'McCall wasn't really much of a hope. He was just a misdirection.'

'What does that mean?'

'I knew McCall would never talk, although there was always a chance. That's why you were there. We knew from his profile that he was emotionally stunted, he has a weakness for a damsel in distress, so if we could put a good-looking female in trouble in there he might come over all Sir Galahad. We were right, but in the end it didn't work.'

'Because you rushed it.'

'True, but I've got to admit the O'Neill killings flustered me somewhat.'

'But what did you mean by a misdirection?'

Vincent sighed. 'McCall was never a serious contender for turning. It might've happened, certainly, and if it had it would've been a bonus, but it was never really part of the plan. He was there to draw Knight's attention.'

'You mean you set him up?'

'In a manner of speaking. I knew Knight would use whatever influence he could to get information, even gain access to my files. So I just greased the way a little bit. I used Donald Simms to let him in, but only left information I wanted him to see. He already knew about MacLeish but I thought I had him safe and sound and well out of Knight's reach.'

'You pointed Knight at Davie? And me?'

'You were never in any danger. Knight was many things, but I don't think he'd take action against a fellow officer.'

'You don't think? You mean you weren't certain?'

'Nothing's certain in this life.'

Donna was speechless for a moment. Davie had been used – *she* had been used. She was stunned at how cold-blooded and calculated it all was. 'Why?'

'I'm sorry?'

'Why do all this? Why misdirect Knight?'

'Because I knew Knight would tell McClymont. And while McClymont was paying attention to Davie McCall, it meant my real informant was safe.'

'Your real informant?'

'Yes. You didn't think I was totally dependent on the likes of MacLeish and your boyfriend, did you? There's another man.'

'Stop the car!'

Vincent frowned and checked her rear view before putting her foot on the brake. 'What?' She said before following Donna's gaze out the windscreen. There was a brick wall ahead of them and scrawled in white paint were the words DAVIE MCCALL IS A GRASS.

'Turn the car round,' said Donna.

'Leave it, Donna,' said Vincent.

'Turn the fucking car around!'

'Listen to me, Donna,' said Vincent, twisting in her seat to face her. 'He's not worth it.'

Donna stared at her for a second, her mouth set in a tight line. Then she unhitched her seat belt and grabbed at the door handle. She threw open the door and almost tumbled out in her haste.

'Donna!' Vincent shouted, pulling at her own seatbelt and darting out. 'Donna, he's not worth it!'

But she was already running back along the road.

McCall had watched her through the blinds. He could look at her and feel nothing. The barriers were back and would never been breached again. He saw her talking to Jimsie, who nodded and glanced at his windows. Then she climbed into the other car and Vincent drove off. McCall watched them go. He still felt nothing.

Jimsie rattled the letterbox and McCall let him in.

'Did you know Jimmy Knight's been shot?' Said the young man. There were dark circles under his eyes and he seemed far from his usual buoyant self.

'I'd heard,' said McCall.

'There's a turn-up, eh? Wonder who did it?'

McCall said nothing.

'I met your girlfriend outside, she told me about Knight,' said Jimsie. 'Then she said a funny thing,' Jimsie went on. 'She said it was over as far as she was concerned. She said she'll have nothing more to do with the investigation.'

McCall nodded. It was over as far as he was concerned too.

'She said she was sorry,' said Jimsie. 'Davie, can I ask what all this is about?'

So McCall began to tell him. He saw no reason not to. Not now.

She ran.

She ran like she'd never run before, dodging people in the street, leaping off kerbs, oblivious to traffic, oblivious to everything except the need to get back to Davie, to tell him, to warn him.

Jimsie listened as McCall told him all about Donna and the fact that she was an undercover officer. For the first time ever, Jimsie felt sorry for David McCall. The poor bastard had it bad, but he didn't even know it. He could tell by the way that he spoke about that lassie, even if she was a copper.

And as he listened, he almost forgot what he was there to do.

He felt sick when his mission came back into his head. He wanted to tell McCall, to warn him, but he'd been ordered not to breathe a word. McCall couldn't know what was about to go down, he'd fight against it if he did and they couldn't have that. McCall had to go along with it, otherwise it wouldn't work. And it had to work. It had to be done.

Donna's heart pounded and her lungs burned but she refused to slow her pace. She couldn't slow down, not now, there was too much at stake. That sign meant Davie had been declared fair game. The word was out and he was a legitimate target. She knew Big Rab was behind it, knew he'd already assigned someone to do the job.

And it would be someone he knew who would draw him out.

Jimsie was trying to be supportive. 'Women. Can't live with them, can't lock them in the basement, I tell you, they've just got this knack of cutting the guts out of us men, know what I'm sayin?'

McCall knew what he was saying but doubted the young man had the life experience to really know what he was talking about. 'So what brings you here, Jimsie?'

For some reason, Jimsie tensed and his eyes flicked away from McCall. 'Need a favour, Davie. I've to fetch the cash from Bru...'

McCall shook his head. 'I'm out of it, Jimsie, you know that.'

'I know, I know, but I'd feel better if I had someone with me, you know? Twenty grand, man. And I've to collect another eighty frae Fat Boy McQueen. It's a lot of cash. I need backup, man.'

'Why doesn't Rab send someone with you?'

Again, Jimsie avoided McCall's gaze. 'I don't want anyone else. I trust you to watch my back, you know what I'm sayin? Come on, Davie, just this once. That's all I ask.'

McCall sensed Jimsie was lying but he didn't care. He was tired. He'd killed a man, a man who deserved to die certainly, but he had violated his own basic rule. Never use a gun. Never kill. He'd always felt that as soon as he did that then the Dark would have him. But the Dark was gone. And yet he still felt lost. 'You sure you're up to this?'

The boy shrugged, knowing he was talking about the O'Neill shootings. 'I've got over it, Davie. It's done. This is my life now, you know? I've got to get used to it.'

McCall noted the way the boy's body tensed as he spoke and wondered if this was true.

She had to stop. Just for a second. Just for a breath. She. Couldn't. Keep. It. Up. Not that pace. It wasn't far now. She could see the closemouth. See the car outside. She stood with her hands on her knees, head bent, gasping for air.

When she looked up again, McCall and Jimsie were in the street, heading for the car.

She tried to call out but didn't have the air in her lungs. All she could do was croak out McCall's name.

She forced herself into a run as he walked around to the passenger door.

She swerved out into the street, her legs unsteady.

She raised her hand, trying to attract McCall's attention.

He didn't look her way.

She called out as he ducked into the car.

He didn't hear her and slammed the door shut.

But Jimsie looked up.

Jimsie saw her.

She waved again, called out again, a bit stronger this time, hope rising.

Jimsie looked at her for a brief moment, then climbed into the car and started the motor. She saw his head turn towards McCall before glancing in the rearview to see her running towards them.

Jimsie pulled away.

Donna followed for a few paces then her legs gave way and she slumped to her knees in the street. She looked up as the car disappeared around a corner.

'Davie,' she muttered, a sob escaping between her gasps for air. 'Davie!'

26

JIMSIE FINGERED THE last of the notes and dropped them in the leather sports bag. He looked across the table and smiled.

'It's all there, Bru, old son,' he said.

'Aye, I told you.' Bru's voice had turned nasal thanks to the broken nose and he moved stiffly, his beating still fresh in his bruises. 'You didnae need to count it.'

'Can never be too careful, not where money's concerned.'

'Aye,' said Bru, wrinkling his face. Jimsie zipped up the bag and glanced at McCall, who was leaning against the wall near the door, looking bored. Jimsie looked back at the red-haired dealer and smiled again.

'Pleasure doing business with you, me old mate,' he said. Bru merely nodded. McCall sensed he didn't like dealing with Jimsie and Big Rab, but they were the only game in this part of town and if he wanted to keep his business going he had to buy product from them. But that didn't mean he had to be polite. After all, it was only last week that Jimsie had been kicking seven shades of it out of him, now he was chatting away like a pal.

Jimsie smiled and left the room. McCall followed, hardly paying Bru any notice at all but wondering why Jimsie's manner seemed so forced.

Outside, the bag was tossed unceremoniously in the back of the car and Jimsie climbed into the driver's seat. Seeing the empty seat made McCall think about Arrow, who he'd left back at the flat.

'You know,' Jimsie said, trying keep his voice light but not quite making it. 'I'm kind of sorry he had the cash. I really wanted to pound him a wee bit, know what I'm sayin? Work off some aggression.'

'Get a punch bag.'

'Bru *is* a punch bag.'

Jimsie drove through the remaining streets to Fat Boy's place in silence. They stopped outside the terraced house but Jimsie made no attempt to get out.

'We going in or what?' McCall asked.

'Someone else is pickin it up,' said Jimsie, his voice unusually hoarse. McCall frowned at him and was about to ask what had got into him when he saw a familiar figure walking down the path from the McQueen house. The man's right arm was in a sling and his head was bandaged. In his left hand he carried a sports bag similar to the one in the back seat.

McCall knew then why Jimsie had seemed so tense, why he had asked him to come along. But then, on some level, he'd known all along. That was why he'd left Arrow behind. He looked at the boy, trying to catch his eye, but he just stared straight ahead, his hand gripping the steering wheel so tightly his knuckles gleamed white, a muscle working in his jaw. The rear door opened and the newcomer climbed in, looking at McCall through one eye, the other swollen shut.

Stringer smiled almost pleasantly. McCall didn't return the smile. He kept his eyes on Jimsie's profile. The boy started the car, looking everywhere but at McCall as he pulled out. Stringer chuckled as he settled himself into the seat, clicking on a seatbelt.

'Cannae trust nobody, neither you can,' he wheezed.

They drove out of the city and into the hills, no-one saying a word, although every now and then Stringer coughed up a grunt that might've been a small laugh. McCall gave up trying to catch Jimsie's eye and stared through the side window, watching the streets and buildings give way to trees and hedges. He'd known it would come to this eventually. Strangely enough, he didn't feel anything – no fear, no sadness, no disappointment. He was just tired. Tired and empty. Maybe it was best this way, although he wished it had been anyone but Jimsie.

They'd been driving for about an hour when Jimsie pulled off the road onto a bumpy track. He stopped the car and got out, still without looking at McCall. Stringer leaned forward in his seat. 'Time for a wee walk,' he breathed into McCall's ear. McCall slowly turned his head and stared at Stringer's face. The man was unfazed by the cold look. He smiled back and said, 'You should've killed me when you had the chance.'

McCall climbed out and smelled the air. It was fresh up here. This is what the air would smell like at the cottage in his drawing, fresh and clean. His little piece of heaven.

'Up the track,' Stringer ordered and McCall looked back to see him holding a gun in his left fist. Stringer looked down at it and smiled. 'Don't worry, at this range I can shoot just as well with that hand.'

McCall turned towards the track that followed a small stream between some trees and up the hillside. The grass underfoot was slightly damp and springy and his shoes squeaked as he walked. Stringer was a few feet behind him, Jimsie a few more behind him. They walked in a silence that was broken only by the squeak underfoot and Stringer's laboured breathing through his broken nose. The man had been right. McCall should have finished him off when he had the chance. But then Big Rab would only have sent someone else, and Jimsie would still have been the bait.

After fifteen minutes of walking, the track disappeared into a marshy stretch of ground between two high banks. McCall stopped at the edge and looked over his shoulder at the two men behind.

'That'll do just there,' said Stringer, his breathing heavy after the walk uphill. 'That'll do just fine.'

McCall looked over Stringer's head to Jimsie at the rear but the boy was looking down at his shoes. First Donna, now Jimsie, McCall thought.

'They'll no find you up here in a hurry,' Stringer said. 'In a couple of hours you'll sink into that marsh. The sea'll give up its dead before that will.'

McCall had the impression Stringer had been up here before. How many bodies lay under that green mat, he wondered?

'We'll no bother with any last requests, eh, McCall? We're both professionals,' said Stringer.

'I've got one anyway,' said McCall, looking at Jimsie, who couldn't return his gaze. The boy's eyes searched the ground between them, as if he was looking for a hole to jump into. McCall fished in his pocket and threw his house keys at the youth. They bounced off his chest and landed in the grass. 'Take Arrow to Bobby Newman.'

Jimsie nodded, just once, as he stooped to retrieve the keys. McCall turned away again and closed his eyes. He heard Stringer step closer, could even feel his breath on the back of his neck. McCall knew he could probably take him but there was Jimsie to consider. The boy was too far away and probably armed. Anyway, he was too damned tired.

Just too damned tired.

He felt a soft breeze on his face and the sound of the crows swirled around him. In his mind's eye, he saw his highland cottage and the mountain beyond. He thought he could smell pine and honeysuckle sweet in the air and somewhere the cry of an eagle and the soft lapping of loch waters. He didn't know where he was, he just knew it was anywhere but here.

And then, just before he heard the gunshot, he saw Audrey standing in the doorway, smiling, and he heard her voice, calling him...

Jimsie had never seen Rab so still, so silent. The big man barely moved while he told him that the job was done. His face appeared frozen, a blank mask. Jimsie had expected something from him. He was, after all, telling him that his oldest friend had just been murdered.

'We made sure the body sank into the swamp,' he said, 'put stones in the clothes, shoved it down with branches. He'll no be found, that's for sure.'

Jimsie waited, giving Rab the opportunity to speak, but still nothing.

'I dropped Stringer off at Fat Boy's house so he could pick up his car. He'll be here soon, I think.'

Another pause but more silence from the big guy. He just sat there, staring across the desk, his hands clasped tightly in front of him.

'He took the cash we'd collected, said he'd bring it by.'

Jimsie ran out of things to say. He lingered in the chair for a few moments but couldn't take Rab's blank eyes any longer. He stood, moved to the door, opened it.

'Was it quick and clean?' Rab's voice, softer than he'd ever heard it before.

Jimsie didn't turn. He looked at his hand on the door handle and said, 'He never felt a thing. Your man Stringer went crazy afterwards, though. Smashed up the hand, did a number on the fingers, battered him about the face, said Davie deserved it. He said it was only fair.' He thought he saw the bag man flinch then, just slightly. 'But Davie was gone then, beyond feeling it.'

He paused, but Big Rab was immobile. He pulled the door open, stepped out, nodded to young Joseph who was waiting outside – *weird fucker*, he thought – and left the office.

If he had turned back to close the door, he would've seen Rab's knuckles tighten as he fought a tremor, and his eyes fill with moisture.

Jimsie drove away from the taxi office, made a series of turns and pulled into a car park behind a library. He sat quietly for a few seconds, then wound his window down to face the driver of the car alongside. He saw his grandfather in the passenger seat, his worried eyes searching Jimsie's face for an answer. Jimsie gave him a small smile of reassurance then looked again at the driver, saw his face was also tight with tension, and gave him a brief nod.

Bobby Newman's grip loosened on the steering wheel and he began to breathe easier.

Donovan was eating a tub of strawberry jelly when he became aware of Bannatyne standing in the doorway of his private room.

'You must really like hospital food,' said his old boss, stepping further into the room. 'You're never out of the place.'

'I don't think twice in twenty years amounts to a habit,' said Donovan as Bannatyne pulled a wooden chair closer to the bedside.

'More than I've ever been.' Bannatyne looked around. 'And a private room, too? Have you got connections?'

Donovan laughed. 'I was in a ward but I think the other patients raised a petition about my snoring, so I was banished in here when it became available.'

Bannatyne's face was serious, despite the banter. 'You're a very lucky man, Frank. You shouldn't be here. The doctors say it's a miracle you're alive.'

Donovan felt pain stab at his wound again but he ignored it as best he could. He'd been out of it for almost a week and finally woke up with the agony of a thousand hangovers and yet, strangely enough, ravenously hungry. He felt as if he hadn't stopped eating in the two days since.

Bannatyne pulled a chair closer to the bed and sat down. He cleared his throat and was obviously considering his next words carefully. Donovan gave him space, knowing there was bad news coming. He'd already heard about Jimmy Knight's death – it was all over the papers. A cop's death always made the news, even one as corrupt and as monstrous as the Black Knight. The reports didn't mention that, of course. They never would, even though one or two of the old hands on the news desks had heard rumours.

Whatever his old boss had to say was slow in coming so Donovan filled in the gap with a question. 'Have they questioned the girl? Morrigan?'

Bannatyne blew out his cheeks. 'She says Knight forced her into everything. Threatened her. Held a drug arrest over her head, abused her since she was a teenager. We've got nothing that proves she helped Knight set up the robbery, got nothing that proves Knight had anything to do with it, for that matter, apart from Shoog MacLeish's statement and he's dead. Lang, the scumbag he claims told him, is keeping his mouth shut. We can place her with MacLeish in the pub and leaving with him but other than that, nothing. She says she had no idea Knight meant the boy harm. She'll be charged with something but with her background she'll end up with a suspended sentence. Knight's taking the fall for everything. Nothing like a dead man to shoulder the blame.'

Donovan rolled his eyes. His gut told him there was more to it but he'd never get to the bottom of it. Sometimes justice wasn't just blind, it was deaf and dumb, too.

Bannatyne cleared his throat. 'Your mate Davie McCall is missing.'

Donovan felt shock stab at his wound. 'Define missing?'

'As in believed dead, if the underworld gossip mill is to be believed.'

Donovan swallowed. 'What happened?'

Bannatyne took a breath. 'Okay, some of it I know, some of it I've pieced together by taking educated guesses, okay? I told you about the task force looking into the O'Neill case?' Donovan nodded. 'Well, it seems it went deeper than that. They were looking at corruption, specifically related to Jimmy Knight and his connection with Rab McClymont. They had an informant in relation to the O'Neill case, who is now dead. And with O'Neill and his family also gone that looks like it may well just be filed away under "The Game's a Bogey". O'Neill's conviction will stand, for now anyway, not that he's bothering.'

'And what about the Jimmy Knight angle?'

'That's where it all gets a bit mysterious. They had a tout inside Rab's crew who looked to set to burst the whole thing wide open for them.'

'Davie?' Donovan didn't believe it but he asked the question anyway.

'No. They tried to turn him, apparently they placed a female officer close to him in a bid to have him open up.'

Donna, thought Donovan. Jesus.

'Didn't work, it seems,' Bannatyne said. 'No, their man inside was a bloke called Stringer. You know him?'

Donovan nodded. 'Knew of him. Davie never liked him.'

'Well, they had something on him – some murder down in Girvan years ago. The body had been dumped at sea but it surfaced in a fishing net last year. The boffins managed to glean a contact trace, or at least that's what Vincent told this bloke Stringer. Find it hard to believe myself. Stringer used to work for the victim, small-time dealer called Mulvey, went missing ten years ago. Soon after Stringer began working for McClymont, so the theory is he did his old boss in to curry favour with his new one. He was also an old tout of Knight's, it being a small world and all that. Anyway, Vincent managed to turn him and used your pal as a diversionary tactic should McClymont ever get wind of it, which he must have because McCall's gone. No sign of him.'

Donovan found this hard to process. He stared at his half-finished jelly tub, his appetite having suddenly evaporated. 'Maybe he's gone away. He used to talk about that. He wanted out of The Life.'

'Maybe,' said Bannatyne but Donovan could tell he didn't believe it. 'But the word on the street is that he'd turned grass – and you know what that means when it suits guys like McClymont.'

Donovan knew what it meant and the blatant hypocrisy of it sickened him. McClymont and those like him survived by inform-ing on others and having bent cops like Knight on their payroll. It was less than a handful of cops but it was enough. Yet when they wanted someone out of the way they labelled them a grass and had them killed. Davie McCall was no-one's tout, Donovan would stake his life on it.

Bannatyne went on, 'The undercover said she saw Davie being driven away by that boy Jimsie – old Sammy Williams' grandson, the brother of that lad who was done for the Club Corvus killing a few years ago?' By his inflection Donovan knew Bannatyne was asking if he remembered who he was talking about. He nodded. He'd met Sammy during the Corvus investigation. That had been a bad one for all concerned. 'The thing is, a couple of witnesses say they saw McCall two, three days after that, hale and hearty. The chances are they're lying but with no other evidence there's nothing can be done.'

Donovan pushed the jelly cup away from him. He wasn't hungry any more. 'So where's this Stringer then? In protective custody?'

Bannatyne paused, a frown appearing on his face. 'There's the question. Stringer's gone, too, with a chunk of Big Rab's cash, I hear...'

Donovan took this in. McClymont wouldn't have hesitated to have Davie killed if he thought he'd become a liability, old pals or no old pals. There are no old pals when it comes to making a profit. As for Stringer's disappearance, that could be put down to his nerve failing. If he'd turned grass it would only be a matter of time before the writing was on the wall for him. He'd know that. Maybe he'd been true to his name and had been stringing the task force along, just waiting for that big payday to top up his retirement fund.

But Davie, dead? Would he let himself fall into any of Rab's traps?

Another thought occurred to him. 'What about Arrow?' Bannatyne cocked his head. 'Arrow, Davie McCall's dog – where's he?'

Bannatyne shrugged. 'No-one mentioned a dog.'

December 2002

BOBBY NEWMAN LOOKED down and saw the father in the boy's features. The eyes, though, were different. They were blue, like Davie's, but there were no ghosts to cast a shadow on their brilliance. The boy stared up at him with an intensity that Bobby recognised, though. 'Pleased to meet you, Davie,' he said, holding out his hand. 'My name's Bobby.'

The boy politely took his hand and gave it a single tug. Then the hand was drawn away and his gaze shifted to the knot of mourners milling outside the crematorium. Vari followed her son's stare and Bobby saw the tears in her own eyes. She cared for Davie back then and she cared for him now, even though they hadn't seen each other for years. Bobby looked at the people waiting for them, saw Connie and his daughter, Jimsie and Sammy, Frank Donovan with his old boss, Gentleman Jack Bannatyne. There were others, people Davie had helped, people he'd saved. People whose lives he'd impacted in a positive way. The people he'd hurt weren't there, of course. Some of them deserved it, some of them didn't, but that was the burden Davie carried. For he was not a good man.

She asked, 'What happened, Bobby?'

Bobby looked over his shoulder at the funeral party. He wondered what to say. Stringer's plan was that the body was never meant to be discovered. He'd chosen the spot well but he'd forgotten that nothing stays the same forever. The land was sold and someone wanted to turn it into a paintballing centre. Two months ago, the swamp had been drained and gave up its secrets. There had been some decomposition but the mud had preserved it well enough to reveal the face was almost gone, partly through the exit wound of a bullet which had entered through the back of the head and blown away most of the teeth. The flesh had also proved to be quite a buffet for whatever insects and bacteria made a life for themselves in the swampy ground. The bones of the right hand had been broken by blunt force trauma, the fingers of each hand cut off and nowhere to be found. A bank card found in the pocket was Davie McCall's. He had no family, no close relatives apart from a drunken aunt who wanted nothing to do with him. It fell to Bobby to identify the body, which he did. He recognised the remnants of clothing, and told the bored officials that the scar faintly visible on the putrid flesh clinging to the chest had been left there by Danny McCall years ago. The police had decided that David McCall had been killed in 2000 so it was all good enough for them and the case was closed.

He didn't say any of that to Vari. She didn't need to hear. Instead he said, quietly. 'The Life just caught up with him, Vari. He always knew it would.'

She lowered her head and raised a hand to wipe something away. Bobby remained silent, his eyes roaming around the grave-yard. He didn't know what he expected to see. A familiar figure, maybe, with a dog at his feet. Not too tall, powerfully built but no muscleman, black hair fading to grey. And the blue eyes. Piercing blue eyes.

Davie McCall was not a good man but he was his friend. And always would be.

Maybe, on some plane he couldn't see, there were other old friends from the past there. Joe Klein, perhaps even Luca, Mouthy Grant – thinking his name sent a pulse of guilt through Bobby, for he had unwittingly been involved in the young man's death. And Audrey, always Audrey.

Bobby felt a hand tug at his and he looked down to see another pair of blue eyes staring up at him. Bobby smiled, 'What's up, pal?' He asked.

'My mum says you knew my dad.'

Bobby looked at Vari, who was smiling though her eyes were a reservoir. So she had mentioned Davie to the boy, after all. The thought pleased him.

'Aye, son, I knew him.'

The boy nodded, satisfied that this was true. Then he said, 'My mum said you'd tell me about him, if I asked.'

Vari gave Bobby another smile and he said, 'Sure, I'll tell you all about him.'

Bobby took the boy's hand, Vari took the other, and they walked towards the waiting crowd. And as they walked, Bobby heard Vari whisper, 'Do you think he's at peace now?'

Bobby squinted against the winter sun as a handful of crows suddenly took to the air, crying out to each other as they rode the thermals upwards. 'I hope so, hen. I really hope, wherever he is, he's found a wee piece of heaven.'

THE END

Author's note and acknowledgements

I HAVE NO IDEA whether there was a heat wave in the summer of 2000 and, as usual, no character here is based on an actual person, no incident on real life. I don't think there ever was a public call box on Huntly Gardens but I needed one – the omnipotence of writing fiction!

I have many people to thank for their help over the four book series.

Joe Jackson, John Carroll, Stephen Wilkie all helped me with the reality of Glasgow's underworld. I've put my own spin on it and any errors in procedures or terminology are all mine.

Graham Turnbull built and administers my website – www.douglasskelton.com. There's no way I could have done it myself and I'm grateful he stepped in and took it out of my hands. As he has done many times in matters technical.

Any author needs a support group, even if only to remind them that they can actually finish what they've started and to buy multiple copies. I have to thank a lot of people who have helped over the past three years, too many to mention by name for fear of missing someone out. So thank you to all the readers, reviewers, bloggers and booksellers. It would not have happened without you all.

Thanks also to the incredibly supportive crime writing community and festival organisers who have made me feel so welcome and part of something bigger than just a messy little room with a PC and lots of books.

Thanks, as usual, to my editor Louise Hutcheson and all at Luath Press, particularly Gavin MacDougall, for allowing me to bring Davie's story to life.

Special thanks are due to Iain Burns for his advice, encouragement and unfailing enthusiasm for the Davie McCall books.

And the Flanagan's Bar of this book does not exist. Don't go looking for it.

Devil's Knock

Douglas Skelton
ISBN: 978-1-910021-81-1 PBK £9.99

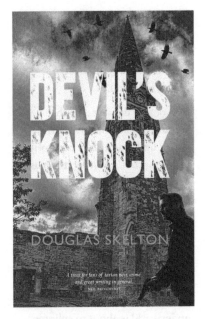

When the devil comes knocking, you either tell that bastard to get the hell away, or you invite him in.

Davie McCall has darkness inside him. A darkness that haunts him, but also helps him do despicable things to those trying to cause him and his friends harm.

When Dickie Himes is killed in a club owned by the Jarvis clan, it sparks a chain of events that Davie knows can only lead to widespread gang war on the streets of mid-'90s Glasgow. The police are falling over themselves to solve the crime, but when justice is so easily bought or corrupted, Davie needs to take matters into his own hands.

Davie has to contend with the ghosts of those he has failed, a persistent Hollywood actor and a scruffy dog with no name. When he finds a target on his back, will Davie be able to suppress the darkness inside him and refuse to kill...

Or will the devil's knock be too tempting?

Blood City

Douglas Skelton

ISBN: 978-1-910021-24-8 PBK £7.99

Meet Davie McCall. Beaten, bloody… brutal.

Irrevocably damaged by the barbaric regime of an abusive father, and haunted by memories of his mother's murder, there is a darkness inside him.

Enter Joe the Tailor. A sophisticated crimelord with morals, he might be the only man in the city Davie can trust. But then the bodies begin to mount…

In 1980s Glasgow, the criminal underworld is about to splinter. Battle lines are drawn, and the gap between friend and enemy blurs as criminals and police alike are caught in a net of lies, murder and revenge that will change the city forever. *Blood City* is the first novel in Douglas Skelton's Davie McCall quartet.

The Glasgow of this period is a great, gritty setting for a crime story, and Skelton's non-fiction work stands him in good stead… he's taken well to fiction… the unexpected twists keep coming.
THE HERALD

Fierce, all too believable.
DAILY MAIL

You follow the plot like an eager dog, nose turning this way and that, not catching every single clue but quivering as you lunge towards a blood-splattered denouement.
DAILY EXPRESS

Crow Bait

Douglas Skelton

ISBN: 978-1-910021-29-3 PBK £9.99

They'll all be crow bait by the time I'm finished...

Jail was hell for Davie McCall. Ten years down the line, freedom's no picnic either. It's 1990, there are new kings in the West of Scotland underworld, and Glasgow is awash with drugs.

Davie can handle himself. What he can't handle is the memory of his mother's death at the hand of his sadistic father. Or the darkness his father implanted deep in his own psyche. Or the nightmares...

Now his father is back in town and after blood, ready to waste anyone who stops him hacking out a piece of the action. There are people in his way. And Davie is one of them.

Crow Bait is the second novel in Douglas Skelton's Davie McCall quartet.

Tense, dark and nerve-wracking... a highly effective thriller.
THE HERALD

This is crime fiction of the strongest quality.
CRIMESQUAD.COM

A gory and razor-sharp crime novel from the start, Douglas Skelton's Crow Bait *moves at breakneck speed like a getaway car on the dark streets of Glasgow.*
THE SKINNY

Skelton has been hiding from his talent for long enough. High time he shared it with the rest of us.
QUINTIN JARDINE

Details of these and other books published by Luath Press can be found at: **www.luath.co.uk**

Luath Press Limited
committed to publishing well written books worth reading

LUATH PRESS takes its name from Robert Burns, whose little collie Luath (*Gael.*, swift or nimble) tripped up Jean Armour at a wedding and gave him the chance to speak to the woman who was to be his wife and the abiding love of his life. Burns called one of 'The Twa Dogs' Luath after Cuchullin's hunting dog in Ossian's *Fingal*. Luath Press was established in 1981 in the heart of Burns country, and now resides a few steps up the road from Burns' first lodgings on Edinburgh's Royal Mile. Luath offers you distinctive writing with a hint of unexpected pleasures.

Most bookshops in the UK, the US, Canada, Australia, New Zealand and parts of Europe either carry our books in stock or can order them for you. To order direct from us, please send a £sterling cheque, postal order, international money order or your credit card details (number, address of cardholder and expiry date) to us at the address below. Please add post and packing as follows: UK – £1.00 per delivery address; overseas surface mail – £2.50 per delivery address; overseas airmail – £3.50 for the first book to each delivery address, plus £1.00 for each additional book by airmail to the same address. If your order is a gift, we will happily enclose your card or message at no extra charge.

Luàth Press Limited
543/2 Castlehill
The Royal Mile
Edinburgh EH1 2ND
Scotland
Telephone: 0131 225 4326 (24 hours)
email: sales@luath.co.uk
Website: www.luath.co.uk

ILLUSTRATION: IAN KELLAS